# DISOBEDIENT

Book Two of
RISE OF THE REALMS

**D. FISCHER**

*Disobedient (Rise of the Realms: Book Two)*

Copyright © 2018 by D. Fischer

All rights reserved.

ASIN: B07B7CVP9H

ISBN-13: 978-1987705317
ISBN-10: 1987705319

BISAC: Fiction / Fantasy / Epic

Everything in this book is fictional. It is not based on true events, persons, or creatures that go bump in the night, no matter how much we wish it were…

*To my husband and two sons, who believe in my dreams and love unconditionally. If it wasn't for them, my world would be absent of hope.*

# CONTENTS

# PROLOGUE

*"A child, who is not embraced by a village,*

*will burn it down to feel its warmth."*

– African Proverb

***AIDEN VANDER***

***THE VOID***

There's a space – a void – between all connecting realms. It's where nothing can fit, and everything has a place. It's where no senses exist, yet I feel it there, scarcely out of reach. This is where I am. That's where we are. We are nothing, and we are everything.

Floating to unknown destinations, passing by other lost souls who sail with no purpose, I hear them whisper, moan, cry, but I can't reach out. I can't touch them, comfort them, bring peace to whatever is left of their souls.

It's impossible – it should be impossible – that I tingle. Every inch of me ripples with a prickling, uncomfortable sensation. I can't see. My mind can't focus on any one thing. I'm nowhere and everywhere, expanded in a time - a place - that doesn't exist. That shouldn't exist. But it does.

A small part of me, the part that grasps this as my new reality, wants revenge. If I could, I'd rip that Fee limb from limb, but even if I was whole, I know I'm no match for him. I have seen his power – he brought me back. He had made my heart beat again, caused blood to flow through my veins and warmth to heat my fingertips. I had felt my veins pulse through my neck with an unrelenting fear.

Life shouldn't be that way. Death shouldn't be that way. Once someone is dead, they shouldn't need to feel fear anymore. They shouldn't be re-given life. Death is death – the end of a cycle and the beginning of a vicious circle of potential regrowth.

*There's no place for the twice dead.*

A sob escapes my nothingness. Where am I?

Images of my life, both as the living and the dead, flick through my mind like shooting stars across the expanse of a black sky. I can't grasp the images; I can't hold onto them for more than a few seconds. It's torture… the consequence I pay for doing nothing wrong.

This is the eternal punishment I don't deserve. But, I'd do it again. For *her*.

# CHAPTER ONE

*KATRIANE DUPONT*

*MYLA'S PAST*

The sun sets in the west, rays of pink and gold painting the clouds as a masterpiece no artist's genius is capable of capturing with a few strokes of a withered brush. But at this moment, one mastermind attempts, his uneven, wooden easel rocking against the dirt with each sway of wind and bump of his wrist.

He is set up not far from my cell beneath the gallows, his left side facing me, his paint brush in hand, and smudges of color covering his bare left cheek.

Observing the barren trees, he angles his head, licking the corners of his lips, attempting to take in the full glory of the view before him. Is he really seeing it? Is he seeing the beauty of what is before him? Or is he simply there to capture something he struggles to scratch the surface of?

I can relate to that. That's the story of my life—not understanding circumstances I've been dealt but trying to live through it anyway.

I breathe deep, watching him as he concentrates, his tongue flicking out again, licking his plump bottom lip this time, and coating it with a fine layer of saliva. He has not a care in the world. Or maybe painting is his escape from it. Maybe he has problems, and he came here for peace. This sublimity may in fact be his escape from the ugliness inside of him.

The sun colors the barren branches, illuminating the grooves of each chunk of bark and every flaw in its grain. A wooden swatch is tucked in his elbow, dotted with different colors of paint. He dips his brush, choosing a color I can't see from where I sit. The bristles swirl and sway to the artist's demand, a slave to a fist, absorbing the liquid of his choosing. He lifts it to the easel, and drops of gold drip on his tattered shoes. With a careful flick of his wrist, he strokes a strip of bland gold onto a blank canvas.

I watch him for a while, attempting to capture the beauty of his time, trying to see what he sees while I'm reminded of my circumstances.

This is his time . . . not mine. I'm stuck here, my back slumped against the cold bars, clothed in Myla's dress, wedged in Myla's time. All around me is a reminder of my failures.

A chilly breeze wafts between the bars, tickling the back of my neck. My skin pricks with goosebumps, and I attempt to soften them by rubbing my hands against my arms.

All those dreams of a damsel being rescued by a handsome prince are fairytale garbage. When it is needed most, no one will be there to aid me, exactly like Myla.

I gulp, swallowing nothing within my dry, parched mouth. *Myla's dead.*

Every breeze that blows through my bars smells of horse manure and human waste as the dark thoughts churn in my head.

People pass my iron cage, their capes or dresses billowing behind them like clouds of mist. Some throw half eaten apples, aiming perfectly to fit the fruit between the bars before they thump to the ground at my feet. They laugh, sauntering away as if they've provoked a captured monkey set here to torment for their amusement. I've been the laughing stock of the village all day, my execution scheduled after dusk.

Mistakenly soiling my face in a layer of grime, I scrub my hand over the sensitive skin, leaving behind smudges that I quickly dismiss. It doesn't matter. Nothing matters anymore.

Corbin has yet to show, and I doubt he will. He abandoned Myla, his own wife, when she was hung for saving the village. What would be any different in the case of my execution? I'm nothing to him.

If he's off trying to find his daughters, he best not attempt. It'd be a waste of time. I don't know Erline well, but the feeling is growing that if she wants to keep something hidden - like dirty little secrets and lies - then she will. Nothing will keep her from doing it.

In my opinion, which doesn't seem to be a popular one of late, it's the ultimate deceit, pretending to be something or someone you're not. Erline's lying to herself, hiding her alternative motives for self-serving reasons, purely to please her own agenda. I've had some time to think about it, stuck here in the gallows with nothing to do but ponder the previous events that ultimately lead to my demise. My death. Soon, I will die. That has yet to settle in. I have yet to accept it. I'm here, sitting in the dirt, my heart beating in my chest. The oxygen enters my lungs, and my chest rises and falls. I exist. How could I go through an event that ends everything I am? How can one living thing exist and then suddenly cease? The thought displeases and disgusts me.

My conscience bucks against the idea that a life can easily be winked from existence by a simple command, a pull of a trigger, or the tightening of a noose. One minute, I'll be there, breathing, living, and the next, I'll be gone. The thoughts rumbling in my head will stop, along with the flow of blood in my veins. My body will be a shell, a cracked nut, hollowed by greedy fingers. I sniff and rub my nose with my wrist. More importantly, how can someone so easily end someone's existence as though it doesn't contribute to the circle of life?

I roll my stiff neck, trying to dispel my focus to simple and easy distractions. It doesn't work though as I ask myself: Will I even go to the death realm?

Time travel wasn't something we learned inside the coven. I didn't even know it was possible, but here I sit, in the dirt, watching a man from the 17th century try to make something out of himself, his paintbrush his muse. I don't know what will happen to me if I die in a time that isn't my own.

Maybe that's what I need – a muse. I chuckle to myself. The painter squints over his shoulder, a scowl furrowing his brows at breaking whatever sliver of futile concentration he's clinging to. I look away, the smile still plastered on my lips, the slight breeze chilling my teeth.

I'm losing my mind. The stress is causing me to have inappropriate reactions to ridiculously terrifying situations. Who knows? Maybe this is an appropriate reaction to an impending death. I wouldn't know.

The only thing I can think of that comes close to a muse is an angel. An angel, my angel, sent me here. Someone who's meant to be divine, to watch over those who cannot protect themselves against the grave vulnerabilities of the mortal world, and she, herself, became the very thing I needed protection from. I was too blind to see it. Maybe I didn't want to see it. Maybe I wanted someone, something, to believe in and call my own. It's no secret that I'm a lonely fool.

My jaw ticks of its own accord, fury driving the motion.

Cutting her wings was a good choice. She'd be a better fit in the demon realm among those who enjoy terror and manipulation – those who specialize in it. She seems to be a master in that area.

I shift my foot and a puff of dirt rises and tickles my nose. My legs are falling asleep. The nerves ripple a painful tingle beneath my skin and the muscles beg to be stretched.

I paced for hours last night, trying to work around how I could possibly live, knowing anything I do will alter the future. Once my ankles grew swollen, I sat and since haven't moved. My stomach grumbles, and my mouth is dry as the dirt below me, parched from lack of water.

A mound of feces lay off in the corner from previous captives, most undeserving I'm sure. Flies buzz from pile to pile, their flight slowing with impending death. I wrinkle my nose every time the breeze carries the stench my direction. I don't dare go myself. Besides, I heard that once you die, you expel all waste from your body. Choosing to go out with a bang, I'll leave them a mess to clean up after they've snapped my neck.

Metal clinks and jingles from off in the distance, and a whistle passes lips I can't see. I startle, my head tilting up to stare into a periwinkle sky. The sun has plunged over the horizon, abandoning me and the stars. They twinkle overhead, seeming brighter tonight than they normally would.

That will be my last sunset. The beats of my heart are numbered.

The painter is long gone. Grooves in the dirt are etched where the pegs of his easel had dug in. I didn't even hear him leave. Did I fall asleep? Was I so lost in my own reflections to watch the sun's final rest?

Footsteps grow closer, the whistling changing tune to an uneven-pitch. Torches glow over the dead leaves littering the ground. The new light reflects on their dry and crumbled silhouettes, casting large shadows against the dark, silent, and morose trees.

A hand curls around the bars before the body comes into full view, a wicked grin matching the face with evil eyes.

"Petite sorciére," he states in French. "Your time has come."

I swallow, my tongue sticking to the roof of my mouth, my heart pumping in my chest, and blood roars in my ears.

I'm not ready for this.

*TEMBER*

*EARTH REALM*

Kat looks peaceful, tucked under her blankets, the hems pulled to her chin. My lips twitch when I remember a story the earth realm has about a princess placed under a sleeping spell. Kat used to watch it when she was nothing but a few feet high, sitting cross-legged in front of a box that flicked bright images across a glass screen. Perched on a tree outside her living room window, I would watch her, chuckle when she giggled, smile when she twirled to the soft instrumental music. I envied her innocence.

Unlike that precious little tale, Kat has no prince to rouse her and no kiss to wake her from an eternal slumber. It's at this moment that I truly see Kat for what she is.

A coven-less witch, no family, no lover . . . She's alone, powerful, and without guidance. I was sent here to do just that while gently discovering the truth. Instead, I manipulated her. I bent her to do as I wished, and she had no idea I was doing it because she craved what I provided – companionship.

I wonder what she speculated when her dreams morphed, blending with Myla's memories. In these few short days, Kat hasn't spoken a word about them.

Guilt rides my back. It seeps through my ribs and wraps my heart in a constricting vice.

I snap back to reality as Corbin bends, his torso looming over the bed. He reaches and slides the back of his hand against her dusky pink cheek. It's an affectionate touch, one I wouldn't have believed to come from Corbin. I expect her to twitch, to wrinkle her brows, but she doesn't – her slumber is too deep.

Erline struggles to contain herself, whether in a jealous rage or hatred, I cannot tell. Her jaw ticks at a frantic pace, and her body is rigid as stone. The vibes wafting from her are not of the friendly sort.

"Pick her up, Demon Creator," Erma barks behind me.

I frown, the skin pinching on my forehead. Erma never behaves this way.

Corbin shifts his head, swiveling in slow motion, and raises a silent, perfect eyebrow. "Pushy," he tsks. "And rude."

With gentle ease, he lowers her purple comforter, exposing Kat's body wrapped in cotton, cherry-patterned pajamas. Sliding one hand under her neck and the other under her knees, he lifts with ease as though she's nothing but a feather.

I watch him with interest as he drinks in the sight of her like he's trying to remember every detail, the perfections and flaws. Or maybe he's recalling memories that are forming in the past. What I would give to learn of those memories. He hasn't been forthcoming as the new memories form. Whatever reason he regards her, it causes me to pause, rooting a seed of suspicion.

Corbin is a self-centered fee, the most absorbed as they come. Perhaps more so than Sureen or Kheelan. Like his demons, he enjoys the mind games, the twisting of stories, and acting as though life is a puzzle piece of his own construction. I shouldn't expect more from the creator of terror and demonic activity.

Spinning to face us, his scent wafts in my direction. It's an alluring aroma, tinged with sulfur. He steps forward, his large shoe creaking the wood boards below our feet. "Who would like to direct this band of misfits?"

Erline pushes past me and places herself in front of Corbin. Her body refuses to touch mine as she passes, and it's then I understand how upset she truly is with me. She doesn't have to be. No one can be more of a critic to this angel than me.

I can't see her face, but her shoulders are bunched, pulled back with stiff posture. Such a challenge in the stare she's surely giving him if Corbin's face, alight with delight, is anything to go by. The skin wrapped around his eyes is that of an internal jest.

"Erline," I begin when it doesn't look as though she plans to move. "Erline, we must get going. If we want to save Kat . . ."

Corbin's bottom lip pouts with a mocking quiver. "Yes, Erline. If you want to save Kat from a most certain and agonizing death, we best move forward with our half-witted plan."

Erline's fingers curl into her palms, and she huffs, the breath passing through her teeth like a kitten hiss.

Attempting to not roll my eyes, I scratch the back of my neck and urge once more. "Erline, you have to touch him – to touch all of us – if we plan to go."

We don't have time to dig deeper into Corbin's agenda. We don't have time for childish, petty behavior. Digging up the past isn't in our plans. We must move onward and bring that sliver of the past back to us.

Erline lifts her hand, uncurls her fist, and rests her palm on Corbin's elbow. Her touch is light, narrowly connecting to the long-sleeved button-down encasing his arm. Erma, with a level of maturity she's always shown despite her obvious displeasure, reaches to grip my hand while grasping Erline's.

The wind trickles in from seemingly nowhere, smelling of fresh, wet earth. It howls through the short hallway and enters the room. It's gentle, caressing, before picking up pace with vigorous force. Papers fly from the book shelf; the clothes whip inside the closet, dangling from their hangers, and the blinds sway back and forth with such strength – I fear they'll become weapons once unhinged from their hold along the wall. The room begins to blur, my body being tugged this way and that, and my eyes sting enough for them to be forced closed.

# CHAPTER TWO

*TEMBER*

*DREAM REALM*

Yanking my hand from Erma's, I bend over, coughing and wheezing with no relief. I steady myself, placing my hands against something solid and rough to the right of me. My vision is still blurry though dark, and I blink several times, waiting for it to refocus. Erline's portals are brutal to a body. I imagine if I were sucked into a tornado, it would feel the same.

The black fades as small retreating dots, and I attempt to focus on my surroundings, on the jagged edges digging into my palm. My lips firm, feeling as though they're bunching into a tight rose.

Supporting my weight is black, jagged rock. The stone sparkles bright, lighting the otherwise dark space around me. They're like stars adorning the night sky with endless, moving twinkles, but there are trillions of them. The Milky Way holds no comparison.

Sweat trickles down my forehead, but I disregard it, rubbing my index finger in small circles along the shimmering, rough, rock wall. My breaths come heavy, and I straighten my spine, expanding my torso, and step closer to examine what's before my eyes. I scrape a nail against one of the many sparkles. It detaches from the rock with ease, like a mote of dust, and I bring it closer to my eye, tip my head to the side.

"Careful," Erma mutters behind me. "Ingest that dust, and you'll hallucinate. Angels aren't built for dreams."

I turn to face her, bringing the speck with me. "This is dream dust?"

She grasps my hand and leans forward, blowing it off the tip of my finger. It twinkles, floating like a feather, before it rests against the matching black rock beneath my feet.

"Yes," she says with simplicity before twisting back to the group.

Her movements are graceful and elegant, something I've taken for granted until now. It's such a small trait, yet I'm hyper-aware. I lost something, something I love, and due to the loss, my mind's eye is becoming more focused and sharpened, noticing things I didn't before. The finer details I've been missing are a hammer to my gut, an unnamable emotion I thought I'd never experience.

Taking in a shuddering breath, I release it, expelling some of the non-existent pressure that's metaphorically swelled around my aching heart.

Erline and Corbin are yards ahead, already marching to the destination they have in mind. Kat's bare feet dangle from Corbin's cradled arms. Each step he takes jostles her calves, and her feet sway to the movement. The black paint on her toenails matches the rock surrounding us.

Another pang stabs my chest, my guilt so thick it constricts my lungs. It's a sharp, invisible knife that my brain has conjured, reminding me of my betrayal.

That is two people I've let down in such a short amount of time. It's an emotion that feels like I won't survive as it consumes my heart. They're new to me, all these feelings. I feel naked, as though I was skinned alive and there's nothing left but bones. Yet, I'm the one who caused all of this. I am to blame.

I swallow, my chin jutting out as I attempt to expel the knot that's formed there. Shaking my head, my brown curls tickling the curve of my neck, I take in my surroundings, focusing on anything else but what my mind is forcing me to endure.

We're in a cave or what seems like a cave. The tunnel is long but tall, several people's length, and it curves at the top. Large, spiked rocks protrude from the curved ceiling, giving it a perilous appearance, as though those spikes will drop and be our demise.

The surfaces that make up the walls aren't smooth but instead, jagged, bumpy, yet hold much beauty and character. These tunnels are mined works of art.

"What is the black rock?" I ask, my voice a whisper.

"Inferaze," Corbin answers.

I turn to the group. "Inferaze?"

Erma nods. "Like coal, only…different."

I purse my lips and catch up to the group in a jog. Every sparkle, every speck of dream dust, lights our way as we walk down the tunnel, each mote a tiny sun, and the Inferaze the night sky. The contrast is breathtaking, a cave that can't be replicated.

My head swivels, absorbing the details of the tunnel, before I look at my shoes silently treading the solid ground. I frown and stop mid-step, my foot falling soundless. The surface surrounding my shoes is lit – bright white surrounding the edges like a puddle of light. I spin, glancing behind me.

With every stride we have taken, our feet have left the evidence, like a bread crumb trail, in the same brilliant glow. It's as if applying pressure to the Inferaze brightens the specks, merges them together. I look a little farther back from where we started, noticing how the prints fade, and I heave a sigh of relief. We can't be conspicuous if we're leaving a trail that'll lead right to us. Not that this is a mission of secrecy, but it's best to find Sureen before she runs. She's known to flee like the defenseless coward she is.

"Tember!" Erma barks.

The muscles along my neck bunch, and I grind my teeth. Whirling back to the group, I jog to them. Her voice should have echoed through the open space, but it's as if the Inferaze absorbed it. It makes me question: What is the purpose of this magical rock? What can it do?

Erline tilts her head, her chin touching the point of her shoulder. Her long white hair ripples against her back. "Keep up, or I'll send you back."

Erma's eyes snap to mine before they wander along the rocks, roaming its surface but not absorbing the detail. Her arms sway slightly beside her as if she doesn't want anyone to know she fights an internal war. She doesn't want to be here. She detests Sureen; this I know.

All the nights we shared a bed, she would tell me stories, and each one would end with Sureen's name passing her lips with a snarl. Not only is Erma uncomfortable with where we are, she's uncomfortable with my sacrifice, even in the face of my self-absorbed missions. It's crass of her to forget my very purpose, to want me only for herself. It's a hint of jealousy, and she's angry about having such emotions. I believe she places this blame on me. I do deserve the full brunt of her silent, vindictive wrath.

A rumbling along the cave wall causes our group to stop in its tracks, wary. It travels down the tunnel, the roar of the rock running its length like ripples of an earthquake. The walls visibly vibrate, and I glance up, watching the questionable, deadly spikes.

"What's happening?" I ask, raising my voice above the sound while keeping the fright from my tone.

Erma sidesteps to the tunnel wall, placing her palm on a ridge of protruding black rock. Her eyebrows dip and she swivels back to Erline, questions on the edge of her twitching lips.

"Don't fear," Erline begins, her eyes running the length of the tunnel. Her inspection halts when a portion of the wall ripples like still water after a gentle poke. "It's the cave's magic. Sureen's magic."

The wall transforms before my eyes, each rock folding back in on itself like the churning of vicious, angry clouds.

I clear my throat. "She knows we're here?"

"No," Corbin supplies. "It's another pathway, conjured here for the purpose of mining."

Sarcasm in the face of danger drips from my lips. "How do you know?"

He stretches his neck, impatience straining the muscles that line his spine. "Must I be forced to share all my knowledge?"

The archway fully forms, the rocks ceasing their movement, and the rumbling quiets, leaving behind echoes of vibrations inside my eardrums, stiff, like an over-flexed muscle.

## *DYSON COLEMAN*

## *DEATH REALM*


Rubbing my hands up and down my bare arms, my teeth chatter, slamming against one another. I huddle in the corner of my cell, trying to contain my own warmth. Oddly, there's a draft that floats through this dungeon, seeping between the bars of my cell like a slithering snake.

Reaper's Breath moved like this, only visible. It was always a warm welcome to see that creature, to have something constant. It was a familiarity in a place filled with sorrow and death, of people and beings unable to move on because the after-life holds nothing for them. But I haven't seen Reaper's Breath since the night I was thrown in here. It abandoned me, finding me a lost cause within its own agenda.

I quickly scratch the back of my neck, agitated. Maybe I am. Since I couldn't, and can't, lead a rebellion against its creator, I can only come to the conclusion that it chooses to stay away because I no longer benefit its uses. I'll probably be dead soon anyway. That frustrates me – to be abandoned and discarded.

Cursing under my breath, I drop my hand and hug my legs tighter against my torso. I guess I'll never know. I should stop worrying about things I can't change and instead, focus on survival so I can find a way out of this hellhole. Literally.

I glance around, seeing nothing but black, and frustration bubbles across my chest. Even with my shifter vision, it's difficult to see past my neighboring cells. No ideas filter into my mind; my stomach's grumbling and cramping, consuming my coherent thoughts instead.

In the cell next to me, Gan pulls me from my self-pity. I can hear him mumble to himself, words I can't understand besides, "devil." He often speaks in French, occasionally switching back to English when he isn't worked into a bundle of smothering emotions.

When he gets like that, it works me up, making me feel as crazy as he is. It's difficult to tell my own feelings apart from his.

I wonder what it'd be like to be him. What's his story? What happened to him to make him this way? It's obvious he's been here for a while, and I'm positive he's older than I care to imagine. Thinking about it makes my head throb. Even as I freeze to death, even as my stomach grumbles louder than his mumbling words, I pity him. Something bad happened to him, and I'm not sure if I want to know the truth behind his tortured soul.

I've tried working with him more, to get him to haunt the witch, but my efforts are pointless. It's a dying dream to think I'll ever make it out of here alive. He hasn't listened to me since he rambled about a beast. Something about the beginning and the end? I rub my hands over my strained eyes.

"Oh, the freaking insanity," I murmur.

My wolf is still and silent as the day he killed Aiden, his remorse and self-loathing smothering. Behind my closed eyelids, images pop up before I can squash them, his inner dysfunction my own.

*Blood splattering stone. Screams echoing through the room. Vampire spittle slapping my cheek. The vibrations of my wolf's agonized howl.*

I drop my hands and open my eyes, forcing the past away before it swallows me whole.

How many days has it been? There are no stones here to act as a chisel, marking the passing of time against the solid wall. Not that I'd be able to. The death realm doesn't have a sun. There's no bright daylight passing to a darkening night. It's a solidified yet continuous cycle of fog and misery. Besides, time passes differently in each realm. Maybe Kheelan created this realm that way on purpose. There's no point in obsessing over time when you're dead. Or maybe, it's one more thing he can take away from us.

A smell reaches my nose, a foul one. I can't work out what it is, but my stomach doesn't care. Any scent smells good at this point, whether it's edible or not.

Shifting my weight, I distract myself once more. "Come on, Dyson. Pull it together," I growl. I refuse to end up like Gan. For my wolf, I can't say the same.

I've tried to talk to my wolf, to get him to see reason, but he refuses to unbundle himself from a curled position inside me. He doesn't want to exist. He doesn't want to acknowledge what he was forced to do. I've never been so at odds with him in any of my lives.

How do I stir a wolf that wants to die and isn't allowed to? He and I are one. If he dies, I die. There is no in-between. He can't have it both ways, no matter how much I wish he could. More than anything, I feel terrible for wanting to give him what he wants. His emotions and trying to live with himself are suffocating and choke me right where my voice box should remain constriction free. But I can't give in to him. Not when there's hope, and that hope rests on a witch's shoulders. I have to find a way to make her aware of it.

A whole new level of rage boils my blood. If only I could use that rage to heat myself. I begin to blame my wolf. While he's dealing with his emotions, I'm dealing with the very real possibility of a second death. A circumstance I refuse to let happen.

Damn it – if he'd grow a pair, I'd be able to shift and save myself from all of this. From being . . . absolutely nothing. I shouldn't blame him. But in this moment, as I dream of warm fires and hot food, I am.

Footsteps echo through the cells, the soundwaves coming from the tunnels that lead to the main floor. Voices follow, along with pleas from the other cells somewhere down here, but the new-comers are still far enough away that I can't make out the words.

I slam my fist against the stone beneath me. It's frustrating, being this helpless.

# CHAPTER THREE

*TEMBER*

*DREAM REALM*

Bustling is an understatement. No words are spoken between each roaming Sandman as they walk through the newly-formed archway. They pass us with determination, heading back the way from which we came. There is an abundance of them, and we're left with no choice but to scoot out of their way, hugging the wall while continuing to make our way to our destination.

Their skin is as dark as night, camouflaging them with their realm, and their eyes are as luminescent as the twinkling specks of dust. The prominent muscles lining their faces are relaxed, void of curiosity and passion, precisely as they were designed. I envy them.

I tilt my head, speculating, watching them continue down the tunnel. They're silent, like a predator, but they're anything but. I'd wager they're the prey - the prey of their creator, forever bound to do her bidding.

It is said Sureen draws her magic from the conjuring of dreams. The sandmen deliver the dreams in the form of dust to those who sleep, and it finds its way back, feeding her. I don't understand the logistics, and I'm not sure I want to. The images that float through a human brain during a sleeping state travel back to this realm. That is all I know. It is not a lot of power in which dreams deliver back to Sureen, but it's enough to keep her afloat I imagine.

The sandmen don't care that we're here. If an enemy came onto the Angel's Ground on the guardian realm, a swarm would be escorting them and inquiring why they're there. We protect our realm, our creator, and our kind. Not all but some.

Through the archway, huddled along the walls, short men use the smallest of chisels to gently scrape away the flecks of dust. Their height does not reach my breast, but their build is impressive. There are areas where the specks of sparkling dust have been fully removed.

While some gather the dust, others use large chiseling axes to chip away at the Inferaze, piling the chunks in the middle of the tunnel walkway. That answers my earlier question: there is a purpose for Inferaze if it's being chipped and gathered.

Large rusted machines, the size of boulders and in the form of butterflies with their backs in the shape of a scoop, pick up the rocks. Their wings remain in an expanded position, and once they're manually loaded, one short male presses a button, and a blue flame, almost clear, exits the bottom of the expanded metal wings. A rush of heat carries our direction, the temperature smoldering, along with the scent of burning sage. The machine lifts, hovering above the ground, and jets forward, traveling down the large tunnel with its load, rounding a curve and disappearing from sight.

We step through another arch, continuing this new path while my mind soaks additional knowledge and observations, compartmentalizing and categorizing. I've never been here before. I've never had a reason to enter this realm.

"Interesting," I whisper to myself. I sidestep a haphazard pile, trying to keep my uneasy, churning stomach at bay. It flip-flops like a fish stuck on a sandbank. I have a terrible feeling, and I can't seem to shake it. Every part of me wants to turn around, to go back the direction from which we came, and not enter this tunnel which will surely lead us to the Dream Queen herself.

I care for Kat, and I want this spell to be lifted from her, but something about this plan feels off. A sense of dread overcomes me, threatening to halt my determination. I want to rip Kat from Corbin's arms and run. Perhaps it's due to my unease, based off the platform of the unknown.

My stride falls silent as I watch the short men mining this section of the cave. Each fragment floats in slow motion until it settles inside the burlap bag another holds, and each soundwave from the swing and connection of axe is absorbed by the walls. They sweat, they grunt, but it's far quieter than it should be. The walls are the gravity.

The fascination of the Inferaze diminishes, replaced by a new object to study. "They're Dwarves," I whisper, slowing my pace.

Comparable to the guardian realm, I knew other creations roamed the realms, but witnessing it first-hand piques my never-ending curiosity. We were Erma's second creations, taught abundantly in wisdom of the realms, however, not to the extent I had previously assumed. Creatures of other realms were part of our studies, but that was a long time ago for me. Perhaps the knowledge has been forgotten or evaporated until now.

The four tribes of elves were Erma's first creations. Built for the same purpose as angels, they protect the grounds of her realm but nothing more.

As Erma and Erline's relationship blossomed into true sisterhood, Erma wanted the elves to assist in protecting Erline's realm. She had approached the elves to provide it, but they had refused and still do. They have no wish to leave our realm and their home.

No matter how much she begged, she didn't wish to strip them of their will. Upon their refusal, Erma had no choice but to create more creatures: the angels. That choice was a double-edged knife, and Erma has been paying for it ever since.

A dwarf catches my eye, observing me with the same white, sparkling orbs the sandmen have, but larger, more rounded and disproportionate to his smaller, yet square and bulky features.

His lips thin into a fine line as he observes me, his eyes roaming my body, my make, with such wisdom. I swallow as he looks to my shoulders, searching for my wings. He knows what I am.

Wrinkles line his pale forehead, bunching his bushy eyebrows. His partner nudges him after briefly glancing at us, reminding him to keep focused on the task before him.

Dwarfs' strength is in their hands and brute force as well as their minds. They're sharp thinkers and obsessive inventors. Constant recalculations, for minimal effort versus maximum impact, describe them best.

For a moment, I wonder why they chisel by hand – why they haven't invented an easier way to extract the dust. Perhaps the sleep dust must be removed with care.

They're loyal to their work; this much is clear, but I wonder how loyal they are to their creator. They work as a team, as one unit, a family of sorts. One chisels, one catches the dust. They care for one another, and I wonder how. Love is an emotion. Perhaps working in such close proximity to the dream dust allows them to find the strength for loyalty and morals. After all, Sandmen are loyal to their charges.

The dwarf's hands are as small as a child's but thick with muscles roping up their arms. Every inch of his shirtless torso is lined with exaggerated strength. His brown hair is long, tied back at the nape with straps of leather, and his skin is white as snow due to lack of UV rays.

"They mine these?" I ask, the question obvious, but the need to fill the silence is intense.

Erma, who has stopped ahead, turns her body toward me. She closes her eyes in a brief blink of affirmation. Her long, red eyelashes fan her cheekbones, and I study her instead. She opens them, and we study one another, holding our ground in a silent battle of will and unvoiced communication. I look away, my jaw ticking as I remember my place, and I force myself to think of something else.

"How do the dwarves not hallucinate?" I ask, walking back to Erma while averting my focus from her.

"Dwarves were made for this and only this," Erline answers.

I chuff.

Erma's teeth snap together, her nostrils flaring as she reaches the end of her patience. "Everyone is a slave, Tember. It's just a matter of who or what is the master. No one is free. Not even from themselves." Her voice drops an octave to a deadly hiss. "Not even you."

## AIDEN VANDER

## THE VOID

If I could cry, I would. My tear ducts aren't too proud. I don't have any. There's no bravado necessary to keep up my image when there's no one to impress.

My mind, or what is left of it, conjures brief memories of Eliza and rotates through them like a restless TV scanner. She was my everything, even with the short time we had together.

In my mind's eye, her hair floats around her head unnaturally, waving in a non-existent breeze like a flag on a pole, obscuring her features from my desperate eyes. Her face is pinched, eyes closed, but her image is blurred like a cartoon picture colored outside the lines by a careless hand. Something blue crackles along her skin - lightning, her body the center of a thunderstorm. It confuses me, and I try to grasp what my mind summons to save this distorted memory, to allow me a sliver of comfort.

The picture of her face reverses and changes. The blue electric tracery along her skin disappear, and her waving red hair stills. She opens her eyes. I can make out her tiny button nose and liquid green irises that sparkle with an underlying wit she tries to hide.

There is a crumbling, unidentifiable, stone wall behind her, and black smoke trickles in the picture, swirling in puffs traveling closer until it, too, pauses just as her hair. I can almost smell the smoke.

I panic. *What's happening?*

Her face still moves, her eyes searching mine. She attempts a smile, but before it can reach past her teeth, it fades, deteriorating to a frown. Those eyes that have captured mine widen, fearful. I break inside. I died, gave my life to make sure she'd hold no fear. I sacrificed myself, to save her. I don't want her to be scared.

Her lips move, but no sound comes out. The slight laugh lines at the edge of her cheekbones relax, her skin angelic, precisely as I remember. But she's frightened, the sparkle within her eyes gaining the moisture of tears, and her lips move faster. She's worried. Why? She's safe. Right?

The prickling, tingling torment intensifies. I'm nothing, but I feel a tugging sensation. A yanking around me, a sudden, unexplainable pull, until my body is ablaze.

*My body.* My body.

Is this my new torture? A level of hell I haven't reached yet, tormenting me by dangling the memory of touch?

Pain worth a thousand licking flames seeps through me. Heat courses along my veins, lines my organs as they solidify and reform. I feel it. I feel their regrowth. It's slow, sluggish, taking its time in a whole new bane.

Thick, hot goop surrounds me, threatening to pull me further inside its depths. One minute I'm floating, and the next, heavy heat engulfs me. My leg muscles quiver and twitch, and I seize the moment, whatever this moment may be, and kick with all the force I can muster.

My head breaks free of a surface, the searing-hot liquid sliding down my cheeks and spilling inside my mouth. I take a large gulp of air before this pit swallows me again.

*What is this?*

As my head goes below the liquid once more, I thrash my arms side to side, desperate to remain afloat. Emotions I once had surface, one by one. Each time they do, they leave me, winking out of my body before I can even name them, until I feel nothing. No love. No sorrow. Nothing, besides the need for survival.

With everything I have, I kick once more, my arms forcing the goop down while I push for another breath. The possibility of self-preservation drives me.

This time, I hear my inhale. Like a drowning man, the gulp of oxygen is a gasp of relief to my burning lungs. Blindly, my hand reaches out in front of me, searching for an object to hold me afloat.

Something firm, hard, grasps my hand, yanking me from this pool that drags me under. I'm lifted in the air as though I weigh nothing but a feather. The goop drips from my toes before I'm placed on my feet.

"Aiden Vander," a voice rumbles in front of me, holding my hand until I regain balance.

Swallowing, confused and desperate, I slowly open my eyes, seeing nothing but black. My eyelids flutter, blinking rapidly, expelling the goop that keeps me blind. Images, objects, and the person standing in front of me, come to light, taking shape, and confusing me further.

The creature before me releases my hand, and my eyes jerk to my newly reformed fingers outstretched in front of me. I still look like me – the knuckles are the same thickness, and the curve of my nails are exactly as I remember. I twist it, checking for abnormalities, testing how real this is.

*This can't be real.*

The goop coating my skin is black. It slides off, dripping and splatting to the ground, but I don't hear it hit. I'm too absorbed in the wonder of this impossibility.

I lower my hand and look around. "Where am I?" I mumble, my voice deeper, darker, void of emotion. I don't recognize it, but I don't fear it. Fear isn't an emotion I can call upon anymore, even if I tried.

I'm standing on what looks to be black flowing lava, orange glowing veins slithering throughout the endless, dark body of liquid. When the veins reach the surface, they break and pop, creating a small puff of smoke which floats and raises in the air. It reaches my nose, the aroma as thick as the contents, and the smell of sulfur coats my tongue as it passes through on its way to my lungs. The black lava is like a river, held in by cliffs on both sides. Waterfalls . . . lavafalls trickle from the cliffs, sluggishly slipping back into the main body.

No one else is around. No one except this man . . . this thing before me, and the flaming black pits that make this landscape.

I turn back to him, and he smiles, a wicked, mischievous grin that would curl the toes of an innocent. I know I should care what his plans are; I know he's up to no good. But the only thing filling me is . . . nothing.

He doesn't answer my question, possibly thinking it obvious. "Aiden Vander," he repeats. "The Thrice Born."

His words are slurred, his lips moving carefully over rows of sharp, pointed teeth. Skin, sagging and shredded, hangs from each bone on his body, like fragments of a tattered t-shirt. His left cheek is missing altogether, showing the expanse of the razors inside his mouth. A black hole exists where his right eye should be. No clothes cover his body to hide the sight that would turn any stomach and leave nothing to the imagination.

"Who are you?" My voice is automatic, robotic, and careless. I only wish to know if he's friend or foe.

The skin along his rotting-flesh arms flaps as he folds them behind his back. He hunches his shoulders, sagging toward me. "Power is within a name. A demon never speaks his name." He narrows his eye. "I am a demon of Corbin, the fee of this realm. You, Thrice Born . . . You will be his ultimate weapon – his first experiment of many."

"Weapon?"

He slants his head, jutting his chin to the side, and the wicked smile returns. "Are you ready to serve, Demon?"

Demon? Is that what I am? Is that what this is? This is hell. This is the Demon Realm.

I nod my head, no care for my well-being or of what is to come for me.

"Good," he laughs, the sound like a child shrilling. "Follow me."

He walks past me, and I swivel on the balls of my feet, following him to his destination.

"Corbin will be along shortly. His plans are mighty."

# CHAPTER FOUR

*ELIZA PLAATS*

*DEATH REALM*

Rounding the corner from the kitchen, I walk the short distance to the obscenely large formal dining area, a tray made of bones balancing in my hands with a goblet of black, shimmering oil placed atop.

As the goblet teeters, my nostrils flare, the smell rolling my stomach. It's not that oil bothers me. It's the fact that it's held within a cup, its purpose to slide past crude lips and be swallowed by a man who deserves the worst of deaths.

My jaw snaps closed at the notion of him calling me his queen one more time, a whole new wave of revulsion.

There's nothing formal about this large room. Some sort of dust webs cling to the high ceilings and the large candlelight fixture dangling over the table. A stone, round table sits in the middle, surrounded by chairs made of bones like the tray in my hands.

I've been through the entire Keep. There aren't any pictures on the walls, and much to my dismay, there's nothing to show that this fee has any soul or a sliver of care for love or life. A small part of me hoped there would be. Maybe, if there was any insight from this man I'm to marry, I could somehow find a way to understand him since I'm to spend eternity at his beck and call.

Instead of mementos, candles line the walls, sporadic and out of order, with flickering flames lit on their tops. A large fireplace, made of crumbling, white bricks, is embedded against one wall, though it doesn't look like it's ever been used. Kheelan prefers the cold, just as his soul. Black rocks sit inside, and I've often wondered why? Is it décor?

Shifting my shoulders, I attempt to relieve an itch from the tag along my neck. I'm still dressed in the scrubs I was wearing when I died not too long ago. Though it seems ages, it has, in fact, only been a few days. I've aged far beyond my years since the day the train hit my car, and I've been through more than I deserve since I've died. Life isn't fair. Even a second life isn't any better.

My mother is held prisoner below, my lover is gone forever, leaving my heart in shattered pieces within my chest, and his mother is held captive with mine. The man, who was forced to deliver my lover's death, rots below my feet. In my eyes, it's a small victory – a small repayment for the debt the murderer owes me. But, he and I have

43

something in common. Kheelan forced us to remain human.

I wonder what's going through Dyson's head, locked below with no one to talk to. I wonder what that's like - to feel. I wouldn't know. Numbness creeps through my body, betraying everything I am with a chemical my glands produce, an anesthetic to emotions. I know what this is – the stages of grief - but I'm powerless to control or stop it.

My gait slows as I reach the round table, Kheelan watching my every step with his hands clasped and folded under his chin. A small smirk plays against his harsh, thin lips. He's enjoying the fact that I have no wish to be anywhere near him – to have anything to do with the man, the fee, who holds me captive. When he calls me his queen, I hold back a gag. I belong to him, and he knows it, choosing to torment me with a title I want no part in. I'm human now; my heart beats. Humans don't belong with the dead. Humans should never wed a fee.

His smile widens, more forced, as he reads my thoughts. I keep eye contact, refusing to show how much hatred is held within the chambers of my heart. I relish this emotion. It's true, one I can trust in this shell which I've become.

"Sweet Eliza," he sugar-coats. "There's no need for such hostility. Come. Bring me my beverage."

I swallow, glancing at the goblet rocking against the uneven surface that makes the bone tray. The shimmering black contents bubble with each sickening slosh. I don't know why he drinks this stuff. Does he enjoy the taste? Or does he enjoy how much it nauseates me? My stomach rolls, and I gag.

Setting the tray down in front of him, I take a step back and fold my arms behind my back. He eyes my skin and the goosebumps that've been tattooed there since my new transformation back to the living.

His jaw ticks, his smile fading like a ghost in the night. "You'll have to excuse my ignorance and insensitivity. I'm not used to the company of those who feel cold."

One of the folded hands under his chin snaps, sending a bolt of blue electricity from his fingertips to the charred, black rock within the fireplace. He resettles his hand, propping his head once more. I barely notice the movement, my gaze on the fire instead.

I've never seen rock like this, especially rock which ignites. It engulfs in flames, the tips of each flame black mixed with bright blue. It sends a blast of warmth throughout the room. I scowl and bite my bottom lip, expecting black smoke to travel up the chimney, but no smoke comes from the unnatural fire.

"Inferaze," Kheelan comments, following my gaze. "Useful rock. Extremely explosive."

With a delicate hand, he swiftly reaches forward, causing me to jump, and grasps my bare wrist. "Your thoughts are unkind, Eliza. Shield them when you're around me. I won't tolerate insubordination from my queen much longer."

My nostrils flare, and my top lip twitches. "I wouldn't be disobedient if it weren't for you uprooting my life and sending my thoughts into chaos. You're a cruel man, one for whom I feel nothing but disdain, forcing judgements to cross my mind." I quiet my voice. "I will never be your queen."

I yank my wrist from his grasp while he uses his free hand to grip the goblet, bringing the oil to his lips. With a content sigh, he slurps a sip.

"Then perhaps, you should watch the company you keep, young one."

Curling my fingers into my palm, I straighten my spine and blurt my next words. "What company? The company you slaughtered? Or the ones held in eternal prison? Do you think I chose this? Do you honestly think this is what I asked for?"

The oil leaves behind a stain on his top lip, his tongue snaking out to capture a drop before it dribbles on his black robe.

A chill runs up my spine.

He smacks his lips, savoring the flavor. "Of course not. No one asks for death." His tone is chipper and misplaced for such a retort. "No one is in control of what happens to their fate. I know this as well as you. I have, in fact, lived for a long time, learning such insignificant lessons you mortals deal with."

"Then why do you keep me here?"

He twirls a finger over the rim of his glass goblet. "To remind you, to remind them – the rebellion that's rising to uproot me from my very throne – that I am in charge. I can choose what happens to you, what happens to them, because this is my realm." His fingers curl tighter around the spine of the goblet, the whites of his knuckles straining against the bones beneath the skin's surface. "They dwell here by my say so. They walk that stone because I, and only I, wish it. They, and you, have no say."

Kheelan lifts his eyes to mine, one brow quirked in challenge, begging for me to retort.

A soulless man hovers inside those black eyes. There's no mask that hides his true nature. It's right there, open for display, leaving the person who stares back in them lost, afraid, and unsure of what he'll do next. He's a man without morals. A man without a little voice in his head that screams when he's tipped the scale to an unusual amount of unjustifiable cruelty.

I internally sigh. The scale doesn't tip. It's superglued to one side, cemented there . . . forever in his favor.

He continues, his tone a deep, deadly rumble, "I will do with you as I please. If I want to scrape the skin, inch by inch, from your bones with the dullest knife I can conjure, I will. I'll watch the blood drip from your exposed muscle and puddle along the floor in a river of red. If I want to deliver a treat to my vampires, I'll stick a bow on your forehead, and let them suckle from your neck. If I want to kill your boyfriend for my own entertainment and pleasure, I will. You have no choice. You have no say. This is no longer your life." He reclines into his chair. "Best you grow accustomed to it, my queen."

I swallow a thick lump inside my throat, my hands uncurling from my palms. "May I go?" I whisper.

"No." He takes another sip.

Ticking my jaw, I watch him with disgust. He slurps obnoxiously, knowing it'll make me gag, and this time, I can't hold it back. I turn my back to him and away from the revolting sight he portrays, bending over with my hands gripping my thighs. Dry heaves arch my back and buckle my knees.

Kheelan chuckles like a chirping hyena. "Yaris," he beckons.

I wipe the spit from my mouth, a wave of exhaustion sagging my shoulders. With reluctance, I swivel around.

Faster than my human eyes can register, a figure blurs into the room and halts on Kheelan's left side, opposite of me. A gust of wind follows, tickling my hair. Yaris, Kheelan's vampire assistant, folds his hands in front of him. His arms are veined with black ropes beneath skin so white, it's almost translucent.

"Sir," he acknowledges, his deep red eyes lifting to mine. His gaze wanders my body and halts on my hammering pulse against my neck. I recall Kheelan's earlier threat, and I gulp, worried that this summoning of his minion is deliverance.

Swallowing with what I can only imagine is intense thirst, Yaris manages to lift his blood-red eyes to mine. A weird thought crosses my mind. *Does it hurt to be forever hungry?*

I panic inside. Kheelan gave him no permission to touch me, to drink from me, yet I can feel how hungry he is, thick in the air of this stuffy, dusty dining room. It's a predator stalking a cornered prey. My heart quickens with erratic beats, adrenaline releasing and coursing through my body, pinpricking my eyes with unshed tears.

"Bring her in," Kheelan mumbles, waving his free hand in the air.

Yaris disappears the way he came, his speed ruffling the ends of Kheelan's long, greasy, black hair. I blink hard, confusion temporarily lifting the curse of anxiety.

"Bring who?"

Spinning a falsely puzzled expression to me, he replies with innocence, "Didn't I tell you? I found a companion for you. Humans need a support system I've learned. I'm sure you know her. You could use some friends since you refuse to visit the one in the dungeon."

"Dyson isn't my friend," I snarl, nostrils flared.

"No?" Kheelan presses. "You wish him death?"

"Well," I whisper, fidgeting and twisting away. "No."

For several seconds, he's quiet, watching me as my anxiety builds under his gaze. "Curious. Very curious."

I close my eyes and pinch the bridge of my nose, a headache forming behind them. "What is?"

He pauses for dramatic effect. "You oversee feeding poor Dyson. Of giving him sustenance. Yet you haven't since he was placed there. You starve him." He slopes his head. "Do you do so in punishment?"

I don't answer him.

"Ah, I see." He lifts himself from his stone dining chair. Coming to stand beside me, he rests his rump on the solid table. "How does this make you any different than me, sweet Eliza? To starve a man for revenge?" He tsks. "I believe you're well on your way to becoming the very thing you despise."

"I will never be anything like you," I force out between clenched teeth. How dare he suggest otherwise. "Dyson killed the man I love."

He slants his head back and releases a boisterous laugh, which reverberates throughout the room. "Eyesight matters not. You, Eliza, are a blind woman. Grudges are becoming on you."

Our conversation is interrupted when a throat hums behind us, a false cough.

"Sir?"

We turn. A woman stands beside Yaris, her fiddling with each of her fingers, pulling them at the knuckles. I gasp, my heart breaking once more.

I knew she'd be here as well as all of those involved with death after being placed on my surgical table. But seeing her transparent and dead, yet here, right in front of me, seizes the breath in my lungs with painful pressure. It compliments my inner turmoil so well.

I want to run. I want to apologize. I want to beg for forgiveness. I convinced her to undergo that surgery; I told her she needed it. I'm the reason she's here.

"Mrs. Tiller," I breathe, and a wave of numbness crawls across my skin.

Dressed in a hospital gown, like so many other shades in the death realm, she fidgets with the seam at the collar.

"What...," she begins in surprise. "What's going on. Dr. Plaats? What are you doing here?"

Kheelan claps his hands together like a delighted toddler. "How wonderful. You two do know each other. Do tell. How did you meet?"

I eye Kheelan, wanting to throw curses his direction, but I know he won't drop the subject until I answer verbally. He did this on purpose. He knew who she was, what her presence would do to me.

"I killed her, but you already knew that."

His hand flies to his chest, hovering where his heart should be with false surprise. "The sweet Eliza, the Eliza who does no wrong, killed a human?"

"Yes," I answer, squaring my shoulders and directing my attention back to Mrs. Tiller. "I'm here because I'm being punished."

Mrs. Tiller, Wanda, stutters before her lips force the words from her mouth. "Punished for what?"

My manners fly out the non-existent window, my emotions raw, exposed, and painful. I hurl them at Kheelan in the form of words before I fully consider the possible complications. "For knowing the wrong people. For being in the wrong place at the wrong time. For loving a man who was dead. You'll have to ask King of Death over here." I flick my thumb in his direction. "His majesty is all about torture for fun, emotional or otherwise."

A flash of light comes from the corner of my eye, and unimaginable pain overtakes my body. It hits me in my shoulder, spiderwebbing like a cracked windshield. At first, my brain doesn't understand what's happening. The intensity, the sensation, is controlling, rippling a surge of shocking heat to every extremity with no place to exit. I remain its slave, its unwilling victim, even as I drop to the floor.

My eyes are forced to remain open. The ceiling is the only object I see, and I mentally grasp it, desperate to anchor myself, to keep me from descending into darkness.

Electric bolts zap their way across my skin, seeping into my bones like a sponge soaking water, cracking my joints. My thoughts seize. The only thing controlling my mind is how to extinguish the pain, to make it go away. Grunts hoarse my throat and leave my lips of their own accord, foam forming at the corners of my mouth. I convulse, the back of my head repeatedly slamming against the floor.

And then it stops, my skin prickling due to chills, to the freedom of blissful relief. I'm left in a puddle of my own sweat, and my heart is pounding in my ears like bunny's feet stomping against a forest floor. I pant for air, blinking repeatedly to clear the tears clouding my vision. They spill from my lids, trailing cool paths along my heated cheeks before dripping in the hollows of my ears.

Kheelan rests against the table, sipping his goblet of black. His face twists, his mouth pinching toward his nose. Such anger . . . such malice . . . such vengeance. His hand flares with another round of bolts, and he flicks his wrist.

I scream, watching the blue lines head my direction once more, feeling the pain ripple all over again. It doesn't last as long as it did the first time, and for that, I allow myself a small amount of relief when he finally releases me from his torture.

Mrs. Tiller weeps beside the vampire, her plump, transparent hand covering her mouth. Her pinched eyes roam my face, her cheeks flushed. Genuine concern for my well-being has replaced her previous slight animosity and sense of betrayal.

"Did you not hear me before, sweet Eliza?" Kheelan coos. He sets the goblet on the table behind him and grasps the front of his robe. Bending his knees, he lowers himself to the ground, looming over me. "When I told you I owned you?" He quiets his voice so only I may hear. "Disrespect me again – cross me again – and I'll call your heart to me. It'll rip from your chest so it hovers in front of you as it beats for the very last time. You'll feel your life ending. You'll feel the spirit fading from your body, leaving you nothing but a shell. You'll be unable to control it, begging me to save you. But I won't, sweet girl. I'll watch as the light leaves your eyes. Your fear, your sense of betrayal, will be my reward. Then, and only then, can you truly join your lover in a place where nothing exists."

I manage to narrow my eyes. A tingling sensation trailing along my skin is the lasting reminder of this threat, driving home his point.

He stands and props himself back against the table. "Get up. Mrs. Tiller is your responsibility. Show her around, teach her what she needs to know. And feed the prisoner if you so choose."

# CHAPTER FIVE

*DYSON COLEMAN*

*DEATH REALM*

I shimmy my bare rear across the floor to get a better look at the newcomer. The skin snags on a few cracks etched in the stone, but the cold has numbed the skin.

This is becoming a habit lately. They've been bringing in shades who were involved with the rebellion. I'm guessing Kheelan read who was involved when he probed my mind. I wonder what these new prisoners told them. Did they flake and tattle? Or did they keep quiet so the undiscovered shades could continue in their absence?

I guess it doesn't matter. It's not like I can do anything about the rebellion or what happens to me while I'm stuck here. Chances are, I won't live long enough to see what happens next.

The vampires don't dare allow them a cell next to mine. In fact, they pretend I don't exist. It's a good tactic – uprooting my norm and replacing it with total silence and darkness. Not to mention the babbling crazy shade next to me. I'm sure they believe I'll turn out to be exactly like him. I suppose if the dripping water continues, I will be.

I prepare myself for the vampires to lead them further into the tunnels where I'm sure they have Jane and Tanya stored like grandma's little nick knacks inside a dusty glass cabinet, forever forgotten.

My new home is the section of eternal punishment. Should that give me hope? That Gan and I are the only ones in here, the only ones meant to rot to the end of time? Jane and Tanya could be set free someday, along with the rest of the rebellion. They could continue our work, without me. Why doesn't that give me hope?

As I'm wallowing in self-pity, sure the new arrivers will turn left once their torches come into view, they don't. Shocked, I scoot closer to the bars, my frozen cheeks almost pressed against their cold surface. I wipe my dribbling nose with the back of my hand.

A tall man, transparent as the rest of the shades, enters between two vampires. He dwarfs them, and even with the flames dancing on the tips of the torches, his skin is so dark I can barely make him out. It's as though he's a shadow. If it weren't for his clothes and strange white eyes, I'd never see him.

They walk past me, and a vampire kicks out his foot, striking the bars next to my cheek. My head snaps back as a reflex as the bars crackle with energy from the assault, ringing my ears. I narrow my eyes, wanting to lash back, but know it won't do any good. I still have fight left in me.

Their footfalls halt at the cell directly next to mine. I lower my head back in their direction, holding my breath in case this is a mistake, in case they're doing this to toy with me by dangling this man in front of me like a thanksgiving feast to a starving man.

Conversation – any conversation – will do.

## KATRIANE DUPONT

## THE PAST

My legs wobble like flexing rubber as I'm escorted from below the gallows and begin the march of death to the wooden stairs. A group circles me, crowds me, shouts in my ears until they ring.

"No. No please. You don't understand," I plead with the man dragging me along by the elbow. He won't listen to me. It's as if I'm not even here. Like he's running on autopilot and I'm a simple girl begging her daddy for candy one too many times. My pleas fall on deaf ears and a black heart.

Spittle hits my neck, leaving the curled lips of an angry mob, their voices curdling my insides. So much hate in their words, so much disdain. They don't even know me. I doubt they know my name, where I came from, that I'm somebody's somebody.

I pull against the ropes bound around my wrists. The strands cut into the skin, leaving painful slivers behind. A drop of blood falls and hits my bare foot mid-stride, chilling the skin as the cold breeze tickles it. They took my shoes from me, forcing me to walk in shame, to feel low. It's working.

A hot tear trails down my cheek, and I attempt to wipe it with my shoulder.

My voice cracks as I shout at the group gathered for my death. "I'm not supposed to be here!"

The man ahead of me spins on the balls of his feet, a blank look on his face. "You are exactly where the devil's child is meant to be." He swivels to a man beside him. "Where is Gandalf?"

His friend shrugs, shouting over the voices. "I haven't seen him all day."

My escort nods, his lips pursing as though he sucked on a lemon. "Find him."

Obeying, the dutiful friend twists, lifting his foot and picking up to a jog. He disappears into the crowd as they part for him.

It's not as though I expected anyone to put a stop to this. I can almost feel how much this is feeding them and their black souls.

Hot blood drips from my wrists down to my pinky finger, the heat against my freezing skin stealing a moment of focus.

My elbow is yanked once more. He drags me up the small flight of stairs, and I resist, veering back and using my weight to slow our advance. He tugs again, and I stumble, my knee hitting the edge of the last wooden step with a pop as the joint gives way. Adrenaline chases away the pain.

The noose dangles in the slight breeze, it's presence forces imagery of my body sagging from it, lifeless, a shell. It'd be almost pretty, the way it sways, conducted by the wind, if it weren't the symbol of death.

Torches are placed around the platform like a theatrical stage waiting for the show to begin. A spotlight, a beacon to my last performance.

I swallow as I come to the realization that it's their show – the crowd gathered around, waiting for the next death to unfold before their eyes. They can't get enough of sick and twisted entertainment. It's the beginning of the era – the era of death and destruction for all those who practice – or are believed to practice – witchcraft. They have no idea the damage they're about to cause, the ripple they've placed in time.

The man who spat his words in my face isn't wrong – he's only misinformed. I'm not the devil's child. I'm the granddaughter of the King of the dead, the Fee of the Death Realm. And I'm so, so much more than that. I'm related to the very fee who turned vampire's loose on their village. At this moment, I don't feel guilty about it, wishing instead that I had my own hoard of blood-thirsty creatures to unleash.

"Please," I beg, my tone pitiful.

My will to stay alive multiplies with each step across the cracking, wood planks. They creak under my feet, under the weight, like drums sounding for a climax in an epic film.

Burning my insides, my internal fire swirls as the dragon half of me threatens to surface. I'm relieved to feel it still there, molded with me as one like Myla . . . But as I watch the dangling rope getting ever so close, metaphorical ice water douses my sense of relief. It doesn't matter that the dragon is still within me – doesn't matter that Myla left a part of herself behind so I may pick up the pieces. There will be no pieces left to pick up. I'll be dead. The dead can't do much, and I can't change history.

A chuckle rumbles inside the leader's chest as he watches the color drain from my cheeks and pushes me toward the center of the platform. I trip on a nail poking from the board and stumble, losing my footing.

Surrounded by all of these people, their voices screaming above the other sounds of the night, I feel like a mouse cornered in an alleyway by a starving, stray cat.

There's nowhere for me to go. There is no escape. If I tried, people would die, and the future would change. The damage that would cause is far worse than a single death.

He places his hands on my shoulders, his nails digging into my skin, and swivels me to face the crowd. Behind me, someone slips a rope over my head, snagging his rough and cracked skin on a few strands of my short hair.

The rope is thick and coarse, scratching along the skin of my cheekbones before it settles over my collar, heavy and foreboding. The knot resting against the nape of my neck is substantial, forcing me back and straining my muscles along my spine.

The man before me turns, showing me his backside. I'm no threat to him – that's how he sees me. Outrage coils in my stomach, his lack of respect as chafing as the rope.

*Oh, what I could do to him if only I choose to.* I could make him beg for mercy, make him wish he was never born. I could light him on fire and watch the village burn while I stand on his ashes.

He lifts his hands in the air, palms facing out, and announces to the crowd, "Let this be a message to all those dealing with the Devil. Witches are not welcome."

The crowd erupts in cheers and the wind along with it. It tickles the inside of my ear, every sense hyper-aware. Smells of burning oils, the spice of dead leaves, the stench of human body odor – all sharpened. The little things I've dismissed all my life, or simply overlooked, call my attention, begging for one last look - one last whiff. The blood pumps in my ears, dulling the sounds around me so that all I hear is the beat and my breath.

"We will scrape through every home, every corner, every unholy citizen, and we will rid this town of those who wish to plague us."

He gazes at me from over his shoulder, a wicked smile crossing his lips and exposing teeth that have never seen a tooth brush.

"Le diable n'est pas le bienvenu ici," he growls.

I snarl like a rabid dog for being called something I am not. *Maybe I should show you who the devil is, buddy.*


## *TEMBER*

## *DREAM REALM*


The end of the tunnel is near, the archway to an open space is feet ahead. Corbin strides through first and continues, but the rest of us stop. It is clear that he has been here before, completely unaffected by the sight before us.

Sandmen and dwarves roam, weaving through a large expanding forest of . . .

"Willow trees?" I murmur, tilting my head. It's a whole forest of them, but they're different than what I've grown to expect from them.

Corbin turns his head over his shoulder, the stubble of hair scratching against the cloth of his shirt. "Incubators," he corrects.

The cave reaches up, a night sky captured in another realm, and deep yellow clouds like northern lights twist and spiral around each spike. The butterfly machines zip through the trees, some even hovering in the air, as though they're real creatures with physical minds.

The incubator trees and the path crawling between them pulse with a white light. In the center of the open cave, a large, glowing dome sustains these veins, acting as the heart of their life. Occasionally, and at random, the yellow auroras dip and caress the dome before the walls absorb them.

"Sureen has been busy," Erma mumbles.

Erline turns her body, reaching out and touching a vine of the willow incubator with a careful stroke. Her fingers travel down, running the length of a glowing, pulsing, crystal leaf. "It would seem so," she replies.

"This is life," I mumble. "She's creating life."

"Not yet," Erline whispers, releasing the crystal leaf and crossing her arms. The smallest of smiles raises at the corner of her lips, and she raises her voice. "The dome is the only thing feeding it. These creatures do not hold hearts. If the dome was destroyed, the same would happen to everything it built." She unfolds one arm and points to the yellow auroras. "Those are dreams, absorbed from my realm, waiting to feed that dome."

I study the dome. It looks oddly like a half moon, holding the attention of everything else in the large expanse of a cave. Gears turn, running it, the grind audible but not echoing like it should. I don't see the gears, but I can hear them. Perhaps they're underground?

"Where do we find her?" I ask.

Ahead, Corbin waits, adjusting Kat inside his arms, and a look of frustration crosses his face.

Erma points. "Inside the dome."

I sidestep as a dwarf hobbles past me, leather satchels gathered in his arms. Erma starts walking first, and the rest of us follow, distracted by the objects and creatures milling about.

Passing a handful of willows, a moan causes me to pause. I twist to the noise, curious, coming face to face with the vines of the willow. Using both hands to separate the curtain of branches, I walk through. The tinkling of crystal leaves clink together as it closes behind me.

The trunk of the tree is made of roughly sculptured Inferaze, exactly as the ground below me. The pulsing veins crawl up, weaving between the protruding rocks. In the middle of the trunk, a jagged, oval opening is carved, and a face rests inside it. I gasp and slowly shuffle closer.

Erline enters and stops beside me. She reaches and strokes the black skin of the creature encased inside.

"That's a sandman," I whisper.

Erline ignores me, caressing the man's cheek one more time. Her movements are slow and deliberate, such passion behind a touch. He sags against her touch, his eyes closed and pinched with pain.

"So that's how she does it," Erline mumbles to herself.

"Does what?" I growl, furious that this man, this sandman, is imprisoned inside.

"That is what Corbin meant by incubator. This is how she creates the sandmen." She shimmies back, looking the tree up and down. "She plants them inside the willows."

"Plants them?" I ask, a chuckle to my tone. "Where would she get the seed for each new growth?"

Erline looks around, her eyes landing on the crystal leaves. "Those," she points. "The trees are her womb, the crystal the seed. The veins and dome are what feed it, and the aurora of dreams are what feed them. It's a cycle." She lowers her voice. "A beautiful cycle."

I turn to face her. Her arms are crossed as she watches the tree.

"He's in pain –"

She rolls her eyes, the action against her normal composure. "He'll be fine, Tember. He's not being tortured inside there. His body is being built and constructed to that of his make."

"Yes," I grumble with dripping sarcasm. My fingers tightening into fists at my side. "He sure looks fine to me."

"If you women are done with the circle of absent life, I'd like to continue," Corbin exclaims on the other side of the vines. His tone is utterly bored, his patience dampening. "I have other concerns to attend to today, aside from saving a damsel in distress."

I open the curtain of vines and crystals, holding it for Erline before I follow her through.

Erline spins to him. "You should have never come."

"And yet, here I stand. Kat's knight in shining armor." A smirk plays at his lips.

He huffs when she doesn't play along. "Reason, Erline. You need me, or you would have never beckoned me. I'm the only one who knows which time period Kat is held in. I'm the only one who's the keeper of the beasts Sureen is afraid of." He leans toward her. "And let's not forget the contract still holds. Kat is bound to me as is Myla."

I turn to Erma. "Sureen is afraid of demons?"

Erma's eyes narrow at Corbin. "Yes. Aside from Sureen and the sandmen, demons are the only ones who can conquer a dream." Her arms tighten over her chest. "How did you accomplish that one, Corbin?"

He simply shrugs. "I'm a fee of many talents."

Erline steps forward. "You don't get to act like the hero here, Corbin. We know exactly what you are. We know you're not here for Kat. You're here for yourself. Let's not pretend otherwise."

His face morphs to a cold and heartless expression, the features relaxing as he stares at her with soulless eyes. "Be cautious what you request, Erline."

She glides toward him once more, toe to toe. "You may be the fee of terror, Corbin," she begins, dropping her voice to a deadly whisper. "But let's not forget who can successfully create life. Those who can create life are strong enough to deliver your death."

He slants his head to the side, biting his bottom lip with a grin. "Is that a threat?"

"Always," she snarls through gritted teeth.

I clear my throat, glancing around. A few dwarves have halted, watching the heated exchange. "Let's keep moving."

I push past them, purposefully marching right between them, and continue down the path, ignoring the groans from the willow wombs. The pulsing veins mess with my eyes as the tree forest thickens, forcing me to see things that aren't there; shadows which play tricks on my mind.

As we go farther in, I notice satchels gathered in groups outside the willow vines, piled hip high. Perhaps that's where they're left so the freshly born sandmen can grab them as they leave.

"Dream dust collections?" I ask my group, their strides matching mine.

"So observant," Corbin retorts with sarcasm.

"Stop with the questions," Erline barks.

I grind my teeth, flexing my jaw, but remain silent the rest of the way. Corbin walks with confidence, leading the group as if we aren't on enemy territory. I try not to notice his cocky demeanor, but focusing on my surroundings doesn't help the conflicting emotions settled in the pit of my gut. Again, dread overcomes me.

I don't have a good feeling about this.

# CHAPTER SIX

*ELIZA PLAATS*

*DEATH REALM*

"I don't understand," Mrs. Tiller mumbles, her transparent body standing in the middle of the kitchen. "How are you here? How are you . . . alive? And here?" Her arm sweeps out.

Busying myself, pacing across the floor, I rub my arms up and down my sides, desperate to bring normal feeling back to my tingling limbs.

It's a small kitchen. A large fireplace is on the far end with a stone-like cave on the other, holding cold, perishable items. The cave is a refrigerator of sorts, somehow retaining a cool temperature and keeping the blood and food from spoiling within.

The kitchen counters are made of the same stone we walk on. I'm so sick of seeing the color grey. Everything is stone. A dull shade of lifeless color.

Placing a hand on my forehead, I rub the tension from between my eyebrows and lean against the counter. The rock digs into my hip, and I relish the pain. At least I feel something. The distraction is freeing and welcome.

"I wasn't alive when I came here," I murmur.

"How – But – You're – I don't understand Dr. Plaats." Her tone is on the edge of hysterics.

I drop my hand and close my eyes. "Call me Eliza. I'm not a doctor anymore."

Patience wearing thin, Mrs. Tiller slams her fists at her sides. "Tell me what's going on, Eliza."

Sighing, I cross my arms, keeping my eyes on the floor. "I died not long after you. It was a car crash." I incline my head, reliving the memory. The noises were ear-splitting, the smells robust. My heart skips a beat, remembering the fear I endured during my last moments. "It's sort of poetic justice." I shake my head, clearing my dark memories, and continue my story. "I didn't survive and crossed over before an ambulance could get there. Not that they could have done anything for me. There's no way I would have lived through it."

I bring my gaze to hers. Confusion etches her once motherly features, right around the eyes. "When I crossed over," I whisper, "a group of shades led me back. This group was a part of a rebellion, one I knew nothing about."

Her eyebrows pinch tighter together. "I was guided by a reaper," she shudders. "Terrifying creatures, they are."

I nod my head. "It's against the rules for shades to guide shades. Something had shifted the realms to make it possible. When we arrived here, that's when I learned of the rebellion. I knew nothing about it before. Kheelan killed the man I loved after bringing three of us back to life."

Biting her bottom lip, she quiets, processing the information I've told. "So, if you're here . . . where are the other two?"

I sigh, the breath fanning a stray red hair from my cheek. "One is dead – I don't know exactly what happens to the twice dead, but I know there's no realm for them." She gasps, but I ignore it. "The other is below our feet, imprisoned in the dungeon until the day he dies."

Her throat constricts as she swallows her bubbling emotions. "I see. Is this the man Kheelan was talking about?"

I tuck my chin. "It is."

"And it's your job to keep him alive?"

"It is."

She crosses her plump arms, frowning. "And why aren't you?"

Hanging my head, I stretch my neck in shame. Voicing it aloud to someone so caring sends a jolt of regret through me. I blow out a breath, choosing to communicate

71

instead of burying. "Because he was forced to kill the man I loved."

"I see." She slinks closer to me, mulling over her next words in silence. "I loathe you at this moment, Eliza. You pushed me to have a surgery that was supposed to save my life, and it ended instead. You took everything from me," she snarls. "You took my husband, my family, and who knows how many years."

"I'm sorry," I mumble, cutting her off.

She shushes me, a rude passing of wind between clenched teeth. "I wasn't finished. I've heard the rumors, Eliza. I witnessed it. I've seen what Kheelan is made of. If the living man in the dungeon was forced to kill the man you loved, it wasn't his fault. You shouldn't make him suffer." She slips closer to me, lowering her voice to a more intimate, personal tone. "You're all he has left. Chances are, you'll kill him by trying so hard to hate him."

Lifting my head, I chew the inside of my lip as her words bounce around my thoughts, categorizing them, shuffling so they fit just so. It wasn't too long ago I believed all lives under my care deserved a chance. I was a fighter – the only fighter – for the broken lives under my capable hands. That's who I want to be. I want to be the one who saves the helpless, not this insignificant human roaming a realm I don't belong in.

"Will you go with me?" I mumble, my eyes tipping to the box that holds food and blood.

She nods. "Yes."

## DYSON COLEMAN

## DEATH REALM

The tall shade dressed in burlap is completely cooperative. The way he holds himself, his build – straight, narrow, and stocky – You'd think he'd put up more of a fight. Maybe he has too much pride. Or maybe he's accepted his fate. If I could do it over again, I would have fought harder. I would have gone down swinging. This man doesn't understand his new reality.

He enters the cell and turns as the vampire snaps the door closed behind him. The sound of metal scraping against metal vibrates within my ears. One vampire hisses though I can't see who.

A shiver runs down my spine. I've never liked vampires. They give me the creeps. And being as I now have blood and a fully functioning heart, with zero self-defense and naked as the day I was born, it stands to reason they should do more than give me the creeps. I should fear for my life. Somehow, the cold and starvation sound like a far worse fate than a couple vampire fangs.

This mysteriously calm man places his hands between the bars, and they unshackle his transparent cuffs from his wrists. As soon as the metal leaves the shade's skin, it returns to solidity, clinking together in the clawed palms of the vampire's hand.

It's one of Kheelan's spells or magic, or whatever he possesses. For having an enemy, I don't know enough about him to seek my revenge to the fullest extent. That's what I plan to do I realize. My purpose: I will make him pay.

It's hard to learn his weaknesses though, stuck here with no insider information. And it's not like I'd ever get the chance.

The fire atop their torches glitters and roars like a deep baritone of authority. The vampires whip around, taking their leave in a blur. A gust of cold wind blasts my skin.

The dark man watches where they once stood before swiveling white, radiant eyes to mine. He juts his chin to the side, curious, as I hold back a wheeze. The floating, disturbed dust tickles my parched throat.

I sniff. "What are you?"

His movements are slow and deliberate. I don't know if it's due to his size, an attempt at intimidation, or if he's still in shock for being imprisoned in the armpit of the death realm. His voice is so low, hollow, that I cock my ear closer in his direction, catching his next word. "Sandman."

My head jolts back in surprise. I wasn't expecting that answer. "A sandman?" I question, the words difficult to form around numb and quivering lips. "They're – you're real? What are you doing in this realm?"

"A human," he throws back at me, placing a hand on the bar closest to my head. His large fingers wrap around it before a shock wave lights his skin. Without a twinge of pain crossing his features, he drops his hand with ease back to his side. "What are you doing in this realm?"

I blow out a breath and look away. "Ah, I see. Deflection. That won't help you down here." I sigh and wrap my arms tighter around my torso, rubbing the skin with hopes of creating my own warmth. "I live here."

"How does a human live with the dead?"

"Well." I sniff again. "I heard there was a rave, so I broke in to check it out. Turns out, breaking and entering is frowned upon." He doesn't respond, not even a twitch along his lips. Narrowing my eyes, I bark the truth. "Because this human was once dead."

He blinks, slow and exaggerated, his mind working to connect the dots. Shuffling closer, he gets a better look at me. It may be dark here, but his eyes act as a flashlight, transparent though they may be. "That can't be," he mumbles.

"But, so it is," I mumble with sarcasm, trying to mimic his tone but failing and embarrassing myself instead. I clear my throat. "Are you going to answer my question?"

I watch his lips move, the light from his eyes highlighting their outline. "You do not understand. Kheelan holds no power to create life."

"And yet, here I stand!" I shout, flinging out my arms. I regret it, the cold pricking the skin I've managed to keep somewhat warm.

For a moment, I see the reflection of my eyes glowing green in the white of the Sandman's eyes, the color of my wolf's as his annoyance matches my own. It's the first time I've felt something other than sorrow. I try to

75

grasp it in an emotional tug-o-war, but as a slippery fish, he burrows down inside me once more, taking the glow with him.

The sandman watches my eyes, speculating.

I lower my voice. "Why are you here?"

He retreats deeper inside his cell until I can barely make out his eyes. Sighing, I hobble to the wall on numb feet and sit in the corner.

As I resign myself to the fact he won't answer, he speaks, his voice quiet enough that only my shifter hearing can pick it up. "You are a shifter."

Sarcasm drips from my tone. "And you're a fictional character."

To my surprise, he answers my pressing question. "I disobeyed my maker, Sureen. I assisted an angel with her charge. The angel and I have – had – the same charge. A witch."

I puff out my lips and sigh, leaning my head against the wall. "The plot thickens. Witches. Witches seem to be the theme song lately." I scratch my chin. "Sounds interesting, dude," I mumble.

"Not interesting. Miraculous."

"A mythical creature of dreams isn't enough to be miraculous?" I click my tongue. "Come on Sandy, we've got nothing but time. You'll have to give me a few more details than tiny sentences."

"I gained emotions," he whispers right away, shame filling his tone.

"Whoa, don't shout, man." I blink slowly and bark out a laugh. "How does that work? Gained emotions?"

He shuffles in his seated position, uncomfortable. "Sandmen aren't built with them. Sureen and I were close . . . too close, perhaps. I was unable to hide my emotions while bedding my creator."

"You've lost me." I purse my lips. "What made this witch so special? How do you not have basic functions like emotions? Wait . . ." My eyes widen and my eyebrows pinch. "You slept with a fee?"

Shifting again, I hear his nails tunelessly tap against the stone. Much to my dismay, he only answers one question. "As the price to pay for a simple request, the witch was reborn with two souls: her soul and the soul of Kheelan and Erline's daughter."

Eyebrows dipping, I blink as my eyes widen. "Myla? Kheelan's daughter? She's alive?"

"Yes," he whispers. "Inside the body of Katriane Dupont."

Unfolding myself from the huddled ball I've curled up in, I start crawling my way closer to his cell, shocked by the recognition of the name.

"Beasty! End-inning. End-inning!" Gan cackles, making my back arch in fright. He's been so quiet, I forgot he was here.

"Who is that man?" Sandman asks as Gan quiets.

Frustrated that I'm unable to ask my questions, to share what I know, I blurt an introduction. "Gan meet Sandy. Sandy, meet Gan. Gan is a crazy shade from another time. Satisfied? Now, tell me about Kat."

"You know her?"

"Yes." I slap the stone with a flat palm. "What do you know?"

"Gan," Sandman whispers, as if he's refreshing his memory. "Gandalf. I know him."

Confused, I tilt my head to the side. "What?"

"I know that man." He points, his fingernail, shining by the light in his eyes. "That shade."

I sigh and slip back into a seated position. "How could you possibly know him? What? Was he your charge, too?"

Slowly, he swivels his head back to me. "Are you always this crass?"

"Prison changes you, dude."

He sighs, answering my question. "Yes, but only once. Several hundred years ago, I was asked to deliver him a specific dream."

I wheeze in fake shock.

"Kheelan had visited Sureen." His eyelids narrow at me, taking most of the light with it. "Kheelan sought to find his daughter, but she was protected by Erline. Kheelan could not reach her by his own means. He asked my creator to do it for him. He wanted to bring her to the death realm by force."

We halt our conversation when half a dozen vampires blur into the cell's walkway, the one leading deeper into the dungeon. One torch lit in a vampire's hand. It's scarcely enough to see them and the shadows they cast along the wall.

They stop in front of one of the walls with no cells. Two vampires hold a human in between them, whether she was human to begin with or Kheelan made her that way, it doesn't matter. I know the purpose of her being here.

She's quiet, making me believe she's unconscious. It's a small mercy for her, to have no idea what's about to happen. That heart in her chest will soon be drained of blood.

A vampire presses against the wall with a flat palm. I puff my lips and bite the inside of my cheek, confused. It's not a wall but a hidden door. The stone moves, scraping against the floor, and I cringe at the sound. The vampires are as quiet as a deadly predator as they enter the hidden room behind the wall. Light flows out as someone lights a candle, illuminating the walkway between cells.

Gan, sitting in his cell, huddled in a ball, doesn't seem to notice, but his rocking accelerates. It's the first time I've actually seen him. A part of me wishes I never had. His tormented expression makes it impossible not to sympathize, to want to save him from himself. What did they do to him to make him this way?

With finality, the stone wall closes, taking the sliver of light with it. My eyes stay glued to the spot though it's dark, and I can no longer see it. Listening as closely as I can, I gulp, waiting for the screams of pain from the human, but they never come. The only thing that fills the quiet is the constant ring of dripping water.

"What'd Kheelan do?" I ask distractedly.

The sandman's voice is lower, remorseful, as he processes the reality and potential hazards of living amongst vampires. "He struck a deal with Sureen. He wanted to expose his daughter to the humans, to bring her to him by death. I was told to deliver a false dream, one that created speculation within Gan's thoughts surrounding Myla's witchcraft."

"I'm guessing it worked," I comment, my tone dry.

"It did. It always does." He pauses, revisiting his past. "Kheelan then sent his vampires to the village after he grew impatient with human suspicions. He is not one for tolerance."

"I'm fully aware."

His voice raises above my own. "The vampires attacked the village, and Myla was forced to expose who she was. They hung her."

Sighing, a grunt rumbles up my chest. "What happened to her after? She didn't arrive here."

"I do not know," he whispers. "Perchance, Erline kept her daughter's soul. She's a powerful fee, maybe more so than the rest. It is difficult to tell when the fee mask their true nature to fool the others."

I sit there, thinking about the horrors Myla endured, the imagery of such an event filtering through my mind. I went through it as well, hung for crimes that weren't my own, fear and dominance at root.

His speculations of the fee keeping their strength hidden is an interesting theory, one which makes perfect sense. It's always wise to let your enemies underestimate you.

A question pops in my head, a half-witted plan forming. "Do you know where Kat is now?"

# CHAPTER SEVEN

*TEMBER*

*DREAM REALM*

"Wait here," a female sandman mumbles. There's no tone to her voice, no emotions. It's eerie. The whispers slithering past her barely moving lips are as slender as her build. Her gestures and speech are automatic.

Long, braided, black hair sways at her waist, her legs stiff as she walks from the main area of the dome.

This dome is bright and blinding, the light pulsing and reflecting off her dark skin seeming to be the smoothest of chocolates. It casts glows of gold over every surface. It's captivating, and I watch her stroll until she disappears down a main hall, her footprints alighting along the rock floor, disappearing after she does.

The dome is like walking into a pulsing star. It's larger than I expected, much larger. It must be expanded inside by magic. The inside sounds . . . hollow, similar to placing my ear against the scoop of a seashell.

"How long do we wait?" I ask, frustrated that we don't already have an immediate audience. Kat's life could be on the line, and Corbin has been silent, refusing to give insight on what's happening in the past as the memories form and surface.

"As long as Her Majesty wants," Corbin responds. His voice is chipper.

Examining Kat within his arms, her head resting against the collar of his striped, long-sleeved shirt, my heart aches within my wrist. If it weren't for the slight rise and fall of her chest, I'd believe she was dead.

I suck in a breath when I take in her wrists. Abrasions and deep cuts line them, blood trailing down her hands. "Corbin," I whisper.

He brings his bright eyes to mine before following the direction of my horrified, pinned gaze. His jaw ticks once, and he looks away. "It's almost time."

"Time for what?" Erline demands, stepping forward.

He doesn't answer, swallowing instead, and for a moment, I see worry cross the crease of his full lips. What is Kat to him?

"The hostility of this room is smothering. I'm growing quite bored of it."

I whip around to the voice. My eyes narrow when I catch sight of the fee who put Kat under this sleeping spell in the first place. Sureen delicately sits on a throne, a chair that wasn't there before. Stomping forward, I'm halted by Erline's gentle hand placed on my forearm.

"You did this," I hiss between clenched teeth, my torso leaning frontward. My nerves are raw and my emotions foreign but driving.

Sureen smiles, exposing white teeth. She's satisfied with herself, and judging by the grin, I can tell she has been expecting our visit.

Reclining back in her throne, she responds, "I did. You forced my hand, Angel of Erma. My sandmen are not at your disposal."

A thought crosses my mind. "What'd you do with him? Where is he?"

Tilting her head back, a beautiful laugh sings from her throat, the Inferaze cave floors absorbing the sound with unnerving captivity. "Eternal punishment." She pauses, her eyes sweeping the fee beside me. "As a shade."

"How bold of you, to collaborate with my one and only enemy," Erline states, her tone quiet and deadly.

"Interesting. I had considered myself at the top of your enemy list." Sureen slouches and props her chin on her fist, her elbow placed on the arm of the throne. She lowers her voice, raising it toward the end of her speech. "Have you forgotten, dear sister? Have you discarded your kind? Have your creations made you as soft as they are? I suppose when you create beating hearts, their emotions become contagious. That is why you and I despise each other, is it not? Did emotions get in the way when you denied me the strength for beating hearts?"

Dropping my wrist, Erline advances, her fingers curling into her palm. I debate holding her back as she did for me but think better of it. An angel in the middle of a fee war wouldn't survive.

A gentle breeze whistles in from nowhere in a threatening manner, displaying Erline's might and smite. "That's correct, *sister*," Erline snarls. "I know you best. I'm aware of your intentions. I see how you treat the creatures you've created in the absence of life. They're your slaves, not your cherished, otherwise, you'd never sentence one to eternal punishment. You would have shown mercy and ended him to prevent further torment."

"Did you know," Sureen whispers. "Did you know your daughter reborn would shift the realms? Your little power play – keeping your daughter's soul and breaking the cycle He had designed by inserting her into another – is what caused all of this. My sandman paid the price. He experienced emotion and heartache which he was never capable of withstanding. He was my favorite you know. That's the result of your power play, Erline. The sandman grew emotions by proximity to your sweet daughter."

Erline glances away, her jaw firm.

"What other ways have you disobeyed?" Sureen snarls. "What is this daughter of yours? What does she mean to you I wonder."

Erline refuses to answer, the wind whipping her white hair over her shoulders.

"Ah, I see." Sureen reclines into the back of her throne, a ghost of a smile playing at her lips as she draws some sort of conclusion. "She's your ultimate weapon."

Erma squints at Erline. "What does she mean?"

"In order to shift the realms, a creature must be most powerful. She must hold more power than a single fee," Sureen answers. "You've always been the jealous sort, Erline. We began creating our own creations, and you grew envious. And perhaps a little frightened. You procreated with the intent of the ultimate weapon to use at your disposal. After all, there's no stronger bond than a mother and daughter. When she died, you took her soul for yourself so that someday, you could rebuild her. You kept your weapon in your pocket." She lowers her voice. "But I bet you didn't bank on the consequences. I wonder what He will say when He finds out."

I cock my head to the side, unsure of this *He* they're discussing. It must be someone they fear for Sureen to use him as a scare tactic.

Corbin chuckles, shaking his head while Erma's body tenses. "Is this true? Did you birth a daughter for selfish acts? For strength?"

Laying Kat on the ground of the cave, Corbin tsks with humor. "Let us not fight. We all know Erline has terrible judgment. We can bicker over this later."

Sureen's bottom lip pouts, and she sighs. "But we were just getting started."

Corbin dips his head, tucking his chin with a grin. I want to wipe that grin from his skin. "As you wish. However, we came to speak to you about different, but related, matters."

"You want your beloved woken." Sureen points to Kat, lying on the ground.

"Yes," Erline and I hiss as one.

She steeples her fingers and brings them to her lips, her eyes turning to Corbin's. I know she fears him. His demons outrank her sandmen. Yet, she hides it well behind the steel of her black eyes, the purse of her lips, and the snarl of her words.

The group holds its collective breath, waiting for her decision. She could easily direct us away, and there wouldn't be a thing we could do about it. They could kill her, try to force it, but that could do more harm than good.

"I will grant your frivolous request," Sureen proclaims behind her hands. Her attention flashes back and forth between Erline and Erma. "On one condition. Give me the power to build life."

They glance at each other, their eyebrows dipping, and a silent conversation passes between them. Erline and

Erma are close – closer than the rest of the fee combined, and most of the time, their intentions are pure and equal, their thought processes on the same wavelength.

Swallowing in fear, I bend down to Kat's sleeping body, fixing a wrinkle in her cherry-printed pajama shirt. The cotton is smooth, fuzzy, and I rub it between my fingertips. My movements feel slow, and I'm hyperaware of every sensation, including the breath leaving my lungs. For the first time, I'm truly frightened.

They won't agree to this. Even I know the terrible plagues of her pending request. Sureen doesn't wish to have life to cherish. She wishes to have life that'll aid her in whatever her agenda may be. Perhaps revenge.

"We agree to your terms," Erma announces, her tone final and sure. I peek up at her, eyes wide in shock, and my lips part.

Holding up a finger, Erline glares. "After you return Katriane Dupont from the past."


## ELIZA PLAATS

## DEATH REALM


The kitchen fireplace crepitates before us, heating my bones from the never-ending frozen state they've been forced to endure. Inferaze feeds the fire, the tips of the flame the same brilliant black and blue. The smoke's aroma is strong, smelling oddly like sage.

"He's a what?" Mrs. Tiller asks, her voice filled with disbelief. She tilts her chin toward me with a listening ear, eyebrows pinched, and picks up the wooden spoon to stir inside the pot once more.

The contents inside the heated pot bubble and roar. It's uncanny how much it sounds like a waterfall. If I close my eyes, I can almost see one. The colors of blues, greens and whites, flowing over rocks and crashing into the body of water below. I miss it.

I was shocked at how fast the liquid began to boil compared to heating over normal fire. It took seconds, not minutes. The pot is cast-iron though I've never held one quite this large or heavy before. It's situated over the small black and blue fire inside the kitchen fireplace, supported by metal chains attached to the wall of the chimney, which remain unaffected by the heat.

There aren't any regular ingredients here for normal dishes, but luckily, Mrs. Tiller is used to making up new recipes. In the time we've spent together, I've learned a lot about her. She is frugal with what she's offered. Without her, Dyson may be eating hot mush.

Reaper's Breath hovers above us, my explanation already given for the creature before Mrs. Tiller had time to ask. She's more curious about Dyson than she is about the foggy snake floating above our heads, though.

Lifting my hand, I run my fingertips over the mantle made of stone, a layer of grime and dust sticking to my skin. I pull it away, rubbing the goopy dust bunnies between my fingers, and watch them plummet to the floor.

Reaper's Breath has remained absent for the last few days, possibly laying low. I believe it's afraid, as odd as that theory is. It was caught helping and aiding a rebellion against its creator. I am surprised the creature still exists.

Resting my shoulder against the wall next to the fireplace, I bite into a green apple, grimacing as the sour taste slides over my tongue. My teeth slice through with ease, the juices activating my salivary glands, and my stomach growls, eager to greet the nourishment.

"He's a wolf shifter," I explain with a full mouth. "I saw it with my own eyes. He turned into a wolf, and that's what Kheelan used to kill Aiden."

"I see," Mrs. Tiller mumbles, her tongue snaking out to lick the corner of her lips. Her eyebrows are pinched together, and stress wrinkles the skin around her firm lips. "Aiden, you say?"

Tilting my head, I watch worry lines crease her transparent skin. I wish I could read minds – that'd make life much easier. It's no wonder Kheelan uses it to his advantage.

I can tell her thoughts are overwhelmed with all the new information she's learning. It took me a long time to come to terms with it as well. But something in her face, something in those eyes, is troublesome.

Shaking her head, she dispels whatever thoughts were there, leaving me to wonder what caused them, but I know that look. It's the look of grief.

When I was alive – the first time – losing my mother was the hardest thing that ever happened to me. My father was never in the picture. I have no idea what happened to him after he skipped out on my mother while she was pregnant. However, sorrow swimming in the depths of watery eyes isn't hard to miss. That feeling – that emotion – lingers in the air. It's as smothering as a hot and humid mid-summer day.

I shove the emotional reminiscences aside. Her grief threatens to ramp up mine. Whatever she's dealing with, she clearly wants to do it privately, or she would have voiced her concerns aloud. She begins to talk again, but I shush her when I hear male voices inside the dining hall. I place my index finger up to my lips. Her jaw snaps shut, and she turns her head in the direction of the sound. With stealth, I tiptoe to the archway opening that leads to the dining hall and place my back against the wall before it, waiting for a better listen.

"Excellent, Yaris," Kheelan beams, his voice chipper and shrill as a child. I cringe, my shoulders bunching at the same time my nostrils flare. Even his glee is repulsively dark.

Everyone has a dark side, a scale that has the potential to tip from good to evil. I can feel it lurking, waiting for me to be desperate enough to press my finger and tip the scales in favor of the dark. All it takes is desperation, and once you taste the dark, there is no return. It's too easy to give in, especially when it's so tempting.

Sometimes, that is what I fear most – what I'd be capable of if I were to slip. I don't think I'd make it back from that, and the call to glide from good to evil is more tempting now than it has ever been. I would never be the same. I would never be me again. But if that's what it takes to survive...

Kheelan continues, "And what of my brother Corbin?"

"I've sent a message to our contact within the demon realm," Yaris begins. "Corbin is unavailable but will return to his realm shortly. He has one matter to attend to, and then he will arrive with a guest."

Kheelan doesn't speak for several seconds, and my mind conjures images of disappointment etched on his face. Kheelan doesn't like secrets, surprises, or to be kept waiting.

"A guest?" he rumbles. "Did he say whom?"

"No. He did not."

Kheelan's robes rustle, a sound I'm all too familiar with. "Very well. And what of the Colosseum?"

Footsteps echo through the dining hall, my heart skipping beats as I debate whether I should move or stay and listen.

"We have rehoused the shades as you instructed," Yaris reveals, his voice fading. "All that must be done is removal of the buildings and the structure built by you, sir."

"Excellent." Kheelan claps and Mrs. Tiller and I jump. "Excellent. It's about time we liven this place up, don't you think?" Their voices trail off as they head away from the dining hall.

For several breaths, we stand with our backs to the wall, staring at one another. I wait for my heartbeat to return to normal, push back my hair, and wipe the few drops of sweat beaded on my forehead.

"Did I hear him correctly?" Mrs. Tiller whispers.

Placing my sweaty hand over my heart, I match her tone. "I believe you did."

"A Colosseum for what?"

I scan the counters, the display of broken stone bricks which make the wall, but I don't see them. I don't search the crawling expanse of crumbling bricks or the candles that are propped along it. Instead, my imagination replays history lessons I learned as a child.

"For fun," I spit with disgust.

# CHAPTER EIGHT

*KATRIANE DUPONT*

*MYLA'S PAST*

My breaths are slow, exaggerated, and loud to my ears. He continues talking to the crowd, but I don't hear it. I'm abundantly aware of my fate, of what this rope chafing my neck means. Soon, my spine will snap, my heart will stop, and I'll move on. To where, I don't know.

To the left of my theatre, spittle flies from a man's mouth, his cheeks flushed a heated maroon. Shadows dance across his face like the dark intentions blackening his soul. His wife dangles from his arm, her face frightened as she props a toddler on her hip, and her gaze is cemented to mine. The top of her head is the same height as the gallows' platform. I hold her eyes for a moment, but I'm too frightened of my own fate and the developing distress of the crowd to care what plagues her mind right now. Maybe she feels for me – that she's developing some sort of maternal comparison. I could be someone's daughter whom she knows, and she can't help but allow her heart to ache for my demise, or my figurative mother receiving words of childless news. Or maybe she's frightened I'll sprout horns like the demons from hell, bringing about the end of times.

The toddler propped in her arms tucks his head into the crook of her shoulder. His blonde ringlets are in disarray as though he was pulled from his bed to attend my death. He's in distress, the emotions wafting from the others too much for his tiny mind to comprehend. He should be sleeping, far, far away from the terrors of his time's reality. This event – my death – will age him beyond the years of his short life.

A gusty breeze, smelling of fresh earth and horse manure, disrupts the man's flow of words, picking up pace in a dramatic effect. The speaker turns, refusing to acknowledge I stand before him, and nods his head to someone behind me. I attempt to twist my upper torso, to get a glimpse of my killer, but with a groan of rusted metal and cracking wood, the lever is pulled.

The floor gives way below my bare feet. The rope tightens, gathering skin and pinching what it grabs inside each groove of twisted twine.

Gravity's laws take effect, and my body begins to helplessly lower. The rope supports what the wood planks refuse while under the command of a heartless man. The muscles roping my calves - my thighs - quiver, fearful, begging for one more chance.

I lift myself to my toes, splinters burrowing under the nails. My chest heaves as I suck in a large gulp of chilled air. This is it. This is the last time I'll fill my lungs. This is the last beat of my heart, the last pump of blood. I count the beats as my world slows, knowing they're limited . . . I'm limited.

My mind fights it, refusing to acknowledge I'll be nothing more than a carcass swaying in remembrance of my ceased struggle.

Goosebumps light my skin ablaze. In seconds, I'll hear the snap of my spine, then feel the shot of pain to my legs, and my world will cascade in an everlasting darkness like a curtain to the finale of a dramatic show. My heart forces life, pounding with competition – a contest between life and death. My potential future flashes before my eyes – a house, a husband, a flock of children. I'll never get that. It's taken from me.

I know it will do no good, in a few moments, to dream of a life I'll never have. My conscience rips them from me, consuming them with metaphorical bellowing flames. My face twists in horror - eyebrows pinched, eyes wide, mouth contorted.

Bound within their ropes, my hands tighten behind my back, nails digging into palms. A scream bubbles up my chest, blocked from leaving my mouth. It's a bubble of anxiety, a screech of terror, a cry for the choices taken from me.

The rope tightens further, embedding my esophagus inside the muscles of my neck, digging into my spine with painful pressure. Blood soaks the rope, coating my jawline, my life fleeing though my heart fights for it.

And then time stops.

The quivering blaze, devouring the oil-soaked torches, freezes. My body halts in mid-air, and my face swells with the pressure of trapped blood, the rope tight around my neck.

Slipping and sliding, my splintered feet try to gain purchase on the boards. They're half open beneath them, my torso whipping in the absence of wind as I try to maneuver my weight. It feels like the boards are wet, slimy. It takes me a moment to realize they are – they're wet with blood from wounds along the soles of my feet.

I search my surroundings with wild vigor, confused, scared, driven by self-preservation. The rope holds me hostage, constricting me from seeing more than what's in front of me.

In mid-blink, the man's malevolent grin is solidified, just as his body. His cheeks are puffed, his glee black, bleak, the beam of an unstable man. The crowd's fists are raised, lips snarled, eyes unseeing. Their clothes that were whipping in the wind are cemented like a statue, carved by an artist with an eye for detail.

An eerie silence fills the village. Time has stopped, but I have not. I don't understand. The gurgles passing my lips are the only sound filling this void, the only thing that makes sense.

"Poor, poor Katriane Dupont," a voice blurts beside me, shrill and high-pitched. "You would think, for such a powerful being as yourself, you'd be long gone from the current predicament you find yourself in."

The owner of the voice saunters into my peripheral vision, her gait slow and silent, her feet bare. My body sways like a pendulum as I try to turn myself to no avail.

"I do not understand what they see in you. You're frail. Weak. An insignificant bug. You're unworthy of the oxygen held captive within your lungs, of that heart beating in your chest." She tilts her head, eyeing my chest. "I can hear it, you know. It pleads."

Her dark skin matches the night shadows cast by frozen, glowing flames against the houses, shining with a dewy residue reflected by the bright moon.

Dressed in a stiff burlap dress, one strap fastened over her slender shoulder and the length purposely frayed at the tops of her knees, confidence rolls off her in waves. Black hair weaves thick braids against her scalp, the ends reaching her hips and swaying with each graceful sashay she takes. Dark, dusky eyes take me in; her head slopes the other direction as she watches me struggle for air. She finds it fascinating, the twinkle in her black eyes, obvious.

Twitching her firm lips, they barely move as she whispers, "I don't know why they are infatuated with you."

Hot tears, filled with physical and emotional pain, trickle down the slopes of my cheeks, mixing with the strands of bloody twined rope. They leave behind a salty, burning trail. I fight for oxygen, my lungs filling to capacity to keep my soul flowing within me. Black and green dots form in my sight, smothering my blurry vision with a speckled fog.

She rolls her eyes as my lids close, in slow exaggeration, against their will. My heart, the blood pumping in my neck, decelerates, and I know this is the end for me. My speculations concerning her timely visit coinciding with the frozen citizens are moot. My only concern is my despair. I'm young, my life unfinished, but my fate is sealed. I have so much left to do with my life and many things I'm meant to accomplish with many wrongs to right . . .

My knees hit the wood first when the rope around my neck and hands disappears. One minute it's there, squeezing the life from me, and the next, it's gone.

Painfully gulping for air, I cough and splutter. Deep bruising lingers along my neck, the skin tender as I lower my head, while my lungs fill with fire. My fingernails dig into the wood planks, slivers embedding under them. The pain from each wooden needle is nothing compared to my other concerns and injuries. In fact, I relish it.

I glance up. The crowd is still frozen, mid-rant, the little blonde boy tucked into his mother's nape, his cheeks wet with tears.

The mysterious woman in burlap leans her back against the post behind her, watching me like a bug, her fingers clenching and unclenching at her sides. She hates me, but for what reason, I can't fathom. I don't know her.

The black of her eyes tells me she's a Fee, but that's the extent of my knowledge. There needs to be an encyclopedia for this subject. I briefly consider creating one before I shove away the irrational concern and force my disorientation to focus.

"Who are you?" I ask, my voice hoarse and quiet.

Her bare feet begin to sparkle, a swirling white tornado across the surface of her skin, fading from their rooted spot. Transparency is all that's left behind. "Someone who is upholding her end of a deal."

I double blink, clearing my vision from watery, tear-filled eyes. Each speck erases her, traveling up her legs and fading each section of her body it comes across. My eyes snap to hers, looking for any fear within them that may match the sliver of dread tumbling in the pit of my stomach. Her smile is wide, though. Vengeful, almost. It's tilted at the corners in a sly sort of way. It takes me a moment to realize she's doing this – she's causing herself to fade.

In less than a few seconds, all that's left is her head and the braids dangling in the air. I gasp when her head stretches and expands, her smile wickedly detailed. Her black eyes become the size of basketballs; almond-shaped pools sparkling menace and silent threats.

On shaky, deprived legs and sore, bleeding feet, I push myself from the wood and stand. That smile and confidence, her magic, it tells me she's no friend of mine. She may have taken away my ropes, she may have saved my life, but evil is hard to dismiss or rationalize. Especially when the prickle of skin and the trepidation within my heart beg to run the other direction.

Holding my hand out, palm up, a small ball of fire forms, advancing to the size I beckon it. The fire flashes and pops against my frayed and bleeding skin, heating the chill within. The familiarity, the protection, settles and anchors me with renowned purpose.

My throat constricts, and I attempt to swallow past a sore throat. A scream rips from the fee woman's expanded mouth, catching me off guard. I take two steps back, almost dropping the ball of flames.

"What the hell," I mutter.

Dumbstruck and frozen in place, I feel powerless as her head flies toward me, traveling at an alarming speed. I duck, and she continues, her path jagged, swirling around the scene and weaving over the citizens' heads. Her head gathers speed, the same sparkles that made her disappear flake through the scene, accelerating in number like a blizzard at the tail of winter.

The flakes cloud my vision, infect my eyes, and I cover them with my free hand to stave off the burn. Like a sandstorm, it bites into my skin, the pain of flames I should be able to bear.

The high-pitch scream that deafens my ears fades yet resounds through the village, traveling through the trees beyond, and the bite of the sparkling sand along with it.

## AIDEN VANDER

## DEMON REALM

I don't know how I know it. The information settles in my mind, a pocket of knowledge as if it belonged there since the beginning of time. It's etched like the carving of rough stone, a picture of scripture chiseled by the hand from an ancient era.

The black lavafalls, riddled with veins of fire, is a portal. Many portals, actually. Only the strong may shimmer away at will, feeding on the unsuspecting, consuming fear from the purest of souls.

I feel the power build within me, reconstructing everything I once was. I know without a doubt I will never have to lumber through a lavafall to reach the Earth Realm - to gain the terror I'd need to survive, to feed. Even now I can feel it beg to find my first meal. I'm a starving demon. However, something wants me to meet my master, the fee who made my third life transpire. One topic drives me: Why me? What does he want from me? What purpose do I hold in his agenda?

As we leave my place of birth in this realm farther behind, parading along the lava as if it were paved, rocks begin to poke through, small at first, until they seat closer together and grow to the size of three men. They create a path of sorts, guiding us to a destination I know nothing of. I can feel him as we near. His power is great, almost smothering yet charming. It's thick like humidity on a warm day after a heavy rain. Maybe it's not him. Maybe it's a call for a demon to find his way home. Only time will tell.

My guide struggles to maintain an even speed. His dangling skin and disjointed limbs bob and sway with each wobble though he seems accustomed to it. Contradictory to nature's laws, it's not handicapping him.

I falter when I glance beyond the demon hobbling in front of me, taking in the scene and structure before him.

Ahead, the ocean of lava flows upward at a sluggish speed, creating the structure of a castle from fairy tales. Though, I'm not sure a castle in a child's tale would be built within the realm of demons, constructed by the black lava with bolts of fire riddled throughout. That would frighten any child. The idea of this untainted fear tickles me and begs me to explore it. That may be what my master was going for when he envisioned his home: a house built upon fear.

The demon before me turns, his arms swinging, limp due to his lack of joints and connecting skin. "What is it?" he grumbles like a testy old man. "What halts you?"

My eyes jerk to him in annoyance. He may not know it, or maybe he does and is choosing to ignore it, but I know I'm a greater demon than him. I relish the feeling of superiority while nodding to the castle. "What is it?"

He spins, his arms flapping against his torso. "Domus Timore."

I recognize the language as Latin, even understand the words, though I've never learned it. Odd how demons naturally come to this language even when freshly made.

"House of Terror?" I ask.

"It be said Corbin built it from a thousand sins. He feeds from that, ya know – terror and sin. It be where he draws his power - what makes him so mighty."

I keep my face impassive. "And what's his weakness?"

Slow and considering, he turns his head, his eyebrows speculating. "Why do you wish to know?"

I shrug; memories and strategies of my first life as a boxer come to the forefront. "Everyone has one. Knowledge is power."

He sighs, mumbling his next words. "It is said that only the tear of a dragon can bring the King of Demons to his knees."

"There are no dragons," I mumble, continuing our walk and lumbering past him.

He wobbles, desperate to maintain my pace. "Not anymore."

I stop, twisting on my heel. He bumps into me with a snarl, his skin flaps hitting my skin, coating it in a slime. I resist the urge to push him away. "Not anymore? What happened?"

"The Dragon was slain by her village."

# CHAPTER NINE

*ELIZA PLAATS*

*DEATH REALM*

The dark is intense, even with the torch lit within my hand. It's like the dark swallows the light, consuming it, desperate for it. The torch within my hand cannot keep up with its appetite.

We travel down the tunnel to the cells, my footsteps echoing, bouncing off the crumbling stone walls. The soles of my shoes gritting against dust. Mrs. Tiller follows close behind, fearful that something will pop out at any moment and eat her. I don't know why she's so worried. She's already dead. It frustrates me a little. I'm more vulnerable than she is.

Reaper's Breath follows us down, hovering between us, the darkness threatening to consume it, too.

Dripping water guides our path. The farther in we travel, the louder it is; a drumroll to our demise. My foot catches on a loose, stray stone, and I stumble, almost dropping the bone tray held by my other hand.

"Careful," Mrs. Tiller whispers.

I grit my teeth and bite my tongue from lashing out in distress. "How far is this tunnel?"

"I don't know."

"Eliza?" A male voice calls.

I stop in my tracks. The owner of the voice isn't one I immediately recognize.

"Hello?" I call back in a tentative whisper.

"Over here." A throat clears. "It's Dyson."

"Dyson?"

I pick up my pace, feeling the wall with my shoulder until it points to a corner, opening to a larger room. My breaths are freer here, but they don't come easier. I feel more exposed, placed in danger by being out in the open.

"What are you doing here?" he asks, panic in his voice.

With brief contemplation, I wonder how he can see me, but then again, he's been living in the dark. His vision has probably grown accustomed to it.

"Which cell are you?" I ask, swaying my arm out in front of me, taking tentative baby steps. My voice echoes, parallel with a constant drip of water.

"Down here. Look for my hand."

Gritting my teeth against my own doubts and short-comings, Mrs. Tiller and I shimmy down the small alley between two rows of cells while I use my shoulders to guide us like a cat with whiskers. It's not an easy feat, my heart thudding in my chest, worried what monster I'll come across.

The temperature is freezing, and with the light from my torch, I can see the breath mist out in front of me before it's swallowed by the dark.

I stumble once more, my shoulder banging into a bar of a cell. I scream as I'm jolted with a bite of electricity, the bar's defense mechanism. A screech matching my own, coming from within that cell, causes me to jump and the tray teeters in my hand.

"Don't touch, don't touch!" the hysterical high-pitched voice screams within.

"GAN!" Dyson yells overtop the noise. "Be quiet Gan! Do you want every vampire down here?"

I take a few calming breaths, Mrs. Tiller shocked still behind me. I wait until her eyes meet mine once more, and we continue, slinking through the walkway. Dyson's hand comes into view, his dirty fingers wiggling to get my attention. A relieved breath escapes Mrs. Tiller's nose. She still hasn't learned that shades have no reason for oxygen. I suppose it's an uncontrollable habit when startled.

We stand before the cage, my lit torch casting shadows over Dyson's naked frame. He's dirty, black smudges along his cheekbones and the bridge of his nose. I force my eyes to remain on his face, on his eyes and blue, quivering lips which shiver.

Desperate to let him maintain some sort of modesty, I square my jaw, refusing to drop my gaze. My nose stings with the sour smell of urine, like taking a whiff of a freshly sliced onion, and my eyes prick with tears. I breathe through my mouth instead, a pang of sympathy stabbing my heart. I have it much better than he does.

"What are you doing here?" he asks.

I swallow, gulping down a lump in my throat. I didn't mentally prepare myself for a conversation with Dyson, and I'm not ready to answer questions yet. It's difficult to shove my grudge aside even if I am aware it wasn't his fault.

Holding up the tray, my tone is weak. "I came with food."

As if he hadn't noticed the tray wobbling in one of my nervous hands – maybe he didn't – his expression widens, and his chin tucks, looking down. He swallows, and I envision his mouth pooling with saliva at the thought of whatever food is placed on this tray.

"Here," I mumble, angling the tray and sliding it through the hole in the bars meant for de-cuffing a prisoner. "It isn't much, but at least it's food."

He unwraps his arms from his body and reaches for the tray. I watch as he picks up a spoon with trembling fingers, shoveling the contents in his mouth so fast I barely see it enter.

"Slow down, Dyson. You'll make yourself ill." Startled by a new voice, my mouth snaps shut, capturing another scream. The words came from next to Dyson's cell, from an unknown voice so low and deep it rumbles like a lion's roar.

Eyes wide, I look to my left at the cell that I assumed was empty next to Dyson's. A figure floats forward, or at least it looks that way, his eyes the only thing I can see. Mrs. Tiller and I gasp, the sparkling orbs of white breathtakingly beautiful yet frightening at the same time.

"What are you?" I whisper, retreating.

Around a mouth full of food, Dyson answers, "Sandman. Sandy, this is Eliza. Eliza, Sandy."

"A real sandman?" Mrs. Tiller asks, shuffling closer and squinting her eyes. She's hard to see. The light plays with her transparency, making her look like wisps of mist.

"Yes," he answers, now fully flush to the gate. I almost warn him not to touch it, but I figure he's already tested the bars. I assume a man that size wouldn't sit here in peace, absent of curiosity.

Dyson slows, eating in a more civilized manner. Satisfied, I glance around, bringing my torch with me in hopes of attaining a better view of the dungeon. There's nothing to see. Nothing except empty cells, stone, and endless dust.

"My mother? And Jane?" I ask.

"Further in," Dyson answers, pointing with his bent elbow. "Down quite a ways with the others they've captured from the attempted rebellion." He slurps his mushed food from the provided silver spoon.

I scowl, confused, and spin on my heel to face him once more. My red hair whips my face, a strand sticking to my lips. "Why? Why are they capturing and detaining them?"

"What do you mean?" Dyson asks.

"What's the point to it?" I shrug, and it wiggles my hand. The flames bounce atop the torch. "They'll never die. In fact, they're probably receiving better treatment down here than up there. What's the point of keeping them here?"

Dyson sets down his spoon, the metal clanking against the bones that construct the tray. The dip of his eyebrows matches my own. "That's a good point," he mumbles. "I don't know."

We're silent, our minds working to unravel Kheelan's plan. The dripping water is our only evidence of the passing of time.

"The Colosseum," Mrs. Tiller whispers.

My face muscles wilt, and my heart skips a beat. "Oh my . . ."

"The what?" Sandy asks.

Cursing, I lift my hand and rake my nails against my forehead. The words I heard earlier, from the dining room, replay in my head. "Corbin – the Fee guy from the Demon Realm – he's coming to visit. Kheelan said something about needing entertainment and a Colosseum."

The group is quiet as the prisoner, Gan, cackles and hoots within his cell.

I swivel on the balls of my feet, directing my frown at Gan. "What's wrong with him?"

"That's a long story," Dyson murmurs, pauses, and goes back to the subject. "It would make sense . . . to keep them, us, down here. Do you think he'd use shades for his new sick and twisted game?"

"Yes," the sandman rumbles.

Reaper's Breath chooses this moment to swoop in, from wherever it was hiding, and twirls around Dyson's shoulders. Dyson gapes, flabbergasted. "I thought this little guy was dead."

"No, but he's been laying low." I smirk, watching the creature caress Dyson like a welcoming pet.

Dyson squints, stress hardening the edges of his eyes. "There's something we need to talk about."

I sigh and look away. "No, we don't. You don't need to explain yourself. What happened the other day –"

He cuts me off. "Look Eliza, I'm sorry about that. I'm sorry you had to go through what you went through, to witness that, to be a part of it. It's my fault. But we don't have a lot of time." He turns his head, looking back to the tunnel from which we came. "Vampires patrol down here, and if they catch us talking, if they catch the Reaper's Breath . . ." he glances at his shoulder where the white fog sits, firming his lips in determination. "There's a witch. Sandy and I are working on his skill to cross over and contact her, but she may be our only hope."

"Our only hope for what?"

He glances up while stumbling closer to the bars. His foot knocks against the tray and it slides an inch. "To our freedom."

## KATRIANE DUPONT

## DREAM REALM

Pressure lines my back, and jagged edges dig into the skin along my spine, poking the spaces in my ribcage. It's uncomfortable, and I shift my shoulders against it, hoping to relieve the discomfort. The wood planks are old but not uneven, like rock. Where am I? Did I fall from the platform? This foreign sensation piques a temporary curiosity, replacing it with a river of fear flowing straight to my heart. My skin pricks with tiny needles of dread.

A portal . . . I was taken through a portal.

I inhale a deep breath. The scent of musky moss and a tang of sage tickle over my tongue as I try to get a grasp on where I'm at. It's frightening to not have a drop of knowledge concerning your surroundings – on where an insane fee took you within her sparkling sandstorm. I don't want to know where I am. I know I'm not home, tucked in my bed. I know I'm not back in the past.

Is this a punishment? I could be in a dungeon somewhere. I seem to be a magnet for fee chastisement lately. I wouldn't be surprised if I am taken prisoner, waiting for a creature of the night to eat me as soon as I stand. Clenching my teeth, I force my fear to subside, swiping it away like it's an unwanted closed curtain, and open my eyes.

As upon waking from a full night's rest, my vision is fuzzy, and my muscles and joints feel weak and fallow. A rock ceiling, too bright, drifts high in the air, taking most of my peripheral vision. Specks of black and sparkling dust float aimlessly between me and the ceiling, the bright light reflecting off them, creating an illusion of a disco ball. There's no wind to blow them, so they drift like noiseless snow. All at once, I take in the ceiling pulsing an even rhythm – it's almost too much, a shock to my system.

Averting my gaze, I look at the floor. My back rests along black rock, each shift of muscle explaining the bite as the uneven, rigid edges dig deeper. It smells unfamiliar

113

here – stale and unlike the natural air I was breathing back in the village.

I run my hands along my torso, feeling the familiarity of the fleece that weaves my pajamas. The raw flesh on my wrists snag against the soft cloth, and I wince, my lips grimacing.

My palms feel like they're on fire, spiked with splinters from the wood planks on the gallows. For a moment, my mind conjures the image of my almost death, taking me to a place I no longer wish to hold as a memory.

I marvel at the fact that I'm in my future body, but my injuries are from the past. It must be a loophole of some sort – a side effect or consequence.

Sitting up, I stand, and spin in a full circle, temporarily ignoring the people observing me. It's a large room, a dome-like structure. The cave's rock floor contains thin, tiny rivers. They look like strings weaving between each rise and fall of the protruding edges and uneven surfaces. The strings pulse at the same rhythm as the dome.

Tucking my chin, I look at my feet, my eyebrows raising to my forehead. The space around my bare feet is lit with a brilliant white light. I bend a knee and lift the opposite foot a few inches from the ground, seeing a perfect print. Huffing, I place it back down, forcing myself to remain calm.

Tember, Erline, Corbin, and a woman with short red curls, Erma I'm guessing, stand to the left, their expressions concerned, except for Corbin. He looks . . . oddly delighted. Is this why he didn't save me from my almost death? Was his future-self planning a rescue?

The woman who released me from certain death sits upon a throne, not far from us. She's smug, her elbows resting against the arms of the chair, and her black eyes twinkle in certain victory.

The throne looks like it's weaved the same way a dreamcatcher is. Vines with crystal leaves flow over the back and reach the floor like a peacock's tail. It's beautiful... a masterpiece of art. In the light of the dome, the crystals sparkle a gold hue.

Piles of satchels are stacked behind the throne. It's like a stash of treasure, and she protects it. For a moment, I wonder what's in those satchels before my mind shoves it aside, deeming it unnecessary to know. Sometimes, it suits me to remain oblivious. I don't need, or want, my hand in every cookie jar. I have enough to deal with as it is.

The victorious throne-sitter shimmies her rump further back in her chair, watching the scene unfold with hooded eyes filled with triumph. I wonder what she thinks I'm going to do. Back in the past, she was sure I was nothing more than a bug. That judgmental intolerance heats my insides, the beginnings of a trembling fire of barely contained emotions.

I look to Corbin, his movements distracting as he rocks on the back of his heels. "Where am I?" I bark, directing my question at him.

With all eyes on me, I feel open and exposed, placed in a territory that isn't my own. The unfamiliarity brands me hostile. Rationality and inquisition are out the window. No one in this room deserves the benefit of my doubt. Self-preservation kicks in, my earlier fear receding while confidence soars to the lead.

Lifting my right hand, I allow a ball of fire to shimmer within my palm, covering and surrounding the skin as I manipulate its evolution. It licks up my wrist to my elbow, a sleeve afire. It's a small comfort to root me, grounding me and filling me with a safety that only I can provide myself. After all, it's all for one, right?

The orange, smoldering flames lick my wounds like a loving pet, and a single tear spills from my eye, leaving a hot trail as it slumps from my cheek. It drops into the flame, landing directly on the ripped and bleeding skin of my wrist. A tugging sensation initiates there, the wound knitting the skin back together.

Without glancing at it, I marvel at my self-healing. I can do it without being a dragon, something that had never occurred when the dragon morphed with me. The dragon and I are one, though two. This last gift, which Myla granted me, is more than I could ask for, or deserve, upon her demise.

Fear and exasperated resentment override the guilt placed on my shoulders. I could have saved her. I could have changed the future and preserved her from a fate she didn't deserve. I don't merit this last gift. She died for me – for her daughters, in hopes the sacrifice would end with her.

Tember slinks forward, and Corbin folds his arms across his lean chest, a smile lighting his face in some sort of pride or silent joke.

"You're back, Kat," Tember coos, her voice calm and even. She holds out her hands, desperate to reassure me. Does she think I don't know that already? Does she think I'm afraid? Is this fire, crawling up my arms, ready to launch, because I'm a rabid and unpredictable caged animal? At first, it was. Now . . .

Gulping, Tember licks her bottom lip. It's the first time I've ever seen her nervous. "This is the dream realm."

I flick my attention to the woman, remembering my lessons as a young witch regarding the most significant realms and those who rule them. Her black braids shimmer, momentarily distracting me. "Sureen?"

"Is any other like me?" Sureen quips.

A man in burlap pants, but no shirt, walks through a tunnel connecting to the dome and softly pads to the throne. He's tall and slender with eyes that glitter brighter than diamonds. Sureen glances his direction as he eyes me, no expression or curiosity on his face.

Nervous, my attention divides, causing panic and the heat along my arms to increase.

"He's a sandman," Tember mumbles to me, hoping for reassurance. "Not a threat."

The sandman bends, whispering words into her ear. She styles no expression to what she's being told, keeping her cold, black eyes settled on me. They're soulless, life-sucking, and unsympathetic. Fire curls thick in my belly with the need to be seen more than the weak girl she thinks I am. I know I was smart to not change history. It was the right thing to do for the safety and security of the future. However, in her mind, I was the damsel who needed to be saved.

Rage. That's what this is. Rage. Secrets built on secrets, lies stacked on lies, judgement overlapping judgement.

I look to Tember. "You did this," I threaten and blame between clenched teeth.

She holds up her hands, her jaw ticking in the side of her cheeks. Is that guilt I see? "Some of it, yes."

"Why?" I roar. I expect the cave to echo from the volume of my voice, but it doesn't. The eerie silence sends goosebumps over my skin, the fire crackling along my arms filling the void.

Tember looks over her shoulder to Erma. Erma gives no indication to help Tember in any way, crossing her arms instead, and raises her sculpted red eyebrows. She looks back to me and tucks a brown curl behind her ear. "Because I needed answers."

"Answers?" I murmur distractedly.

My eyes travel over the rest of the entourage. The sandman scurries from the cave as he feels me succumb to an unstable level. For such a large man, he terrifies easily, choosing not to stick around to protect his queen, his maker. I find that curious in the midst of my tantrum.

With a look of satisfaction dimpling Sureen's cheeks, I already know the answer to the question crossing my lips. I tuck my chin, inclining my head toward her and pinning her with a stare. "It was you, wasn't it? You put me in that place."

She moves her elbows to the armrests along her chair, steeples her fingers in front of her, and rests them on her abdomen. Her fingers are long and pointed, a skeletal structure covered by dark, mahogany skin. "Whatever do you mean, child?"

"You put me there!" I scream, the fire reaching my shoulders. "You put me there!" I repeat to Tember. "All of you did!"

My chest heaves, smoke curling from my nostrils, clouding the space in front of me. It's a release to the fire burning within. The group shuffles simultaneously in an attempt to stand before me, and their lips move, passing words I can't hear while blood roars in my ears.

I withdraw, frightened for my lack of control but unwilling to stop it. My skin quivers, scales slicing through like a knife to soft butter as the fire continues to creep across. My bones pop and expand, elongating, transforming to my better, more equipped half.

Grey, black, and green hues take over my vision, accentuating every fine detail of everything around me. My top lip curls, exposing sharp teeth. The fee and Tember's body become rigid, their shoulders bunching and their eye's lifting as I grow.

Bones elongate, cracking, reforming, and the fury inside feeds it. It drives my anger to a whole new level, one that doesn't only belong to me but the beast I am. It doesn't hurt. In fact, it's comforting, like the massage of a scalp. I relish it, bask in it, take comfort like a purring cat.

They'll pay. All of them.

Sucking in a deep breath, my front feet plummet to the ground, heavy, shaking the rock like the boom of thunder against a house. The flames that were licking their way up my arms dissipate, retreating within me to fuel the bigger weapon.

The pulse of light throughout the dome skips to an uneven beat. Sureen lifts her head, concern narrowing her eyes. I'm threatening her home. Did she not expect it?

The muscles along my neck ripple with each sway and shake of my head, relishing freedom. My actions are filled with discontent, and my tail flicks to mirror it. Corbin narrowly misses the contact, disappearing and reappearing as soon as my tail crosses the space where he stood.

I snap my jaw, sharp teeth sliding over sharp teeth, disliking his vanishing act. One second, he was there, and the next, his form started to ripple, shimmering from existence before he reappeared in the same manner.

From the corner of my eye, flames outline each scale along my body, paralleling my inner turmoil. I've never seen it do that before. Could it be since the merge of

120

beast and human, the connection adapted into something entirely different? Would it hurt if someone were to touch me?

I release the inferno building inside me, a bellowing roar so loud the dome walls shake, stopping the pulse altogether. Saliva drips from each razor-sharp tooth, diving to the black rock floor. The pulsing light wavers when I quiet, before beginning its tune once more.

Snorting, I eye each Fee without having to shift my neck. Everything they are reminds me of my fury, reminds me of my purpose. They almost killed me. I don't know the details, but the details don't matter. Each one of the creatures is the root of my plight. They see me as weak, as insignificant as the creatures they create. A pawn between their pinched fingers.

I blink slowly, letting the magic flow through each vein, each scale of my massive towering frame. They look small compared to me. The dome's ceiling doesn't seem so high from my vantage point.

My mother always told me to never seek revenge. Revenge was for the disobedient. "Seek revenge, and dig two graves," she would quote. She promised that life was a cycle, and eventually, they would get what's coming to them. Forgiveness is a time-consuming luxury which rests on patience's shoulders. I hold neither.

When my lids open, I feel flames lick around the lids. I operate on instinct. Erline, Erma, Corbin – they gather a few feet in front of me, shuffling as close as they dare. Sureen is standing behind, angry, contorting her features in a cruel snarl. Tember stands apart from them, a lone angel exiled for her crimes by everyone she holds dear. Or maybe she recognizes untamable emotions.

The fee tuck their chins, watching the ground as their feet leave it, their bodies slowly lifting into the air against their will. They're dumbstruck, unsure of what's happening beyond their control. Erline raises her eyes to mine, fear creasing worry lines around her perfect porcelain face.

I stomp my foot, claws scraping against rock. Magic flows through my bones to the tips of my talons. A tremor travels into the ground and shakes the structure, threatening the dome. Crumbles of tiny pebbles break free, bouncing along and knocking together in the sound of a drumroll. The noise is like an instrument I've never heard, orchestrated by a brilliant mind. It feeds me, urges me in my plan built on a disobedient witch, a rebellious child, a creation that's broken free of constricting chains.

The spikes on my head flatten, propelling my head forward, and a roar rumbles through my chest, up my neck, and through my opening mouth. It releases the magic I've built up inside, slamming into the hovering fee like a cloud of smoke erupting from an unstable volcano.

As if in slow motion, they fly through the air, helpless, their backs crashing into the dome wall. They drop to the ground, landing in a haphazard heap. Turning eyes to me, their faces quiver with a variety of fear. Except for Corbin. He props his top half up with his hands and the corners of his lips raise in a smile. He's feeding from them

– he's consuming their fear. I'm making him stronger, I realize.

I snap my eyes to Tember, my chest heaving with heavy breaths. She stands still, her lips parted in shock, her attention flicking between the fee discarded on the ground and the dragon before her. I had left her untouched. She was my friend, my protector. I am her charge. Nothing can break an angel more than her charge walking away. Sometimes, the best revenge is to show my back.

Erline growls, pulling my attention back to her. My muscles tense, ready for her next move. A rapid swirl of wind cyclones around her, and she disappears, reappearing in a standing position. Flinging her arms out from her side, she tips her head back. Her white-blond hair ripples down to her hips, and she screams. The upsurge of her outrage leaves her mouth, crashing into my chest like a stream of water from a broken fire hydrant.

My dragon form flies through the air. I expand my wings on instinct, flapping them to avoid crashing into the dome wall. Hovering in the air, I drop back to all fours, roaring in her direction. Their clothes and hair ripple with my rumble. I take a deep breath and release it. Streams of scorching flames caress my tongue. It feels like a cool drink of water on a hot, dry, summer day. I hold it for a moment, relishing it. Flames lick from my nostrils in an attempt to escape. I open my mouth, and it exits my muzzle, the torrent of fire heading right for the fee.

Erma quickly stands, throwing her palms forward. The edges of her eyes are harsh and malicious as she directs a challenging stare at me. A blue, transparent wall glimmers and expands from her palms – a shield. The shield is impenetrable, my flames blanketing it, covering it like frosting smothered on a cake.

Erma drops her shield, her chest heaving with the effort to maintain her magic during such an assault. Corbin whistles low, fake-fanning himself when the flames distinguish. I snap my jaw in his direction, threatening him. He holds up his hands and laughs, shirking back against the dome wall.

"Kat," Tember yells, trying to gain my attention. "Kat!"

# CHAPTER TEN

*ELIZA PLAATS*

*DEATH REALM*

I back away from his cell, shaking my head. My red hair tickles my cheek, and I brush it away with a forceful swipe. "I can't . . ." I begin, sorrow drips in my tone.

Dyson tilts his head. "Can't what?"

"She can't leave here," Mrs. Tiller whispers, pulling at her fingers. "She has no freedom."

Understanding dawns on the sandman. "You're the queen. Sureen, my creator, discussed you. You're to wed Kheelan."

I nod my head, a tear trailing down my cheek. I'll never leave this place. I'll be within Kheelan's grasp for the rest of my life. The torment I'll endure . . .

"Do not fret," the sandman mumbles.

Swiveling my head to him, anxiety bubbles within my chest, threatening hyperventilation. "You don't think this," I argue, waving my hand, "warrants worry?"

The sandman's thick lips twist, and his sparkling eyes narrow. He pauses, choosing his words carefully. The dripping noise fills the silence once more as we hang on his every last word. "There is a reason fee do not take mates, little one."

I sniff, angrily swiping my nose on my shoulder. "Why? Because the fee mate suicide rate is off the charts?"

"Don't talk like that," Dyson mumbles. He reaches up, instinct guiding him to touch the bars, to reach out to me, to draw me closer for comfort. He catches himself and drops his hand back to his side.

Sandy continues as though he weren't rudely interrupted with my bout of sarcasm. "Once a fee takes a mate, the mate can draw the power from the fee."

"Is this true?" Mrs. Tiller turns, asking me as if I have all the answers. She often forgets she has been in this realm longer than I have.

I scrape my teeth over my bottom lip and swallow, my eyebrows pinching with anxiety. "Excuse me?"

"Is that true?" Dyson asks. The sandman inclines his head, and Dyson frowns, his lips puckering. I can tell he has a curious mind, constantly absorbing any information he comes across and tucking it in the back of his brain for later evaluation. He would have made an excellent scientist. "How?"

"I do not know exactly how it happens. But there are only three reasons a fee will mate. Love, vengeance, or self-preservation. As you may draw from him, he may draw from you."

My jaw clenches, and I hiss out a breath. My future is uncertain, but a light of hope has been sparked.

"Vengeance," I whisper. Kheelan wants vengeance. It's always at the top of his agenda.

"And what about the witch?" Mrs. Tiller asks.

The sandman glides closer, blinking slowly. "She's the key to end suffering across the realms."

## AIDEN VANDER

### DEMON REALM

A splash in the lava diverts my attention from the demon's tale of fire breathing creatures, just to catch a green tail disappearing beneath the surface. It doesn't splash as it descends. The lava is a thick goop, swallowing the disturbance with easy passage before the surface is flat once more.

"What was that?" I ask before the knowledge floats to me like a whisper between my ears. "Pyren."

The demon giggles though it holds no humor. "Very good, young one. Very good."

"They live in this realm? They're not demons," I state, searching the black depth of ever expanding lava.

"Says who?" he whispers, his gnarled lips an inch behind my ear. A normal being would jump at the sudden closeness, perhaps even wonder how he managed to move undetected, but I hold no fear. I have no soul to fear for.

He continues, "Do not cling to your old lives, young one. It will not serve you well here." He pauses, letting his subtle threat sink in. "Pyrens are not mystical. They be creatures of fear, just like you, just like I. They be crossers between realms, delivering fear to all those who sail the moving waters in their ships made of a life they destroyed."

It takes a moment for my distracted muse to comprehend his words. "You mean wood? Trees aren't life," I retort, watching a head pop from the water. The Pyren claims my attention again, captivates it, enough so that my next sentence is a hushed whisper. "They have no hearts to make them so."

The demon gives a humorless chuckle. As the Pyren floats closer, her arms wading through the lava, his voice quiets, and his words slow. "Oh, they be life. They be life with no voice to protect their continued growth."

I suck in my bottom lip and observe her strange features. Where her tail was green, her flawless smooth skin is dark blue, and her glowing green eyes set in her smooth, flat face surely compliment the mysteries within. She's mesmerizing, the fall of the sun over a beautifully landscaped horizon. Her mysteries call to me, beckon me, suck me in until all I want is her.

He whispers once more. "Captivating, isn't she? Taunting, almost." He pauses, leaning closer. "Never trust anyone. This be the only advice I will ever give you."

The Pyren has some of the same features as a typical mermaid would - a nose, two eyes, two arms, and a fin - but it ends there. Her scalp sprouts thick black tentacles like an octopus'. Two sets of gills line the hollows of her cheeks, and foot-long spikes emerge from her temples, reaching out past the tentacles. The tips of her ears are constructed the same, appearing as though she wears a thorny crown when seen altogether.

Thick, full lips, like a fish, drown her subtle nose, and when she speaks, I almost miss it, hypnotized by her presence. Her voice is a song, beautiful and heartbreaking at the same time. "You're late," she sings.

"For what?" I ask, my voice husky. Her pull continues to drown me. It's near impossible to fight. My mind hopes that I'm late for her, and my arrival is untimely to the agenda she has mapped out for me. My conscious screams of the danger her lure truly is. Bending closer, I catch myself being sucked into her presence. I give my head a shake, unnerved by how much she's consuming me, taking over my desires, overpowering me.

Even though her eyes stare at me, it takes me a moment to realize she isn't speaking to me.

"He's arrived back?" The demon asks, his voice farther away from my ear.

Her tentacles move, squirming along her scalp and dipping into the lava like extra limbs seeking warmth. They play with the surface, each its own finger. "Soon," she reveals. "He will wish to know where his thrice born child is."

"We'll be along shortly," he responds, his voice low and threatening. I sense his hostility toward the Pyren, and it naturally piques my interest. Where there is hostility, there is fear.

She tilts her head, her eyes wandering my body. "So, it's true then. You truly are thrice born?"

"His heart does beat within his chest, Ferox. But he be demon."

A small smile brightens her cheeks with questionable humor, showing the pointed tips of her teeth within. The gills along her cheeks wrinkle, contorting their flawless slatted lines. "Not an ordinary demon. It's . . . fascinating, isn't it? Corbin holds the power the other fee do not."

"And what is that?" I ask, my voice husky, wanting her attention on me and only me. I want to own her, to call her mine, to be the only thing she wants. What does she feel like, I wonder? Is she as smooth as she looks? As wise as she speaks?

Privy to the effect she's having on me, her grin widens. "Some of the others can create life. But the next feat is pulling back a life already lost. To pull a soul from the void, to create life from a place that no one understands, not even the fee, is strength beyond anyone's imagination.

I cross my arms. "And where did he get this newfound strength?"

Her smile widens, reaching both sides of her face, a giddy tone to her sing-song voice. "From the rebirth of his dragon queen."

The demon wobbles, walking to stand side by side with me. "She be reborn? The dragon lives?"

Ferox rolls her eyes, blinking two sets of eyelids – the normal one and a transparent one underneath. "Do you know nothing?"

He looks away. The shredded skin along his cheeks flaps. "He enjoys talking to you finned-folk better than demon."

"Perhaps it's because we are better company." She twists to face me, wading through the lava. She's close enough now that I can smell her vanilla scent. "Though his marriage stopped when his wife died, the contract still holds despite her being reborn inside another. He feeds off his wedded, Thrice Born." The demon splutters, but she cuts him off, raising her voice. "Before he left for his errand, he said this witch was stuck in the past, weakening her ability while her true body remained in the present.

That is where he drew his strength to create you – her weakened state, her fear and dread, her dragon. He created you by thieving her powers and manipulating them for his own."

I tilt my head. "And he plans to rescue her to keep his power source."

She swims backward, inching away from me. I keep my arms crossed, forcing myself to not reach out to her, to pull her close. "I'm sure that deed is done already," she whispers. "But with a power source such as the Reborn - the dragon - comes great consequence."

The demon nods beside me. "She is his only threat. His only weakness."

I look back and forth between them. "So how does he keep the balance in his favor?"

Ferox smiles, weak and false. "To conquer the dark, one must drown the light."

*KATRIANE DUPONT*

*DREAM REALM*

Faster than I've ever done, my body molds back to human form. The bones have cracked, reshaped, and my back feet curl against the rock. It's cold here, the damp slick air slithering across my naked body that was once heated by the fire of my dragon form - by the fury of my emotions.

I'm done here. Though they convinced me to return to human form, it doesn't mean the war is over, but my fight is gone, replaced by consuming sorrow and self-pity.

I hold out my hand, the flames returning in a swirling ball within my palm. Tember eyes me carefully, her body moving slowly. She opens her mouth to speak, to get me to see reason, but her jaw snaps shut when she watches my next move.

Using my other, I create mist on my own, not bothering to think of a spell. I don't need them anymore, and I have no wish to hear what she has to say. My heart is broken, the fight leaving me like a wisp of wind.

I twirl my finger, mist forming, swirling like a tornado. I guide it to the ball of flames within my palm, cupping it in my hand and blowing through the small space between my thumbs. I open the cup, the ball lifting slightly above my palm, hovering on its own and waiting for further instruction. Ticking my jaw with barely contained grief, I bend, grabbing one of the many pebbles of black rock that broke free. Pinching it between my fingers, I drop it in the flames and the ball expands, shocking me with its blue and black hue.

Erline starts to yell my name, and the fee advance, preparing themselves for another attack.

"You're not leaving here!" Erma shouts over the crackle of my developing portal.

A scream rips from my throat, and I shove both hands in front of me, a quick study from Erline's early moves. I am my fee mother's daughter.

A force of powerful wind shoots from my palms, and Erma slams back into the wall once more. She snarls, rising quicker than a blink, and conjures a bow similar to Tember's.

Propelling myself forward, I tuck my arms to my side and run through the portal. An arrow unleashes, narrowly missing my ear. It whistles past, slamming into the dome behind me. The swirls of blue, firing hues envelop me as I run through, carrying me back to where I wish.

*TEMBER*

*DREAM REALM*

"Where the hell did she go?" Erma asks, whirling to face me. The bow dissipates from her hand, disappearing, along with the arrow discarded on the rock. Her face is scarlet with unleashed rage, her hair in disarray.

I know exactly where she is. A witch always retreats to where she feels most safe. "Home," I murmur.

The slick oil in the pit of my stomach churns. I saw the way she looked at me. I saw the way her eyes held me in contempt. She despises me and with good reason.

Corbin stuffs his hands in his pockets. "Well, that was quite entertaining."

Erline turns to him, her eyes narrow and her nose wrinkled. "You think this humorous?"

"I do," Corbin begins, the smug smile leaving his lips. His face darkens, and a sense of dread overcomes the room; a thick aroma, choking and smothering all at once. I imagine this is what the Angel's Kiss feels like.

With quick thought, due to his overpowering threat, I call upon Ire, the electric bow tremoring within my palm. He's been given a power boost by the fear which layered this dome moments ago.

I bring the arch of the bow to my face, the side of my hand resting against my cheek. I pull the string back, an arrow taking its rightful place, resting on my finger.

"Stop," I huff. Whatever he's doing, whatever magic this is, it'll consume us. It's a magic I've never felt; dark, thick, and slick. I don't know what he's doing, or his plan, but the results surely won't end well. Not with the power boost he's been given.

His head swivels to me, the pits of his black eyes seemingly endless. "You think to stop me, Angel? You're only half of what you should truly be." His eyelids narrow. "Do you think that's enough? To stop the King of Fear?"

It is unnerving to watch his façade drop, to witness the snake beneath a rabbit's skin. It's almost a separate personality to the one I've grown accustomed to. My breaths are harsher and barely contained. His charming demeanor is gone, and we see him for what he truly is: the threat we didn't see coming.

"Enough," Sureen bellows. She's been quiet, absorbing knowledge like a dry sponge dropped into a bucket of water. She's witnessed much this day. "We had a deal," she adds, turning to Erline and Erma. "Your daughter almost destroyed my realm. You came here, begging for my help, asking me to save that *thing*, and now you forget your promise."

It takes them a moment, but they eventually remove their gazes from Corbin's and glance her direction as one. I keep aim, refusing to back down.

"I have a realm to run," Corbin expresses, his charming attitude returning like the flick of a switch. I falter in my statue stance. "If you'll excuse me."

Like the ripple of a finger poking a body of water, Corbin shimmers away, his body waving until there's nothing left, and he's gone. The deal was not his to bargain, but I can't help wondering what matters drive him back to his realm.

Erline nods her head, and Erma glances behind, her attention on me and Ire. "Drop your weapon, Tember. There's no need. Not anymore."

Reluctantly, I do as she wishes, watching the bolts fluctuate and disappear.

"Go wait outside," Erma adds.

"No." My voice is firm and nonnegotiable, my fists clenching. "I'm not leaving your side while we're here."

Her lips thin into a line, and I can tell they hold some sort of crude and hurtful remark. Instead, she carefully blanks her face. It hurts more than the unspoken words.

"Giving Sureen strength will take a lot of power. It will fill this room and kill any living being within. Outside, Tember. Now."

I slouch closer to her, whispering while watching Sureen. She crosses her arms, her foot tapping, impatient. "Giving her what she wants isn't a good idea, Erma."

I don't have time to add anything, to plead my case. Erma screams a frustrated yell, rolls her hand in the air, and I'm outside of the dome.

# CHAPTER ELEVEN

*AIDEN VANDER*

*DEMON REALM*

We stand before the Domus Timore, and the black lava flowing upward sounds like the roar of a slow-moving waterfall. There are no doors, no windows, and no obvious entrances.

"How do we get in?" I ask my demon escort.

He tsks, shaking his head. Without answering me, he hobbles forward, the lava parting as he does so. Looking over my shoulder once more, searching for Ferox who disappeared not long ago, I turn and follow him through.

The sight before me would have been one I'd thought impossible, if I weren't standing here, witnessing it myself. Demons, of all variety, roam and stroll to destinations of their choice while conversing with others. The area we occupy is luxurious and not what I expected. The features are grotesque, gothic, and darkly beautiful.

Black leather couches occupy this room, interspersed with old, wooden chairs that creak under pressure. The room is octagon-shaped, and each corner has a fireplace with no fire. Instead, it drips black lavafalls, surely more portals for demons to travel through.

Above the fireplaces, mantels rest with skulls as décor, and behind it a wall of skulls crawling to the top. Their jaws are frozen in a silent scream, and pillars made of charred, black wood hold up the high tin ceiling, etched with delicate swirling designs. The tin drips, from where I'm not sure, but it's a steady stream of thick black rain. The drops don't dribble from everywhere I realize. They follow each demon, soaking into their skin upon impact.

"What is it?" I ask, glancing at my own arm as the first drop absorbs. Like a bee's thorn, it stings, and I suck in a breath of surprise as sensation changes.

I remember fasting to get my weight down for a boxing match. I remember taking the first bite of real food afterward. The sensation is like no other, a frenzy, when it slides down my throat and plops in my empty stomach. That's what this feels like as the black drop soaks into my skin. It's feeding a starving demon sustenance it needs to survive.

"It's liquid terror," I mumble, mesmerized.

"Very good. Come," the demon demands, impatient.

He begins walking, and I follow his wobbling strides, taking in the demons around me. They watch, whisper, their make vastly different from one another. One is green with grotesque features, short and plump, and hobbles past me. A gargoyle.

Standing by the lava fireplace, a banshee holds her hand out and her long nails obstruct the flow. Her pale white skin is a contrast to the black lava, and her red eyes watch it with interest. Sharp teeth poke past purple lips even as her tongue snakes out, licking them. White hair flows down to the back of her knees and sways with each shift of her impatient hips. The silky locks float like a breeze even though there is none. Her figure would make any woman envious.

Entering a hallway, we come across another room. It's circular and small, the walls made of mirrors. Each mirror flashes between numerous different humans, some sleeping, some in a wakened state though their faces droop with depression.

Stopping in my stride, I lick my lips, hungry for more. It's like a buffet. Momentarily, my eyes catch in one mirror, and I gaze upon them. My normal irises are gone, and in their place is lava, molten and moving. I'm not allowed the time to marvel or question this conundrum before my attention is averted.

A few humans inside the mirrors have a demon resting a hand along their shoulder. They continue along with their daily tasks, unaware they're accompanied by a creature who controls them.

In the middle of the circular room, a small demon - a little boy - stares at one particular mirror. I watch him, interested in the intensity of which he studies the bedroom and the sleeping human through the mirror. Slowly he shuffles, hypnotized and pulled by a force I don't feel from where I stand. The side profile of his face comes into view as he does. His features are angelic, innocent even, but the purple surrounding the skin of his hollow eyes tells me he's anything but an ordinary child.

His gait is automatic and slow, and the mirror ripples like disturbed standing water as he steps through and exits the other side. The mirror is nothing but a curtain I realize.

Climbing on the end of the bed, he stands to full, unwavering height. The mattress doesn't dip, like I'd expect, as though this child is weightless. The red patterned comforter remains unrumpled under his feet. Soundlessly sleeping, the woman he looms over rustles under her covers. She rolls over on her back, tucking a hand under her pillow to prop her head.

Something overcomes her – an internal instinct that tells her she's not alone. First, she wrinkles her nose, surely smelling the sulfur from our realm which wafts from the child. Her eyebrows slide higher, wrinkling her forehead, and she slowly opens her eyelids.

The look in her blue irises, the dilation of her eyes, is recognizable. I'd seen it many times when I was alive.

She blinks, clearing her vision, hoping that what she's seeing isn't real. Her lips part in dread, in consuming fear, and her nostrils flare with doom. What she's seeing is, in fact, there. Her fear trickles from her skin like smoke from a fire with no breeze. It travels along her bed, caresses the child, and floats to the mirror. I can feel it as it travels through. I can feel it from this side of the mirror, feeding me as a small appetizer. Flaring my nostrils, I inhale a deep breath, my eyelids fluttering. My mouth waters, and I swallow while rolling my head and stretching my neck. It's an addictive feeling, one I'll never have enough of.

Why doesn't she run? Scurry? Flee?

She's paralyzed I realize, unable to move as she witnesses a child demon at the end of her bed. He stands there, needing nothing more than to be present for his purpose to be fruitful. He doesn't need to scream; he doesn't need to speak. All he does is shift his stance, and she gasps in horror, her hand flying to her mouth to cover a scream that doesn't rip from her throat. Another wave of terror slams into me, a force of invisible smoke. It leaves her room as though a bomb exploded under her sheets. I hiss in a breath between clenched teeth, and my hands grasp my torso, feeding an unquenchable hunger while gripping the muscles which flexed on impact. I want more. I need more. Like a rabid, starving cheetah, I want to barge through that mirror and take her terror as my own – to rid the child of the scene and claim what's mine.

"Enslaving, isn't it?" my demon escort teases behind me, bringing my mind back to this realm and our current errand. I drop my hands back to my side in hopes of keeping my surprise at bay. "Don't get close to that one. Terrors aren't as friendly as they seem. It's games they enjoy. Games of the mind, you see. Games that drive one mad." I glance over my shoulder, catching him tapping his temple, and I get the distinct feeling he's been a victim of a Terror.

"Right," I mumble, glancing back at the mirror once more. The competitive drive fuels me, begs me to stay and conquer. I want to see what the child is made of, compared to what I'm capable, but only after I take the woman for myself.

"Come," the demon mumbles, leery.

## TEMBER

### DREAM REALM

Roaring with frustration, I slam my hand against the side of the dome, catching a few sandmen off guard as they linger between the willows across the cave's landscape. Their white eyes train on me, the noise distracting from whatever task they're trying to accomplish.

I push my hair out of my face with a huff, debating over ignoring her orders and charging back inside. She shouldn't be alone. Not here.

Resting my head against the wall of the dome, I watch the hues of yellow aurora borealis play with the cave's spikes along the ceiling. It doesn't take long before my distracted mind becomes uninterested, and I begin counting the pulsations to ease the tightness within my chest. No measures of relaxation techniques aid me in my quest to ease my troubled heart.

Erma is in there, unprotected. Erline is in there, unprotected. I know I can't protect from the threat of another fee – I'm not built for it. But what if the worst happens? What if Corbin returns with vengeance? I saw the look in his eyes. The real Corbin is troublesome and thirsty for control.

I close my eyes, breathing deep. Kat's dragon form floats behind my lids; the image of her breathing fire in the direction of those who care for her breaks my heart. It's a feeling I've been unfamiliar with until recently. Each black scale had glittered with flames beneath, illuminating them, outlining them. I don't recall her dragon's scales doing that before. What happened between the night in the alley and now? What happened in the past?

The bitter resentment, wafting from her, was thick and unforgiving. Does she have a reason for being upset? Of course she does. I mentally place myself in her shoes to find a way for me to gain forgiveness, and a voice interrupts the process, coming from beside me.

"You're the angel – the one he helped?"

My eyelids pop open in surprise, and I glance around me, settling on a figure standing to my right – a dwarf. His long black hair is pulled back into a leather loop, fastened at his neck. Bushy, unruly eyebrows dangle above his eyes which have no lashes. He's short but wide with muscle.

"Who?" I ask, frowning.

He nervously shifts, and his scent wafts my direction, thick with sage. "The sandman."

I swallow my guilt. However, I'm more interested in why a dwarf would go out of his way to hold a conversation with me. "The one Sureen is punishing for eternity?"

He nods, his thick square jaw ticking. I find my anxiety matching his own with mild curiosity.

The dwarves we met in the tunnels seemed absent of paranoia, driven by the work they do with their hands and their minds. Perhaps they guard their emotions carefully, fearful of their master, of their creator.

"Yes, I suppose I am. And you are?"

"My name is Nally." He dips his head. The hair tied at his nape falls over his left shoulder. "Do you know where she sent him?"

Placing a hand on his shoulder, I bend my knees, bringing myself eyelevel with him. His muscles are rigid beneath my palm, firm and sculpted from years of hard labor. "To the death realm, eternity as a shade."

Nally sucks in a breath and hangs his head.

I bend a little further, trying to capture his eyes. "Were you two close?"

He shakes his head, keeping his eyes downcast. "Sandmen do not hold emotions, so relationships cannot be built. But at the end – before she took him away – he sought help from me."

"Why you?" I pry, tilting my head.

He rolls his shoulders back, forcing himself to stand upright and proud. His eyes return to mine, and I drop my hand. "I am the eldest of the dwarves," he begins. "He wasn't sure who to turn to when he – when he . . ."

"When he began feeling emotions?" I supply for him.

His nose twitches, wrinkling over the bridge. "How'd you know?"

I lick my bottom lip. "It wasn't difficult to see."

"Right," he murmurs, glancing away at the willow landscape. "There's another world out there you know. Many, I imagine. I do not believe this is where we're meant to be. Not like this. This is no life." He pivots to me, and places a large, calloused hand over my wrist. "Your heart beats here, doesn't it?"

Nervous that he knows such a secret, a secret guarded carefully for optimal survival, I search his face for his true intentions. I see nothing but worry, sorrow, and inquisitiveness of an intelligent mind.

"Yes," I answer, narrowing my eyes.

Nally looks at my wrist, his thumb running over my heart in slow circles. "I wish I had a heart," he mumbles.

I don't know how to answer him, so I remain silent. Sometimes, having a heart is the recipe for a broken one.

He continues, "I heard the commotion from out here. I heard the roar of a dragon. Was she really here – the dragon the sandman assisted?"

A tear wells in my eye, spilling over the edge from the reminder of my failures. "Yes," I whisper. I angrily wipe my cheek with the back of my hand.

"Good," he mumbles, nodding his head and dropping my wrist. "She will save us."

Dumbstruck, my question comes out harsher than intended. "Excuse me?"

He doesn't answer me, his attention flicking over my shoulder. The dome glows brighter and his facial features elongate.

"What's happening?" he shrieks.

I close my eyes, my gut telling me how wrong this feels. "Your creator is getting a power boost."

His gaze shifts from me to the dome and then back again. His lips quivering. "You mustn't."

"Why?" I ask as he takes a shuffle back. "What's wrong, Nally?"

"She will create life!" he screeches. I reach out to him, and he shakes his head. "I must leave. I must leave and tell the others."

Lashing forward, I grip his upper arm with firm fingers. "Wait! Tell me what's wrong!"

Stuttering, he spits out the words as fast as he can as if he were sharing a large secret. He continues to back up even with my grip, his eyes shifting for listeners. "The life she creates isn't a life you've known. There is no love, Angel. I repair the dome when requested. I've heard the desires she and the demon fee have discussed. The creatures she plans to create will be built only for war."

I grit my teeth. "War?" I knew Corbin was up to something. Perhaps not definite, but deep down, my instinct is correct about him. Did he manipulate this situation, perhaps made it work in his favor? If he and Sureen are conspiring together . . .

"Are you ready?" Erma asks from behind me.

I drop my grip on Nally, turn my head, and look over my shoulder. Erma's face is dark, exhaustion and worry taking over her once delicate features. Her red curls are in disarray, this evening's events taking its toll.

Erline exits the dome, running her hand through her long white hair. With little effort, she conjures her winds, leaving in a swirl of visible airstreams, and disappearing from the realm.

"Is it done?" I ask, hesitant to know the answer. Erline isn't happy with her choice, choosing to leave instead of converse, choosing to flee and lick her wounded pride.

"Yes," Erma answers, grasping a stray red hair stuck between her lips and pulling it behind her ear. Her delicately carved brows furrow. "Why are you standing like that?"

I turn back to face forward, to Nally, preparing to bid farewell and perhaps console the stocky paranoid creature, but the dwarf is gone.

Standing up from my bent position, I sigh and face Erma. "We should go," I demand, walking to her. The information I've learned this day will have to be evaluated before I share.

Questions still hover on the edge of her lips, but she chooses not to voice them, gripping my upper arm with cold fingers instead. A yellow portal appears in front of us, swirling and beckoning us to enter. I look to Erma, her troubling thoughts visible on the surface. She ignores my gaze, leading us with a determined march, and we enter together.

# CHAPTER TWELVE

*AIDEN VANDER*

*DEMON REALM*

Hobbling through a dark hallway, the walls lined with black wallpaper with red swirling designs, the demon halts and turns to large double doors. They reach the high ceiling, consisting of heavy dark wood, intricately carved. They still smell freshly crafted.

He looks back at me for a moment, his eyes speculating as he weighs an internal struggle. A sliver of fear curls from his body, tendrils of smoke which remind me of a place I struggle to recall when the opportunity of a meal is presented before me. I wonder: Is it me he fears? Can I bend his will so easily?

My lips tilt in a smug smirk while I hold his stare, my gaze unwavering, a challenge that begs for a victor.

Blinking hard, he reaches out an arm, grasps the brass knob, and twists his wrist. The latch unlocks, and the hinges creak as one large door swings open. Glowing, yellow light spills from the room onto the hallway floor, and I wait, expecting the demon to make a move, to give me a reason.

Impatient under the watch of a predator, he thrusts his arm out, pointing inside the room, and his voice shakes. "I haven't got all day, Thrice Born. Enter." I watch his skin flap against his arm and lift my eyes to him.

I could feed from him. I could consume his terror, taking it for my own. It would be easy, satisfying, a drop of heaven in a place of hell. It would end him. I could end him. That thought alone sends a shiver up my spine, and I lick my bottom lip, ravenous.

The tendrils of his smoky fear increase, traveling to me like an obedient dog who wishes to only please his master. It wakes something in me, something I knew was there, lurking within, waiting for a moment in time.

My muscles tense, and my smile widens, pulling at the skin along my chin. The dark hallway brightens as my eyes smolder inside their sockets, hot yet soothing. It's right. This is right. This is me. This is who I am. *Embrace it.*

His breaths are heavier, and his nostrils flare to allow quick passage. A tightness in his chest threatens to consume him, just to feed me, just to give me what I desire, bowing his torso forward - a puppet string attached to his ribcage. I own his terror. It's mine for the taking, mine to consume, mine to possess.

151

I dip my chin, allowing this inner darkness, my inner demon to take what belongs to me.

His hands shake at his sides, and his one eye widens when he realizes what I'm doing. I'm commanding his body, pulling his emotions as though they never belonged to him in the first place. I could kill him. I could call for all his fear and know it will obey, destroying the host just to please. He would be gone, and I would be *more*.

He quivers, slightly, enough that it's hardly noticeable, but my sharp gaze takes it in. "Don't let it rule you, demon. Consuming your brethren be a slippery slope. You be meant for bigger things than destruction for which there be no return." My eyes narrow, and he stutters out his next words, short of hysterical. "He would not be pleased if you killed me."

I huff, a small chuckle tickling my throat. He begs. He begs and expects me to heed his request. He doesn't move an inch as I stride past him, shaking my head and entering the room. The door closes with a soft click behind me, and to my surprise, the demon didn't enter with me. His mismatched footsteps resound outside the solid door as he shuffles away, taking my meal with him.

I glance around, muscles rigid for the loss of sustenance. The flow of a lava fireplace obscures the sounds of my breaths which quiver with adrenaline – a high of sorts. I force myself to remain rooted, to not hunt down the demon and finish my meal.

*Focus*, I growl to myself.

No one is in here but me, and I take the opportunity, the distraction, to get to know the fee who created me before he arrives.

"Knowledge is power," I mumble, desperate to convince myself.

The walls are painted black, and the ceiling is high. Shelves of old books with worn spines and artifacts from ancient periods are littered throughout, disproportionate and misplaced. It's not a large room, but it's filled with furniture from an era I know nothing about.

A large bed is sits my right, and a canopy of deep red netting surrounds it. It falls past the mattress, waving in a nonexistent breeze. To my left, two red couches with high, curved backs face each other, and a large pool of black oil is puddled on the ground between them.

The puddle is what catches my eye, diverting me from inspecting the belongings within this room. Curious, I slip over to the couch and sit, my weight sinking me into the plush cushion. I lean forward in my seated position, my chest touching my thighs, and stick my finger out, submerging it in the puddle. My skin coats in black oil, and I pull it back, rubbing my thumb against it, eyeing it with suspicion. I look to the ceiling, curious as to how this puddle got here.

"There is no leak," a voice exclaims, loud in this quiet room. "The Oleum has been there since the beginning of time."

Unhurried, I stand and spin toward the voice. Behind the couch, a tall, lanky man leans against a bookshelf, his arms crossed. Light brown hair is disheveled atop his head, and I imagine women would find it charming. Black, wise eyes stare back at me, and carved, sculpted lips tilt in a smile.

"Oleum?" I ask.

He unfolds his arms and walks to the other couch, sitting down and swinging out his arm, inviting me to do the same. "Almost the same consistency as oil," he begins. "Oleum is anything but." He inclines his head, nodding to the double doors. "Did you not wonder what fell from the ceiling?"

I look at the Oleum then to my fingers. The oil is gone, absorbed in my skin. Oleum is what was raining in the common area, feeding the demons a snack as they passed through. "I see."

He lounges back into the couch and points at the puddle. "This is my personal Oleum. I do not share well, and this Oleum does not hold the same purpose as it does in the common areas."

"You're Corbin," I realize.

He inclines his head, tucking his chin into his collar bone. "Thrice Born," he greets. The way he speaks to me, it's adoring, like a child who's come home after a long absence.

I slouch and position my elbows against my knees, prepared to take full advantage of this weakness. "What does it do?"

"I'll show you." He holds up a finger and bends forward enough so that his face reflects within the black puddle. Moments tick by, and nothing happens. I frown and lean closer in hopes of a better view. Maybe I'm missing something.

He holds up a hand once more, halting me from hovering over top. "Don't taint it with your reflection. It must sense my own desires."

As my back rests against the couch, the oil begins to ripple and then bubble. It doesn't make a sound, and my lips part in anticipation.

Slowly, an oval emerges from the oil – a head – constructed by the slippery black liquid, and then a neck, and then two shoulders. A person – I realize – as soon as the full figure forms in front of us. It moves, lifting a slender arm and grabbing something that isn't there. I stand from the couch and lumber around to the other, wonder driving my anticipation.

"A woman?" I ask, recognizing the feminine features. "Who?"

He reclines back in his chair, and the springs squeak as he watches the oil woman continue her invisible task. "Katriane Dupont. My wife, and my relation, though I'm not sure if she's aware of the first."

"The dragon?" I ask, remembering what the Pyren said about a contract.

He tips his head, studying me over his shoulder. "How did you –" he cuts himself off with a sigh. "The Pyrens."

I slide my hands down my thighs, nodding once, encouraging him to continue. "Oleum shows you what you want to see most? Like a magic mirror?"

Twitching his eyebrows, he scratches the side of his jaw. "That and more. It allows me to possess my enemies while they remain unaware."

"How?" I tilt my head.

The woman is doing something, but I can't tell what. Her fingers flex, grasp, and release. How am I to know the purpose of her actions if I can't see her surroundings?

Corbin stands, adjusts his pants, and takes a small stride toward the woman. With a careful hand, he grips her chin and turns her face to him. Oil coats his thumb and knuckles, dribbling down his wrist. The woman freezes like she's having a thought or lost in a daydream. Corbin lowers himself, bending his knees and bowing forward, inching to her, nose to nose. The oil where her temples are ripples, and black tendrils, like fingers, wiggle their way out. They float between them before the oil settles on his forehead like a leech. It disappears, absorbing into his skin, and he inhales a deep breath, his eyelids fluttering.

Releasing the woman, she shakes her head, clearing her thoughts, and returns to whatever task she was doing. Corbin turns to me, a smile on his face. "Understand?"

I sigh, annoyed. "No."

He runs a hand through his hair. "I haven't had a new demon in a while," he mumbles. "Her thoughts, her most prominent thoughts, were shifted from her head to mine. To her, she lost herself in a day dream. She isn't aware her mind was tapped."

My forehead wrinkles, but the rest of my face remains impassive. "I see. Kheelan can read minds, but he can only read them if he's in the same vicinity. Whereas you can conjure any person and pull from them at will."

A wicked smile lights his black eyes with a mischievous glint. "I supply Kheelan with Oleum. He consumes it. If he does not drink it a few times a day, he cannot tell the thoughts within someone else's mind."

Shaking my head, I chuckle with no humor. Before, when I was human, even when I was floating in the void, I deemed Kheelan a powerful being. So powerful that I was an insignificant bug, splattered on his windshield. There was no hope of revenge for me, and now . . . now I couldn't care less about the revenge I wanted to deliver. Here I am, in the presence of a fee who dwarfs Kheelan in every aspect, and it bores me. I want to feed. I want to consume. I wonder . . . What would happen if I consumed a fee? Are they capable of feeling fear?

A question crosses my mind. "And how does Kheelan create life?"

Corbin leaves the pit, walking over to a hip-height side table. With his desires absent to the puddle and his reflection gone, the oil woman melts back into the body of liquid as a rain of droplets.

He picks up a crystal vase and a matching cup, pouring a liquid inside, scented in a familiar aroma - the bitter bite of Brandy. I eye the glass, and he silently gestures with his finger, asking if I care for some. I shake my head.

"I've always been partial to the earth realm's luxuries." He takes a sip, sighing with content. "Kheelan creates life by tying his own to them. If one were to die, it wouldn't affect him much. If they were to all die at once, it would greatly weaken him. If they try to leave, he could force their return." He shrugs. "Or take back the heart he gave them. Whichever he chooses."

"Is that why he doesn't have many humans walking his realm?"

"Such a curious mind for a demon. There's only one reason a demon voices questions: he thirsts for power." He tilts his head. "Do you thirst for power, Thrice Born?" We hold each other's gaze, but I keep my ground. I'm not afraid of him, and I'm unwilling to provide a window into my query. He grimaces while taking another sip before answering my question, "It is. Too much vulnerability is never a good thing when you have many rivals."

"You don't care for Kheelan," I state the obvious.

Pursing his lips, he narrows his eyes. "No. He's weak and egotistical. He has no idea how insignificant he is compared to the rest of us. Sureen and he have this in common. They've tied themselves to something that's easily destroyable," he reveals, placing the glass back down on the small table. "Sureen to her dome. Kheelan to the living."

"Oh?" I cross my arms. "And the others?"

Corbin twitches his eyebrows. "Erline is tied to the humans, and Erma, the fool that she is, tied herself to Erline. Without their ties, they're nothing."

"And you? What did you tie yourself to?"

"Wouldn't you like to know," he says, a chuckle to his tone. He dips his chin, looking at me through his eyelashes. "Kheelan plans to enter a few humanoids into an arena of sorts. He isn't aware what this will cost him, but he enjoys believing he's King."

"An arena?"

He shimmies nearer slyly, and he whispers, "Have you ever heard of a colosseum?"

## KATRIANE DUPONT

## EARTH REALM

The water droplets trickle down my bare back. My hands support me, placed inches below the shower head, my fingers splayed against the tiled wall. I let the water wash my troubles away, the heat diffusing the bubbling anger still inside me. Music plays in the background – soft violins and accented cellos.

I know without a doubt, and by experience, the fee always require payment for favors. Sureen pulled me out of the past, out of the dream and back into my sleeping body, per request. What did they have to give her in return? I wasn't going to wait around and find out.

My body aches with tireless opinions, a migraine threatening to wake. These are theories based on pure speculation, and I'm desperately trying to drown in music. It's not working.

Corbin's smirk invades the back of my eyelids. Seeing that grin tips me to the side of consuming paranoia; what does he want from me? I remember the mischief and charming demeanor which had rolled from him in waves. It was nearly impossible not to be affected. What he has planned in that mind of his, I should probably find out.

This is all too much – the fee pulling at me from all sides, Myla's death, the odd shifting of the Realms. I am to blame. I am the common factor. And I hate myself for the guilt.

I sigh, water dropping from my parted lips. Am I going through the stages of grief?

Scrubbing my face with my hand, I open my eyes. Corbin's smile dissipates as I watch the water drip from my chin in flowing waterfalls, splattering against the porcelain tub. Arching my back, I hold my breath and stretch my neck.

A moment ago, I stared at myself in the mirror as I gathered my toiletries. My mind couldn't focus, day dreams interrupting the troubling thoughts I should be compartmentalizing. I look as though I've aged ten years.

As I gazed within the mirror, tears streaming down my burning cheeks, I touched the wetness with my fingertips, bringing tears to the rest of my wounds. The bruises and the remainder of the cuts healed. The power coursing inside me has woken. It's like a drug – addicting and begging for more. I can feel it traveling through me, adding a renewed life. It'd be exhilarating if I were into that kind of thing. I want to be normal. This has never been what I wanted, and yet, I now have it.

This consequence won't be my last I'm sure. I'm a magnet for trouble.

The music changes songs, breaking me from my trance. I shut off the water, pull the curtain back, and step from the tub. My wet legs drip on my plush purple rug.

Grasping a towel from the hook and patting my face dry, I sigh into it. The smell of the sweet fabric softener calms me while water creates its own path down each slope of my exhausted body.

I groan when I come to the conclusion that I've painted a target on my back. When I took action, when I let my dragon half loose and handled them as if they were nothing but paper, I became something they should fear. The image replays in my head, their bodies flying through the air, the thud as they hit the dome wall, ending with Corbin's smile. Always Corbin's smile. It was the smile of evolutionary plans. What is it that ties me to him?

He fed from them, drinking in their fear and accelerating his powers. It was almost too obvious what he was doing, but he managed it with subtlety. It's a careful plan – to keep his magic hidden. What is this man capable of?

I'm not entirely sure of the logistics of creating a demon or how it's even done, but I suppose I don't want to know. I'm sure it takes some measure of extreme magic to do so. There are many breeds of demon, after all. Most of which I'm sure I only have basic knowledge.

Wrapping the towel around my torso, I reach and open the door to the bathroom, halting in my tracks. Tember rests against the door frame of my bedroom, adjacent to the bathroom. Concern wrinkles her perfect eyebrows.

"Get out," I demand, pointing to the wall as if my finger could poke through and hit the entrance door to my apartment.

Pushing from the door frame, she crosses her arms, uncomfortable with my festering hostility. She quirks an eyebrow. "We need to talk."

"No. No we don't." I push past her and enter my bedroom, dropping my towel. She's already seen me naked, twice. Why care about modesty now? "I've seen enough. I've been through enough to fully understand what you did and how you did it."

"But you preserved me, anyway. Why?"

I yank my clothes from the hangers, choosing to ignore her, and begin getting dressed. It's almost daylight outside, the morning sun rising and peeking through my blinds. I'm exhausted. My body may have rested for who knows how long, but my mind hasn't. My shop is due to open, and I can't afford to lose the income.

"Where are you going?" she asks as I stomp past her, heading down the hall and into the living room.

Slipping on my shoes, I eye her behind my disheveled, wet hair and tie the laces. "I'm running away. I hear Neverland is a good vacation destination. I might try there next since you know, technically, I'm hundreds of years older now. I believe I'm old enough to retire. Traveling to the past does that you know – ages you beyond your years. Maybe if I go to Neverland, I can be young forever."

My subconscious quirks a brow at my petty retort. We should talk, and I should get my answers. But right now, I can't even look at the person who exposed me to such danger.

I open my apartment door and descend the stairs, careful to not let my sarcasm cause me to miss a step. It wouldn't do to exit an argument by a tumble down a flight of stairs.

Tember follows me as I enter the shop, unlock the front door, and flip the sign to 'open.' People already mill about the streets, waking far earlier than I ever would have if I were on vacation. I suppose they must get their breakfast and caffeine fix from somewhere.

Turning from the door, I march to the breakroom, my shoes padding against the wood floor in an even, irritated rhythm. Tember props herself against the doorway after I enter, watching me but remaining silent.

I prepare the coffee and slam the pot into the machine, tapping on the button with a jabbing finger. I purse my lips, knocking my knees as I shake my legs, and my fingers drum along the counter. The tension is thick in the air. Neverland is sounding better and better as the morning progresses.

She clears her throat, and I prepare myself for the motherly instincts and unwanted advice she loves to bestow upon me. "I was trying to gain answers, Kat."

My nostrils flare. "Yeah?" I ask, sarcasm thick, dripping from my curled top lip. "Answers for who? You or Erma? Should we throw Erline into the mix?" I grab a mug from the open cupboard, busying my hands.

"Perhaps both," Tember whispers, her eyebrows pulled down. "I needed to know why Erline brought back her daughter. Why she inserted the dragon into you. Why she hid her daughter's soul. . ."

I spin to face her, my eyes narrow. "I know this isn't familiar to you, to feel love and the desire to protect them, but maybe, just maybe, she did it to bring back a sliver of her daughter." I don't know why I'm defending Erline. Maybe for the sake of keeping the argument flowing? I'm on the defensive with whatever pops out of Tember's untrustworthy mouth.

Tember's eyes roam my face. "You care for Myla, don't you?"

"Of course I did!" I shout. "She was more to me than someone who shared my thoughts and drove half my actions."

She bites the inside of her bottom lip. "Did? Past tense?"

Sighing, I close my eyes, turn, and rest the curve of my back against the counter. "She's dead."

Her arms drop to her sides, shock replacing the tension. "How?"

"The last time I went into the dream, I merged with it as did Myla. We both had full control and corporality of our bodies. They hung her for her crimes, just as in the past, but she was there. *She* was there. It was her they hung this time, not her past self."

165

"You're still a dragon," Tember points out.

I roll my eyes. "I prefer 'scaled warrior.' She left me a piece of her. Actually . . . a lot of her. It's what those who love another do."

Tember remains quiet for a while. "I'm sorry."

I chuckle a humorless laugh, filling my mug with a delicious dark brew. "You should be. How'd you do it?"

"The sandman?" she asks. I nod my head, and she readjusts her position against the doorframe, her throat constricting as she swallows her palpable guilt. "I asked for his assistance – to make you dream of Myla's past since you two were one and the same."

I take a scalding sip of coffee, grimacing as it travels over my tongue. "And Sureen? How does she fit into this?"

"She discovered what the Sandman and I were doing. She put a spell on you and took her sandman."

"And the sandman? What consequences does he have for aiding you in your quest of absolute stupidity?"

Tember rakes a hand through her hair, her fingers pulling on the curls. "Eternal punishment in the death realm."

"Spectacular," I spit, grasping the mug with both hands. "You made a deal with Sureen, who placed me in the past, forced Myla to be killed *again*, and what? What was the tie breaker? What deal did you have to make?"

"Erline and Erma," she licks her bottom lip. "They gave her the ability to create life. They allowed her to temporarily tie herself to them so that she could draw their power."

"Hm. A fee gas pump." I close my eyes, bite my bottom lip, and shake my head. A hysterical chuckle bursts past my front teeth. "Angel of the year goes to – "

"Kat?" Tember mumbles, cutting me off.

"What?" I bark.

"There's more."

My eyelids feel heavy, and my blinks feel gritty. I take the heel of my hand and rub my left eye. "Do tell."

"Erline is using you for a power struggle. We've been made aware that you're her chosen weapon."

Popping my lips, I mumble. "Aren't you all?" I don't have it in me to care anymore. My emotions are spent, my exhaustion is overbearing, and my nerves are raw.

"That's not all," she sighs. "Sureen and Corbin have been collaborating together. For what, I'm not sure. Sureen has been given the power to create life, Kat. Surely the two have something planned – "

I cut her off, rubbing my hand down my face. This is too much to handle at once. I am not the solver of all problems. "How long have I been gone? Asleep?"

"A few days."

Animosity swells within my chest, and I take a hot sip, rubbing the back of my neck with my free hand. It does nothing to distract my mind and the dark thoughts swirling within. I'm nothing but a fly to them, easy to swat away and perfect for cleaning up messes.

The one who started this all, the one who took me from my nice and quiet exiled life, stands not feet from me. She has the nerve to make their problems my problems. She's trying so hard to be innocent, so hard to get me to see reason, by relaying information that deflects her own actions.

My straying gaze drops to the floor, eyeing the many crumbles of dried dirt I have yet to sweep away. I bend and gather a pinch.

"What are you doing?" Tember asks, wary. I ignore her while I debate her very near future. Licking my bottom lip, I come to an easy, yet merciful conclusion and create a portal in record time. I ignore her murderous eyes, and I flick my wrist, sending her through. The smile that lifts my cheeks is one of glee as I hear her growl fade while her body transports to another realm. It feels good to have an unlimited, untapped power. I frown, lift my mug to my mouth, and take another sip. Maybe too good.

# CHAPTER THIRTEEN

*DYSON COLEMAN*

*DEATH REALM*

For the past . . . I don't even know how long . . . Gan has been chirping like a bird, unevenly tuned and sporadic. The longer he does it, the more it sounds like a dying bird. Maybe that means he'll eventually stop . . . and the bird will be dead forever... right?

I need sleep. Humans need sleep. This can't carry on for much longer. If it does, I'll end up chirping along with him, crazy-eyed and google brained. We'd be two peas in a pod, and then –

I smack the side of my head in an attempt to tap out the crazy stirring within.

"Bodily harm will do you no good," Sandy murmurs as he rests his head within his cell.

I shush him, the noise obnoxious and exaggerated. "Can you let me go crazy in peace, please? Is it too much to ask?"

I've tried covering my ears once, but the rebounding chirp bounces within the cells. It doesn't end before he begins again. The sound penetrates through the skin of my hands, determined to drive me to the brink of what's left of my sanity. I'd take the dripping noise over this any day. I can't even hear the leak splattering against the cell bars before sliding off and thumping against the floor. This obnoxious noise is that consuming.

"Think they'll give me a muffin to shove in his mouth?" I ask Sandy, pointing to a vampire traveling by, going deeper into the cells. "If Gan comes a little closer, I could grab him. If I can grab him, we could gag him. If we gag him – "

"There will be no gagging," he interrupts.

The light from the vampire's torch is whisked away once he rounds the corner, leaving us back in the dark. At least we have Sandy's eyes to give us some sort of light.

I open my mouth to retort, but three more vampires travel down the tunnel, slowing for the same corner, before they disappear, following one another. I frown when more arrive in the same fashion, standing once I hear screams deeper in the cells.

"What's happening?" I ask, slinking to the edge of my cell.

Sandy stands, coming to the corner, wedging himself between bars without touching them to get a better look. "I am not sure," he whispers, questions forming on his own tongue.

Hissing and shouts, growls and pleas. Goosebumps raise over my skin, and the breath leaving my flared nostrils is heavy. I wait for the cause, preparing myself for what's to come.

Instead of blurring in their usual speed, a new vampire leisurely pads down the tunnel, torch in hand, followed by two more.

"What's going on?" I ask them.

They approach Gan's cell first. Choosing to ignore my question, they slide a key in the hole and unlock his cell. Gan shouts and giggles as they shackle his wrists and hoist him from the floor.

"Yaris, what about the wolf and sandman?" one asks the vampire standing outside Gan's cell.

He turns to me but speaks to them. "He will put up a fight," he surmises, pursing his lips. "Drain some of his blood first. Then take them both. Kheelan wants all prisoners at the Colosseum."

I back away from the bars, my bare heel catching against the cracks of an uneven floor. My nostrils flare, and despite the cold, my body begins to sweat. The lock to my cell unlatches, and my back hits the wall behind me.

"No," I mumble, hearing the squeal of the metal hinges. "No."

I don't see them coming, their blurs faster than the minimal light Sandy's eyes provide. Their luminosity is swallowed by the dark, pitch-black dungeon. The vampires are snakes striking a blind, misplaced foot, and I'm helpless to defend.

My upper torso is wrapped, constricted by strong arms - vices of impending death. They reek of corpses, of rotting decay. Fear grips my heart, and my eyes widen like a frightened deer, glowing green. My wolf surfaces to defend while my fear holds me captive. I mentally slide aside, allowing him the forefront of my mind. He wastes no time, roaring inside me as he pushes through. Our lives are on the line.

My bones begin to crack, pop, and reshape to that of my wolf. The fingers claw at the vampires' arms, digging into their flesh, my nails now claws. Fur sprouts over my skin, pricking the pores as it pokes through. I tip my head back, a growl ripping from my throat, a threat from my wolf. I'm almost there. My wolf is almost there.

But he's too late . . .

Teeth clamp on both sides of my neck, cutting through the skin and hitting veins. It's all too easy, all too victorious, and I, too weak. Their teeth bruise my skin, puncturing through with a pop. The fangs slide across the large veins, lighting my nerves with intense agony. I feel the pull when the vampires suckle, hear the sickening sound of slurps. The blood leaves my body, flowing

172

through the open wounds into the mouths of thirsty sharks. It weakens me, and I struggle against them with everything I have. My wolf continues to transform, to fight for himself, to fight for me.

Too much blood is lost, his fight fading, and blessed darkness takes us.

## KATRIANE DUPONT

## EARTH REALM

*A black area with no walls encases me. The feeling is eerie like I could fall off and float into nothing for the rest of eternity. That's what this place is – nothing. It's a bridge between minds, held within a dream, where no senses exist.*

*Though I conjured this place with a purpose, it doesn't mean I hold no fear. Everything frightens me these days. I'm capable of the unimaginable, but I can no longer go without the help of someone I trust most – someone who's bound to love me unconditionally . . . I hope.*

*In front of me are two chairs, wooden and antique, facing one another. I cross my legs, stuffing my ankles under my thighs, and close my eyes.*

*"Janine," I whisper to the black abyss. The words leave my lips, too deep to be my normal tone, like the song*

*of a whale as it reverberates under the water. The pressure changes in the atmosphere, thick and heavy. I fight to breathe normally, to calm my panic. I've never conjured a psychic before.*

*In slow transparency, the woman I remember oh so well, enhances to solidity. Her long brunette hair flows as she turns her head, and her chocolate eyes roam our surroundings, confused yet frightened. Her boney fingers grip the wooden seat of her chair, the knuckles white.*

*"Mom," I whisper. Her head snaps to me.*

*I've been longing to speak to her, to hear her words of wisdom that I've missed. The warmth in her tone, the twinkle of love in her eyes, I ache for it. I ache for her . . . for the comfort of a mother.*

*"Katriane?" She blinks, her voice in awe. Her head swivels once more, taking in the pitch black. "How – How did you do this?"*

*I uncross my legs and lean forward, situating my elbows on my knees. I wipe a hand down my face. "I have no idea."*

*She turns her attention back to me, slow and calculating, her brows pinched. "Is this a dream?"*

*I blow out a breath. "Yeah."*

*"But how?" Tilting her head, her eyes roam my length. She reaches forward, before thinking better of it, and pulls back, gripping the seat once more. It's as if she*

*thinks she'll fly from the chair if she doesn't have good purchase.*

*"You look well, mom," I murmur. She does – the last time I saw her, precisely after I saved her, she was practically on her death bed.*

*When she doesn't answer me, I reach, my hand running down her arm past her elbow and to her wrist. I grasp her fingers and tug gently, pulling them from the chair. I fold her fingers in mine. "I – ah -. Mom, I need advice."*

*She visibly droops, her face softening. "Katriane, we shouldn't be talking. You've been banned from the coven. Subconscious or not, this breaks the rules of your banishment."*

*"Will you just listen?" I ask between clenched teeth. I don't know how long I can hold up this conjure. I can already feel myself draining.*

*Chewing on the inside of her lip, she contemplates. "Proceed," she demands, sweeping her free hand out.*

*"I don't know what to do." My shoulders sag. "I believe I was brought back for the wrong reasons. I don't know what I am, I don't know who I am, and I don't know what all I'm capable of." I pause, taking a deep breath. "There's war between light and dark inside me." I place a hand on my chest.*

*"There's a war between light and dark within the realms," she sighs, taking her hand from mine. "This is what I warned you of, Katriane."*

"What?" I ask, looking at her hand as she folds her hands in her lap.

"The beast." She nods to me but more through me. "It's untamable. It's an addiction. The first born is too strong for one body to hold and one fee to try and control."

"Right." I scrape my hand down my face again, steeling myself to break the news. "Myla's dead."

My mom closes her eyes, cursing in French. "There's no place for the twice dead."

"I know," I murmur.

She opens her eyes, her jaw ticking. "You have no idea what this will do. You now hold all the powers of the first born witch, of the dragon. They'll come for you. They'll use you. A war will come if it hasn't already begun."

I exhale, slouching in my chair and glancing away. "This much I've learned already."

Picking up the hand within her lap, she shakes a finger at me. "Do not be cocky, daughter. The realms have already shifted – the entire coven felt it." She takes a calming breath and speaks to me in a stern, hushed tone. "You have no idea the power of the fee."

We stare at one another, paused in silence. "So, what do I do?"

Her answer is swift as if she's already thought this all through. I wouldn't be surprised if she knows more than she leads me to believe. Psychics tend to do that – to withhold information in hopes of not changing the future.

*"You steer clear of them. You flee. You hide. You don't show them what you're capable of."*

*I lick my bottom lip. "I can't."*

*"And why not?" She crosses her arms. Tired of the questioning, she slips into her visions, her eyes rolling into the back of her head until all I see is the whites. It doesn't take long, seconds maybe, before her eyes return to mine, scornful and malicious. Her cheeks burn a bright red. "Katriane Dupont . . . you challenged not one fee but four?"*

*I square my shoulders. "I did. Did you see it all?"*

*"Yes," she hisses, her nostrils flared. "Do you have any idea the target you've painted on your back? The consequences of your disobedience? You showed them a taste of what you can do. They'll come for you. All of them. They'll want you for themselves." She pauses, her jaw snapping. "You've painted a target on all of the earth realm just by being here."*

*My lips firm, the fire curling within my stomach. "I didn't call you here to be chastised. I called you for help, for advice."*

*She shakes her head, closing her eyes. Running her index finger over the bridge of her nose, she continues. "You'll die. I've seen you in the death realm, Katriane. I've seen you a shade."*

*"What if –" I pause, frowning and disliking my train of thought. "What if I kill them? All of them?"*

"You can't do that." She drops her hand, her expression steel. "You can't kill the fee. All the realms will merge. They are the only thing keeping the realms separate. The living, the dead, the warriors and creatures of all likes, cannot live together in harmony."

Frustrated, I sag in my chair. I'm out of ideas.

"I have no advice for you," she adds in a whisper. "But that's not all I've seen." I look at her from under my lashes. "Someone will come for you. Soon. You must go with him."

"Go with him where? You just told me to keep myself hidden!"

"I do not know," she murmurs. "But I know it's important. That's all my vision revealed."

I nod, closing my eyes.

"The future is uncertain, but right now, I can't help you, and I can't hide you." She leans in, tipping my chin up with her knuckle. Her eyes hold such sorrow it breaks my heart. Unshed tears wait within the lids, and her bottom lip quivers. "Do you know how much this hurts, my daughter? To know the life I created will soon dwell with the dead?"

Tears prick my eyes in return and trickle down my cheek. One runs to the corner of my lips, spilling inside my mouth and coating my tongue with the bite of salt.

I sniff as I feel something . . . odd. It's a metaphorical tap on the shoulder, and I feel as though I have eyes on the back of my head. Twisting my torso *against the seat to look behind me, I try to discover the cause, but nothing is there.*

*"It's him," she whispers. I turn back to her. "He's here for you. You must wake."*

*"I'm not ready yet," I confess, my voice on the edge of hysterics.*

*She grabs my jaw with both hands, her fingers brushing my cheeks. "You must. You are strong, Katriane. Even I do not know the strength building within you, the power you have become. But if anyone can fix this wrong, it is you. You must remain strong." She shimmies to the edge of her seat, her mouth inches from my forehead. "Resist the dark," she whispers, placing a kiss on my forehead.*

*With that single peck, the dark dream - my conjure - fades.*

# CHAPTER FOURTEEN

*ELIZA PLAATS*

*DEATH REALM*

I grab the tray from the counter, the smooth bones grinding against the gritty concrete surface. Shuffling toward the dining entryway, I turn to Mrs. Tiller.

She looks so concerned, her eyebrows pulled toward eyes filled with grief and anxiety. She tugs at her fingers. This action has become such a habit with her. I try my best not to comment about it, to let her comfort herself with repetition. She fears for me.

"You should stay here," I whisper.

Swallowing, she nods with reluctance, dropping her fingers to her side and clenching them into fists. I bite my bottom lip and turn from her with a deep sigh.

I know what I'm doing. I know why I have so much concern for the well-being of Mrs. Tiller. I'm grasping for anything - anyone - to protect, to feel like I'm doing something. Everyone around me is fighting for their life and what's to come in the very near future. It's my duty to guard Mrs. Tiller like it's the one thing I'm positive I know how to do. Even if she's already dead, I'm not taking any chances. I failed her once. I'm not doing it again.

In the back of my mind, the sandman's words play on repeat, echoing in the chambers of my skull. If I could figure out how to channel Kheelan's power without him discovering, I may have a chance.

Could I do it, though? Could I marry him for my own revenge? To free myself? I squash the revulsion that's settled in the pit of my stomach.

This could be my part in the rebellion I'm now willing to fight. Aiden would have wanted this for me. He would have wanted me to continue, to fight for the heart within my chest. This is my last chance. There's no other road for me to question if it's the right course.

Taking a deep breath, I totter through a carved, rounded stone arch. The contents on the tray wobble like my inner turmoil. Oh, how much I want to flee right now. That stubbornness I used to have when I was a doctor, a high level of pure determination, has abandoned me. I find myself swimming in a sea of weakness and terrified each breath I take could be my last.

The dining room is brighter than I expected it to be. All the candles are lit, and the stone floor feels smooth beneath my shoes, unlike the last time I came through here. Someone must have cleaned and lit the wicks in record time.

It is difficult to keep up with the vampires that move faster than my eyes can register. It's like trying to see the wind; practically impossible. I'd bet they did this – they cleaned for the visitors.

I swallow with a numb tongue. Kheelan seems to be going out of his way to impress his guests, which does nothing to settle my nerves.

Seated at the table, Kheelan folds his hands in his lap as soon as we catch eyes. He waits for me to deliver the goblets for himself and his arriving guests, to serve him like his willing slave or dutiful wife.

The slapping of shoes grasps my attention, providing the perfect excuse to drop Kheelan's gaze without seeming as weak as I feel.

To my surprise, Yaris walks in at a human pace, straightening his clothes and wiping blood from the corner of his lips with the cuff of his sleeve. He leans against the wall, closest to the arch of the throne room, and scratches his chin as though he's bored. A lit candle above his head reflects in his hair with a dull hue, making his hair seem golden.

My gaze travels across the black veins along his arms to the pointed teeth poking out of his top lip. How long ago were those teeth sunk in innocent skin? A shiver runs up my spine, igniting every nerve with an unpleasant tickle, and goosebumps raise on my skin.

A fire is lit, the blue hues licking the stone within, trying to consume something impenetrable. I'd love to be like the rock right now – I'd love to be that firm and indescribable, both inside and out.

The smell of sage fills the dining room. It's not an unpleasant smell, but it's one I am now associating with cruelty. Every time I smell it, it's when I'm around Kheelan.

Kheelan beats his fingers, one by one, against the table. I gulp and glance at the tray, steadying my shaky grip. It's as though his fingers are a drumroll of what's to come. I do fear him and his impatience. But not as much as what I fear is coming next.

I fear the fee who creates demons and what possible purpose he has here. I'm not entirely used to Kheelan's antics, but I've never met nor heard anything about this newcomer. Something makes him special, something which requires this to be a formal occasion. Or, do they always entertain the other fee this way?

A shade I didn't recognize came to the kitchen earlier, handing me a silky, black, long-sleeved dress with a mandatory corset. I've never seen nor worn anything like it, and I reluctantly slipped it on as soon as he left the room. Mrs. Tiller was kind enough to compliment me, but I could see the worry behind her eyes. Her troubled and questioning expression mirrored my own. What does this man and the colosseum have to do with one another?

The tray clinks as I set it down and begin placing the goblets even with the stone chairs. My hands are trembling with adrenaline. I pause to fumble with the hem of the dress, pulling the sleeves further down my wrists.

The breaths traveling through my nose sound rushed and heavy, and the blood pumps, pulsing within my ears. I try to slow them down, to quiet them and gain better control of my senses. I need to remain sharp. Yaris and Kheelan are watching me like prey. Surely, they can hear my anxiety whistling through my nostrils, too.

Yaris speaks, and I nearly jump out of my skin, the hair prickling on the back of my neck, as goosebumps freckling my skin, harden further. "They've arrived sir," he alerts, his words hissing around his fangs.

With a huff and a final yank on my sleeve, I glance up. His head is averted, watching through the other archway leading to the throne room. Butterflies beat through my stomach, and I fight the urge to run.

Kheelan chuckles, glee glittering his black eyes. "Scared, are we?" He blinks innocently.

I choose to tuck my chin, to busy myself setting the delicate and light foods across the round stone table, than to play his game by giving him the satisfaction of answering his tedious question.

We were told our guest enjoys tiny tea sandwiches, so that's what Mrs. Tiller and I prepared. I grip a small plate within my fingertips, placing it to my left. I set it down as gently as possible, but the sound of china against stone still fills the room.

Their footsteps come first, the pitch changing from a slapping echo to a dead beat once they cross the archway into the dining room. A wave of heat and the smell of sulfur follow, wafting in like a humid breeze.

Turning my head toward the kitchen, I wrinkle my nose discretely, refusing to draw unwanted attention to myself from creatures who master fear. Fear is the only thing consuming me right now.

*Keep calm, Eliza. Set the table and get out of here.*

The scent evolves, replaced by a sweeter aroma I can't name. It's alluring, inviting, promising sweet relief; a hot tongue against chilled skin. I fight with myself to maintain my control instead of the pull these guests summon. I grip my fingers around the edge of the table to steady my balance and center my core.

"Corbin, always a delight," Kheelan greets, pausing after drawing out his last word.

Clenching my jaw, metaphorically holding myself together, I wrap my fingers around the tray, lift, and turn to leave, forcing myself to be fully aware of my actions.

"Is this the guest? But – But," Kheelan splutters. "He looks precisely like -"

Frowning, I stop in my tracks, my lips parting as I hang on the reasoning for Kheelan's unease. He's not a man who's ever caught off guard. But, do I really want to know?

*No*, I answer myself. Yet, I remain rooted, frozen, still as a statue.

"The shade twice dead?" An unfamiliar voice asks.

Oh, that voice, filled with much mischief yet licked with liquid pleasure. Such a poetic tone would turn any girl's legs into jelly. But that's not what causes me to suck in a breath and hold it. The blood drains from my face. Shade twice dead?

The poetic voice continues, "You'd be correct. I'd introduce the two of you, but I hear you've already been acquainted."

Kheelan splutters. The white noise within my ears prevents me from hearing the words slithering from his mouth.

I turn, slow, exaggerated, time standing still. It takes me back to the tween before I died, to the time I met the man of my dreams . . . literal, devastating, heart-quenching dreams.

My eyes find what I'm looking for, the rest of the room blurring in my peripheral vision as though it melts from the background. There, standing with a straight back filled with pride, exactly as I remember him, is my Aiden.

I gasp. The tray leaves my fingers and crashes to the ground.

# TEMBER

## GUARDIAN REALM

I pop through the portal with no grace, my arms flailing. My destination is unknown until I'm buried in a downy drift of deep, wet snow. My fingers curl into the familiar white fluff, packing into my palm and creating a firm ball as I gather my bearings.

The breeze is chilly, a few flakes melting against my skin. It's moments like these that I relish the absence of pain.

Lifting my head, I prop myself up on my elbows and climb to my feet. I feel the portal close behind me, the breeze rushing through the now empty space, and tickling the loose curls on the back of my neck.

I rake a hand through my hair, my fingernails scraping my scalp. I know where I am. I know where she sent me. I stand in the forest belonging to the elves. The woodland smells of the guardian realm are familiar – it's an aroma that's hard to forget, and there isn't another smell like it. I've fought wars here, fought for my people, watched the blood splatter along the mud from both lines of battle.

The fact she knew where to send me is chilling. All except for the fee and most powerful, who transport themselves to wherever they wish, need to have been to a destination in order to travel there on their own via portal, shimmer, or sandstorm. It is why the fee built portals for their own creatures who frequently leave their realm.

Though she may have sent me to my realm, she did not send me to safety. Whether that's on purpose or by accident, I'm not sure.

I glance up and to the east. There, floating in the sky, obscured by a pleasant downfall of snowflakes, is the Angel's ground. A glittering, never-ending night sky looms over it, whereas where I stand, it's bright, the snow descending from nowhere.

This is the realm filled with guardians – with warriors capable of protecting themselves, this realm, and much more. The wars here are brutal, and me being on territory that isn't mine could cause another.

I often wondered why Erma created beings built for war. She and Erline are close. Erline created beings who were defenseless, for reasons I can't fathom. They've thrived and are now capable of such, though it could possibly lead to their own demise someday, but in the beginning, they were weak.

Perhaps Erma created us to defend those who couldn't – to defend Erline's creations, at least in the beginning. Now, we protect them from themselves. However, with the revelations about Sureen and the possible complications of her probable future actions, we could be defending them against their wildest nightmares.

I arch my back, straightening my spine and limbering my muscles. Being tossed from a portal came as a surprise. I didn't have a chance to ease into it, and my muscles suffer the consequences. It won't do me any good to come across an elf, stiff as the trunk of these forest trees.

Erma used to live down here with the Yoki Elves, walking amongst them like she does now on the Angel's Ground. Perhaps that is why they are bitter, why they don't get along well with angels. Jealousy is a root to a gnarled tree.

Scanning the forest, I quiet my breaths and sharpen my eyes. An angel hiking this forest is an angel asking for trouble.

"What are you doing here?" A voice whispers behind me. I whip around and scan the many trees smelling of lemon and sandalwood. My eyes fall on a figure treading my direction.

Erma's tiny red ringlets whip in the wind, a whipplemonk wrapped around her shoulders. She wears a white rawhide, a partial shell of an Oxtra.

I remember the Oxtra well from the battles of the past. They're the animals who carry the freshly chopped wood of the Yoki Elf tribe. Their heads resemble a goat and their bodies are covered in long white fur. As large beasts, several human heights, they stand on their two back legs which adds to their musculature. Oxtra's are equipped for a hardy job, but they are as deadly as they look, and difficult to kill.

A part of me is shocked that the fur adorns her shoulders. Though the Oxtra work for the Yoki, the shawl was gifted to her by the Igna Elves, the hunters, when she walked among the elves. Since then, it has hung in her closet and collected dust.

I tilt my head. If she's wearing it, she wants something from the elves.

The whipplemonk chirps, the sound of a high-pitched tiny bird that ricochets a tiny song with one squeak. I smile, my fondness for the palm-sized animal swelling within my chest. Back when I'd have missions in this area, I always adored them.

Holding many similarities to animals on the earth realm, they have a face like a small monkey, six legs with delicate feet like a tree frog, and a long, whipped tail scaled like a rat. They're loyal and loving, but when crossed, they can be a nightmare just the same. All Erma's creatures are defensible and rightfully so.

Shaking the fresh fallen snowflakes from my hair, I answer distractedly, feigning indifference, "I didn't ask to come here, if that is what you question."

A small smile plays at the corners of her full carmine lips, smugness puffing her cheeks. "She sent you back, did she?"

I flare my nostrils and sniff. "Apologies have never been a skill I excel at."

"Humanity doesn't suit you, Tember," she responds, quick-witted and full of deep sarcasm.

"I'm aware." I pause, disregarding the ping of offense which stabs the heart within my wrist. I frown instead. "What are you doing down here? You know it's not safe."

She laughs, stroking the head of the whipplemonk with her index finger. With each caress, the tiny creature's skin wrinkles, his eyes contently hooded.

"You forget who I am." Her tone is like dripping blood from a fresh wound. "It's not safe for you, but it is for me. I created the Elf Tribes, Tember. I can put them right back where I found them."

Closing my eyes in annoyance, I feel a headache beginning between my pinched eyebrows. "They're hostile, Erma. There's a reason the angels and the elves have no ties with one another."

"Don't you think it's time to rectify that?" she hisses, the wind almost carrying it away. "Time and time again, I've watched the elves and the angels destroy one another. And for what I ask you? The affections of your creator?"

I ignore her questions, because we both know the answers, and instead, ask another. "Why? Why are you here?"

"Do you think me a fool, Tember?" She kisses the whipplemonk on the forehead, his black eyes disappearing when its double-fold eyelids close in affection. She lifts him up until her arm can reach no more and uses her power to lift him in the air, settling him on a white branch above our heads. His body blends so well with the bark, his skin camouflaged from the threats lurking within his forest.

Erma had a sense of drama when she created the creatures who roam this land. Perhaps she was in a dark place. The Erma I know is filled with light and hope. Maybe she wasn't always so. The many creatures who lurk this land would frighten any child.

She continues, "Sureen has never held the power to have warriors herself. With the coming light of Erline's powerful daughter, and the reasoning behind it, she'll be more than determined to build protection for her realm. And that's the least of our worries, Tember. She could do so much more." She begins parading deeper into the forest, and I, traveling behind her, hang on every word.

Whenever we are alone, she makes a point to touch me with affection, but this time, she passes me without a second thought or a moment of hesitation. Does she hold me as dear as she once did? Or is she as angry with me as Katriane?

Searching the forest for danger, I settle into my natural element – a protector. I keep my muscles loose, my body at the ready.

"Myla's dead. Erline's daughter is dead," I blurt.

She whips around, eyes furious. "What?"

I incline my head. "She died in the past. Her second death."

Erma closes her eyes, turns and mutters, "Erline already knows. I had wondered why she seemed filled with sorrow before she left Sureen's realm."

"What do you plan to do? Where are you going?" I ask.

"Well." She blows out a breath and stops. Her foot crunches in the snow as she turns to me once more, her face blank. "It would seem you're intent on traveling along. I suppose you'll find out when we get there."

Erma trudges onward while I'm rooted to the spot, snow up to my mid-calves. Her voice held no malice, but the lack of information said it all. She doesn't wish to speak to me more than she must. I'm a disappointment to her, unworthy of her trust and time.

I roll my neck, popping my spine, and follow with stealth and anxiety. My shoulders bunch, my tension profuse. This is enemy territory, and here I am, walking the land where I've ended the lives of many elves.

I grit my teeth and press my tongue to the roof of my mouth. This is an appalling quest. We're beckoning misfortune.

The snow packs beneath my soles, dense yet forgiving. The layers of crystals shift and vibrate the balls of my feet, a muffled, crisp crunch under each subtle modification of weight. Twigs, buried beneath, spontaneously snap; brittle, fragile, yet merciless, giving way to our location in a way I'm desperate to stifle.

It's ironic, how the snow and the debris beneath it resemble my current dilemma. I accommodate for whom I guard, which is my purpose. But beneath my surface, I am a dead branch, discarded by what created me, buried beneath a frozen land and considered fragments of what I once was.

Eventually, she slows and allows me to match her pace. The heat boiling within her lessens to a simmer, her movements more graceful and less plodding.

"Sureen and Corbin," I begin, trying to find a way to tell her what I've learned from the Nally.

Erma cuts me off with the wave of her hand. "I already know." I frown at her admission, biting the inside of my cheek. Perhaps she's more aware of her fee siblings than I give her credit for.

I don't know why she's choosing to walk. She could use a portal to travel. Perhaps her errand requires more discretion, or maybe a more personal entrance than arriving abruptly, uninvited, to a territory that holds her in contempt.

Wood snaps up ahead. Erma's unaffected by it as though what lurks in this forest will never be the means to her demise. She forgets that she created capable creatures.

I stop and listen, my eyes shifting through the trees, waiting for the branch to drop to the snow. It thumps to the ground moments later, along with other branches it hit on the way down. The solid, frozen soil beneath the snow trembles under its weight.

The blizzard is getting heavy, packing its weight against frail limbs in the dead of a winter season. The scenery – white snow and black bark, makes it difficult to distinguish between nature and beings. The creatures here are built to blend.

I breathe deep, letting my senses roam, calming the swirling emotions within like the dulling of a flame. One more breath, and a vibration in the wind catches the influx as the breeze switches; a whistle within the pockets of the wind. I keep my eyes closed as it travels closer, visualizing it, constructing its direction and shape.

My hand flies to my cheek, catching the arrow before it grazes the skin.

Opening my eyes, my expression blazes, the snowflakes falling against my cheeks melt. I snap the wooden weapon in two. A halo forms around my head, my protection, my nature, coming to the front.

I duck down, glancing at the arrow as it plunges from my hand into the snow, ready for what's to come.

# CHAPTER FIFTEEN

*KATRIANE DUPONT*

*EARTH REALM*

My eyes open, blinking and fluttering, to dispel the layer of oily grime gathered there. I lift my head, taking in my dark room through foggy eyes. Through the doorway, light from the living room filters in, unmoving shadows cemented on the wood floor, highlighting the dark grain.

I couldn't fall asleep without the light. The feeling of vulnerability had kept me awake. For some reason, the light chased away my insecurities.

Something shifts in the corner of my room – a subtle twitch of cloth, enough to alert me I'm not alone. My attention snaps to the corner, and my heart thuds heavily, swelling one dense beat before dropping to my toes.

A figure, dressed as a sandman but transparent like a ghost, nervously fidgets with his fingers. We stare at one another, his jaw firm, while my lips part. I want to scream, to be terrified, but the noise doesn't leave my throat.

Pulling the comforter tighter around me, I gulp. "Who are you?"

Nervous, yet willing, he slinks in my direction. "Your sandman," he murmurs.

My eyelids flutter at the density of his deep voice. He's tall, dark, yet his features are soft, even as his figure's transparency plays with the shadows lingering in the corner. "Excuse me?"

"You were my charge," he gulps. "But . . ." his lips part, a breath hissing through him. His words are slow, calculated and measured. "I am dead."

"Um," I shift, sitting up on the mattress, and scratch my jaw. "I know. I've been told." I shake my head. "I don't know how to help you."

"No." He takes another step, tendrils and wisps floating where he once was before they merge with his body again. "You don't understand why I visit."

I scratch the edge of my jaw, slowly. "Okay?"

"I came to warn you, to caution the dragon. And to ask for help."

I gulp. My secret is no longer hidden. He even knows - a shade... or a sandman... my gosh, what does this make him?

Keeping eye contact with me, he glides, his body connecting with the mattress, which cuts him off at the knees. I frown at the sight. Transparency has its perks I suppose. I double blink, my exhaustion fleeing like an animal in a forest fire. He's a ghost. I have a sandman ghost in my bed . . . through my bed. How weird is my life?

"Warn me of what?" I probe.

His frown dips, matching mine. The light from the living room highlights his bone structure. "He told me you would recognize his name. He said he needs your help."

"Right. Okay. Um." I shake my head a little. "What's his name?"

"The man with the beating heart calls himself Dyson Coleman."

My mouth drops open, my chin tipping to the side in disbelief. "There's a human – a live human – in the death realm?" I pause, the name clicking with reminiscence of the Cloven Pack's territory. My features relax as the memory surfaces.

*The stench of death . . . destruction . . . betrayal. The hiss of vampires . . . the splinter of a wood floor . . . the blood, so much blood.*

"He's not a human," I whisper, raking a hand through my hair. "He's a wolf-shifter." I look up at the sandman, squaring my jaw. "What does he need? What could I possibly do for him? How is he alive?"

He looms over top of me, and as he bends his hips, every part of me wants to recoil. "It's his punishment, to have a beating heart, to die once more. I want you to save him . . . to save them."

I gulp. "Punishment for what?"

"For forming a rebellion." His lips purse. "You don't know what it is like there."

"Shush, okay? Shush, I'm sold. You have me sold. Where do I find him – them – you – in the death realm?

His body begins to fade, and he lifts his arm, marveling at the magic. "The Colosseum."

"What do you want me to do?"

His white, sparkling eyes return to mine, his body disappearing altogether. His last words are a whisper in my room. "Free them."

## DYSON COLEMAN
## DEATH REALM

It's not as dark here as the dungeons of the Keep though there are no windows. The colosseum isn't as dusty and gritty, either. This wasn't here before when I used to stroll the stone streets of the death realm. This is new. A structure this large should have taken years to build, yet here it sits in all its fine glory, waiting for blood to be spilled.

Instead of individually celled, we're bunched in groups. The ground here is made of crushed stone, tiny pebbles of cement. I'm betting it's meant to be uncomfortable, to get the contenders ready, riddled with insanity, for the fight of their lives. That's what Kheelan plans to do; we are all sure of it. He plans to make each of the shades human. What we are to fight against, we aren't sure. None of us is relishing the idea we may be forced to fight friends.

Our cells are barred with electric bolts, crackling in tune to a heartbeat. Rows and rows of electric bars separate the cells and the walkway between them.

Candles are lit, their wax and wick never diminishing or fading. That's the only source of light we've been granted.

I look over to the sandman, his eyes closed. Through his transparent body, the stone wall rests, supporting his back as though he won't fall through it.

He's reaching the witch, trying once more to haunt her, to ask her for help. If we are to survive, she'll have to come here. I can't sit around and wait, knowing all of these shade's around me . . . they're about to be granted life, only to die and float forever in a void which doesn't exist on any realm. There's no coming back from that fate. It's a fate worse than their death, than this realm.

The shades talk in hushed whispers as I sit in front of the sandman, watching his features, waiting for his return. I'm weak from the blood loss, and I know this is going to affect me when it's time to pick up the sword, so to speak. I fainted, and I have no idea where this place is because I woke in this cell.

At least they clothed me. My skin is wrapped in denim and cotton smelling of rotten flesh. No doubt it's a vampire's clothes.

I shiver, my skin pricking with goosebumps at that thought. I hope to live long enough to make them pay for their mistreatment of my people.

My mind wanders, and I miss the sandman opening his eyes, but his gasp brings me back to the present. Reaper's Breath exits him, swirling and caressing his shoulders. It takes a lot out of a shade to haunt the earth realm. The Reaper's Breath was always a comfort, a welcome when returning to this realm.

"Well?" I ask, leaning closer to him, my elbows resting on my knees.

Sandy glances around, his eyes shifting from side to side as he grasps his bearings. "It is done," he nods.

Hanging my head, I breathe a sigh of relief. "She agreed?" I ask, looking at him through my eyelashes.

With a subtle dip of his chin, he nods. Just as I, he knows it's important to not alert the other shades. Giving them hope where there may not be any is cruel. At this point, hope is a treacherous game built by false expectations and delusional courage.

## ELIZA PLAATS

## DEATH REALM

My mind works frantically to absorb this impossibility I'm witnessing. Aiden's woody scent is gone, replaced by a sweet aroma I don't recognize. The edges around his eyes are harder than steel, void of emotion, while molten red drifts within them like flowing lava.

Aiden takes me in, sweeping from my head to my toes, to the tray on the ground, and returns them to mine. "Eliza," he greets with no emotion.

My heart breaks, shatters and scatters inside my soul, and my knees threaten to give, to drop to the floor in a devastated heap. This isn't him. This can't be Aiden. It's like someone scooped out everything he was and replaced it with something else.

"Aiden," I mutter, tears welling in my eyes and blurring my vision. I wipe them with the back of my hand, moisture coating my skin.

Corbin rocks back on his heels, his hands in his back pockets. A smile spreads across his face, exposing straight white teeth. "You must be Eliza. You are more stunning than I thought you'd be."

With reluctance, I turn my stare from Aiden, swiveling my head in Corbin's direction. My lips form a thin, tense line. "What did you do to him?"

Kheelan's head bobs back and forth between us, his mouth parted in distasteful agitation and his greasy hair struggling to sway.

Corbin sucks in his bottom lip. "I made him. Is he not to your liking?"

"No," I spit. "What is he? What did you do?"

His head shakes in a cocky sort of way, and the smile lowers into a smug twist of malice. The skin along his cheeks puffs. "He's a demon."

"No," I deny, shaking my head in exaggeration. I twist my head, seeing the shell of what he once was. "He's not a demon."

"He's feeding from your fear even now," Corbin whispers in my ear.

A screech leaves my throat. I don't know how he's suddenly standing behind me. I didn't see him move. One minute he was standing there, the next, he's behind me, whispering over my shoulder, his chin almost resting on the crook of my neck. Hot breath fans my cheek, the scent as delicious as a taunting chocolate cake.

"How did you do this?" Kheelan demands, ignoring the rest of the conversation. "How did you bring him back from the void?"

Corbin leans away from me. "Haven't you learned already? I always have a trick or two up my sleeve."

Kheelan splutters, his white cheeks changing to a shade of scarlet. I stagger away from Corbin and turn so my back isn't to him.

Corbin holds up a hand, silencing Kheelan, and points to Yaris. "You. What do you hear?"

Yaris frowns and puckers his lips past his fangs. He swings his head to Aiden, the candlelight highlighting his black veins. His blood-red irises twitch, roaming Aiden's large frame. "A heart."

"Well done!" Corbin shouts, slapping his palms against his thighs.

Licking my bottom lip, I turn to Aiden, his molten eyes still locked on me. He angles his head, lines forming between his eyebrows, and his lips twist down in scrutiny. Something crosses his expression. It's momentary, fleeting, but gone before I have a chance to grasp it. Recognition, maybe? An emotion? My heart holds onto it, gluing a broken piece of it together.

Instead of wiping the trail of fresh, hot tears dribbling from my chin, I let them sit. The salt burns sensitive flesh with a prickling pinch as it dries. "Is this why you came here?" I mumble, turning to Corbin. "To torment me? To feed from me?"

Corbin tucks his chin, his lips twitching, holding back a smile. His cheeks pucker in sexy, smug pleasure. "I'd never do such a thing." Even as he says it, I know his words are a lie. I'm the snack, maybe even an appetizer for a feast I'm unaware of. "We came for a wedding, among other things." He arches his shoulders, bowing toward me, and his breath fans over my face. In the candlelight, his black eyes glint with the yellow reflection. Lifting his hand, he runs his fingers over the edge of my jaw. "Your wedding dress looks striking. I've always been fond of black."

Kheelan snaps from his mental stupor while Corbin's eyes remain locked with mine in a silent challenge. "Right." Kheelan smacks his lips, bringing the focus back to him. "Yes. A wedding. Corbin? You and I will discuss this later."

Corbin's eyebrows wiggle once, his only sign of acknowledgement. He leans in a little closer, his scent intoxicating as his breath fans my face, and our lips almost brush. Against my conscious will, I briefly close my eyes, the pull so strong that all I wish to do is bask in it. The undeniable lure drags me underwater, and I'm powerless to wade through it. I know what he's doing, I know what this is, and now, I understand who he is. He's mastered the art of manipulating hormones: fear, paranoia, lust . . . He's fully aware that he's capable of ruffling anyone's feathers because he has the strength to do so.

His lips twitch, and as they do so, they slide over mine, featherlike and sensual. I open my eyes to the black depths which capture mine, and the lust flees, replaced by earlier fear . . . Fear because he can manipulate what I should be able to control.

"You should really do something with that fiery hair," he whispers, his breathy words fanning my face. "It won't do for your wedding."

*TEMBER*

*GUARDIAN REALM*

Calling upon Ire, I feel the familiar grip of carved elven wood settle within my palm. Electricity travels through the solid weapon, lighting my skin with a pleasant tingle. It charges me with adrenaline, forcing ultimate focus.

The wind still howls at my back, shuddering the trees' barren limbs, but the snow declines to a slower rate. My ears pick up the sound as each flake settles to a final rest against the snowbanks. White sparkles twinkle throughout the banks, a subtle yet captivating shimmer as light filters through the branches, reflecting off the crystals. The forest aromas tickle my senses, the breeze carrying the scent of burning wood from the East where one of the tribe's villages had settled. Every brush of hair against my cheek, every melting flake against my skin, makes me feel as if the world is moving in a slower motion.

I scan the woods, blocking out Erma whose resentment could melt icicles. The breeze shifts again, aiding and guiding. It paints an invisible map, pointing me in the direction I seek. I scan each tree and the limbs which sprout from their trunks.

Like the whipplemonk, the Igna Elves blend with their surroundings. That's this tribe; I'm sure of it. The Igna are the only Elves skilled with bows and arrows. They're the hunters. Trained in distant accuracy and aim, they're deadly with the weapons they strap to their back.

My eyes snap to a subtle movement within the branches. The change of wind causes an archer to shift his weight, which was resting, hidden from my view.

An arrow appears in my hand, its make of pure electricity. I lower my body, crouched, back straight and knees angled. Placing the arrow in the correct position, propped atop my finger, I slowly pull back the string with two fingers, resting the curve of my hand against my cold cheek. I blow out a breath through relaxed lips and loosen my fingers, releasing the grip. The string vibrates as Ire's arrow whistles and crackles, soaring and cutting through the falling snow as though it doesn't hinder a sure path.

My target drops from the tree, narrowly missing my arrow's strike. Agile and graceful, he lands in a cat-like drop. Knees bent, back arched, his fingers steeple against the snow, his rump low to the ground, balanced. He tips his head up, hair whipping in the wind as he pins me with a deadly, daring stare. With elegance, like a panther who rules his jungle, he stands. His posture and movements are slow and confident. Skin as white as snow, he's tattooed in black ink that matches the bark of the trees surrounding him. If he stood perfectly still, if the wind didn't grab hold of his dark hair, I would never have seen him.

One side of his head is shaven while hair cascades down the other, reaching his thin waist. His ears point to an exaggerated tip, and horns in a variety of sizes halo his head. His eyes are large and almond-shaped, tilting at an angle like a feline, and dark around the rims. The dark skin

207

around those eyes fades as it travels to the rest of his face, hiding the orbs within their sockets.

Now standing at full height, he spins in my direction. He reaches over his shoulder and grasps another arrow from the leather quiver slung onto his back.

"Igna," I whisper like a curse, my top lip curled in a snarl. I tense my muscles and prepare to fight for my life.

He lifts the bow, the muscles rippling on his bare arms, and slides the new arrow in place. Holding his pose, those dark orbs bore into mine, unwavering and certain. Being his target, I recognize the concentrated focus, his aim sharp and intent as the tip of his arrow.

The elves are breathtaking creatures, their tall frames roped and lined with muscle. It's their way of life – they live off this land and what it provides them. With that kind of survival and lifestyle, it's prudent to have a physique able to withstand it.

His body is still and unbreakable, like cliffs taking the beatings of a remorseless ocean.

"Jaemes," Erma commands, her tone exasperated and clipped. "Put down the bow."

"Nuet neame isu-ate," he mumbles in Elvish.

I stiffen and glare, not recognizing his words, but storing them away anyhow. The language is beautiful, silk, yet roughly clipped. My only knowledge of the basic and simple language is that many words hold double meanings.

Erma translates with a sigh. "He won't until you do."

"No," I snarl.

He shifts his weight enough to set me on edge, and an arrow releases from Ire. Turning the moment it leaves my vicinity, his bow dances with his body, the arch of it blocking my arrow. It rebounds, hitting the tree behind him. The sparks exploding against bark distracts me, giving him time to release his own arrow. I duck and roll but not before the arrow cuts into my shoulder, creating a deep wound as it passes through.

We aim, firing at the same time, before Erma screams in frustration, throwing each hand at one of us. Like sound waves, her magic pulses from her palms, stopping our arrows and throwing our bodies into the air.

My back hits a tree trunk, the wind within my lungs expelling in a quick rush before I drop to the ground. I fling my hair from my face, spit snow from my mouth, and glare at Erma. Jaemes and I climb to our feet, weaseling from the snow drifts each of us landed in.

Erma huffs. The heat of her emotions is enough to prick my skin. "Enough," she growls.

Jaemes keeps his attention settled on me as he speaks to Erma. "What are you doing here?" he asks, his words accented.

My eyebrows lift in surprise. I didn't know elves knew English. I've only ever heard them speak in their own tongue, even on the battle field.

"That does not concern you." She spins to him, her back to me. "You will take me to your council."

"And the angel?" he spits.

Her fingers ball into tight fists, her patience wearing thin. "She will be escorting me."

Jaemes' eyes pinch, his posture stiff. I don't believe him to move, until his lips part enough for a chirp to escape. Cocking my head to the side, I watch as the air quivers beside him. I've never been this close to an elf when it wasn't a fight for my life. Most of them remain on the backs of their Matua, a skeletal two-headed horse, but I've never seen how the Matua are brought about. I assumed they were pets, of sorts.

The air thickens despite the chill, and the two-headed animal appears, snorting and pawing the snow. The breeze sends its scent my direction. The aroma is pleasing like a crisp fall night. It becomes abundantly clear elves conjure them, such as I do with Ire.

The matua's long neck splits at the top, dividing into two heads that connect at the jaw. There is no mane but instead, vertebrae bones stick through the skin, creating flat horns. In contrast to the elves' long-tipped horns haloing their head, the vertebrae along the matua's neck are short, thick, and rounded.

There is no saddle situated along the back. A solid plate of bone replaces it, in the same shape and form. I marvel at the skin which holds no fur, the colors matching the elves' camouflage as though they are one. My eyes skim to the tail, watching the wisps of smoke fidget, unaffected by the breeze of the blizzard. The beast is large and frighteningly so, the hoofs as bulky as a human head.

Sliding the bow up his arm and settling it in the crook of his elbow, Jaemes touches the muzzles of the matua with both hands. "I cannot guarantee her safety once we enter my village," he warns, his tone lighter.

"I'll take my chances," I grumble. He talks as though I do not stand before him.

He swivels his head in my direction. "Do you come by arrogance naturally, or has your ego been boosted throughout time?"

"Jaemes," Erma warns.

He dips his head, his arm swinging out in an exaggerated gesture as he bows. "As you wish," he retorts sarcastically, lowering the bow over his head so it's nestled along his back and chest.

Grasping vertebrae along the animal's neck, he takes a step forward with a bounce in his pace, bends his knee last minute, and flings his body over the back of the Matua. There are no reigns to guide the animal, and as it begins to move in the direction of the village, I question how they communicate. Do they do so telepathically? Or is the matua and elf connected in a way I cannot understand. I refuse to ask. If I were to voice my questions, I'd have to talk directly to the elf. There's no way Erma would answer me, not in close proximity of an elf.

There are four tribes of elves, each as deadly as the next. The Yoki are foresters who chop and collect wood, often building the ships and huts all tribes need. The Inga are hunters, gathering skins and meat. Uji Elves are fisherman, manning the clear ocean on the west side of the guardian realm. The gatherers and crop cultivators are the Kaju Elves, feeding the tribes with the grains they grow.

There is no currency among the elves, but instead, they trade their goods, disbursing and living in parts of the guardian realm that hold necessities to sustain their lives.

Each tribe's tattoos are different colors, matching their trade's surroundings, and a member from each tribe is elected into the Council of Four. They congregate only when needed or summoned. In this case, Erma is demanding a summons, but for what?

# CHAPTER SIXTEEN

*AIDEN VANDER*

*DEATH REALM*

In the arena of the Colosseum, Corbin stands next to Kheelan. Behind them, I watch as Kheelan turns shade by shade, giving them beating hearts, making them human against their will. Their skin changes from transparent to pigmented. They don't want it – they know if they die, they'll be gone forever. It's torture for them. They scream, beg, and plead with the fee, but to no avail. Some even attempt to fight back. The soft sand below our feet rises in puffs of dust as the vampires subdue the shades who do.

I rock my feet from side to side and let the small grains bury my shoes in hopes of rooting me to the spot. It's a struggle to not show the effect their fear is having on me. It's an untamable lust which grips my abdomen, threatening to wake the demon I am. But I can't. I can't show Corbin what I truly am. It's a card which must be played by a careful hand and instructed by a calculating mind. No one can control me. The corners of my lips tilt. If he were to learn this . . .

I wipe the smile from my face and eye the back of Corbin's head, my thoughts traveling to other matters while the innocent scream before us. It's abnormal that I feel no sympathy. A part of me wants to, but I don't know how. Emotion is a weakness that my third birth obliterated. The memories of them are easy to recall, however. It's an oily slickness that was capable of breaking me. Even the ones that feel as though I were drowning . . . I remember them well.

The humans' fear wafts my direction in puffs of smoke that only I can see. It's taunting, like the scent of a turkey cooking in an oven on a Thanksgiving Day. I'm a starving demon, kept from a full feed for this very reason. Corbin knew I'd feed this day, and I also believe he knows I'm holding back from him. To attempt to force me to show him exactly who I am is a careful plan; I'll give him that.

A woman, a shade, is dragged from the tunnel by two vampires, the sand engulfing her toes as she digs them in. She's young, maybe in her twenties, with fiery red hair. I cock my head. She reminds me of Eliza.

*Eliza*, my mind whispers . . . The memory hovers inside me: the love I felt for her and the swell of my heart only by saying her name. It's out of reach, and I'm reluctant to reach inside and grasp it. What kind of demon would I be if I let love rule me?

In the dining hall, the same thing happened, but it was strong. Like fear, I could almost taste it. It was a different kind of feeding, one which I haven't had the pleasure of consuming, and one I knew only she could provide. It was different – it wasn't substance but more of a vitamin I was missing. But as her fear grew in my vicinity, it fed me, squashing every chance I had at this new entre. No matter how hard I mentally tried, I couldn't grasp it, test it, see what it was. Not while I was feasting. It's my nature now even though I saw how much it hurt her. Tears shed from those eyes that once captured my soul. She had wiped them away with hands that once held mine.

I lift my arm and look at my palm, seeing the lines and texture, remembering what it was like, what I felt when it ran over her skin.

My subconscious whispers to me, *You were meant to love her.* My jaw clenches, and I drop my hand, squashing what I see as a weakness. I can't. I won't. I am *more*.

The woman is released from the vampire's grasp and she drops to her knees. The fall is muffled by the sand, and her wrists are shackled behind her back with cuffs that seem as transparent as she is. "Please," she sobs to Kheelan, her bottom lip quivering.

Corbin crosses his arms behind the slope of his back. In fear for herself, the woman tilts her head to the sky which holds nothing but the foggy mist I remember so well. What could she be looking for up there? A savior? There will be none for her. This is the last step to her end.

With only a thought, Kheelan begins the transformation. Her spine arches to an impossible angle, her chest bows, and her mouth opens wider than her eyes. Screams fill the arena, reverberating off the stadium as they rip from her throat. Spittle flies from her mouth, dribbling to the sand, and her face is pinched, contorting in an unimaginable pain.

I twist my midsection and observe the rows and rows of climbing seats, distracting myself from the growing weakness inside me. I doubt any shades will fill them, but from what I've gathered from conversation after Eliza fled the dining hall – this is going to be entertainment for the sadistic minds. Demons and vampires will fill those seats, feeding from terror and leftover blood while a battle ensues across the sands.

Her scream reaches to a new pitch, animalistic and agonizing.

Another fee is to arrive soon; Sureen of the dream realm. I've heard she has a few creatures of her own she plans to transport. I can't imagine what a dream realm would hold when it comes to a capable warrior, but Corbin is giddy about it though tight-lipped.

I look back to the shade, my perusal boring. The solidity starts at her fingers, raising to her arms, her neck, and her face. The process is quick and surprising. I remember the feeling of my new heart beating within my chest. I remember the process. I remember the agony.

Regifting life should be a lengthy process, but as soon as it starts, her screams reaching a pitch that offends my ears, the process is finished. Her breaths come heavy, and her shoulders rise and fall with effort, her lungs refilling with oxygen it needs to feed the new blood pumping in her veins. Her head droops with exhaustion, red hair cascading in a curtain and hiding her features.

Feeling weak at the knees, she needs the vampires to hoist her up by the elbows.

"Where do we put her?" the blonde vampire hisses, his tongue snaking out to lick his bottom lip.

Corbin turns to Kheelan. "This is the twenty-fifth shade you've turned, Kheelan. I believe you owe them the fulfillment of your earlier promise."

Kheelan's greasy hair sways at the ends as he rakes his fingers over his scalp. "Very well," he mumbles, waving a hand in the air.

The woman doesn't see it coming. I knew she wouldn't. As her head dangles from her shoulders, her exhaustion too great, the vampires take advantage. Not that she'd be able to stop them.

In a blur of speed, one vampire is at her back, and the other is at her front. They open their mouths wide, exposing fangs, and strike like a snake, teeth searing into flesh with fascinating ease.

"When does Sureen arrive?" Kheelan asks, watching the vampires grip her skin, their nails digging in. Their claws puncture her, blood welling around their fingers. She struggles at first, like a baby rabbit caught in the mouth of a cat, and then begs in unintelligible whimpers, her hands pulling at their arms.

"After the wedding," Corbin murmurs, consumed with the sight before him. I imagine he doesn't get to witness this often.

He peeks to Corbin. "And she'll bring them?"

"Yes. Their hearts already beat in their chests."

Blood pours from her neck as they feast, their actions animalistic. It trickles down the slope with sluggish speed, pooling at the hollow of her collar bones. The iron scent wafts its way to me, and I shift my weight. If I can smell it, so can the other vampires.

I barely have time to finish the thought before more arrive. They bite into her wrists, her thigh, hissing at one another to feed their hungry bellies. Her moans fill the silence, and the beasts drink their fill. Eyelids fluttering, she raises her gaze to mine. I hold it, watching the light leave her eyes, fading faster than the beats of her new heart.

## KATRIANE DUPONT

## THE TWEEN

I step through my portal and check over my shoulder, watching it swirl into a smaller circle before it disappears altogether.

It's hard to breathe here, like the air is too humid. I swivel my head, taking in my surroundings.

Dead, gnarled trees, so tall I can't see their tops past the fog that dips and sways like an ocean. Brittle twigs and dead foliage crunch beneath my shoes when I begin my hike.

Placing my hand on the bark of a tree next to me, I slide my palm over it, feeling its rough texture. This forest seems so deceased. Is it meant to be this way? It's almost like they hover between life and death – a transition of sorts. And then it hits me – this isn't the earth realm, nor the death realm. This is the tween: the transitional space before the death realm. It's meant to ease, and create a sense of calm, neither of which I'm getting from it.

I close my eyes, chastising myself for the stupidity I'm showing lately.

As my skin prickles with goosebumps, my spine quakes with shivers. It's freezing here, and I shouldn't dawdle. If the sandman was eager to reach me, to beg me to save Dyson and the others, then time must be a factor.

My feet are obnoxiously loud with each footfall in this quiet, dead forest. I cringe with each placement of weight. Gritting my teeth, I force myself into a faster speed.

I don't know much about the tween, but there has to be an entrance to the death realm somewhere. Some sort of portal, maybe, similar to mine. I want the hell out of here.

The farther I go, the more the blanket of fog thickens along the bed of the forest. I trip over something solid, a hard object I can't see in this sea of moving white mist, and I grit my teeth once more, paranoid it's a monster lurking under the fog. I concentrate more on walking, feeling with my toes against the soles of my shoes while I sneak along. My shoulders bunch on their own, my emotions feeding tense muscles.

Despite the cold, the air here is thicker, heavier, and smothering. It's like the midsummer humidity but with a wintery, hefty bite. My foot steps on a rock, and I wobble before placing my hand on a nearby tree to catch my balance. Curiosity overcomes, a momentary weakness in my striving to continue. I bend, dip my hand through the fog, and grasp the object. It looks like the earth realm's rocks.

A breeze, out of place and certainly not nature-made, tickles along my neck, followed by a ragged intake of breath. I freeze. The goosebumps raised against my skin harden, bringing the chill to my bones. My heart thuds in my chest as another breath tickles the back of my neck.

With slow, careful movements, I instinctively clutch the rock, and turn to face the heavy breather behind me while holding my breath. I'm prepared to let a scream rip from my throat. Not that it'd do any good.

I shouldn't have turned. I should have run as soon as I knew someone was here with me.

My gaze lands eyelevel with the chest of a hooded figure. The black robes are tattered with age and sway like the cloth is under water. The creature's boney shoulders protrude under the robe, and a hood covers a head I can't see. Is there a head? The space inside is so black, utterly dark, I can't even make out eyes or the tip of a nose.

It exhales again, the breath fanning my face. It's the unmistakable breath of death, ragged and rotting.

"A reaper," I whisper before gulping.

It hovers over me, looming and reeking of impending demise. I stumble back but too late. A boned hand reaches out quicker than I thought possible and thrusts forward, shoving me against my sternum. My feet leave the ground, and I fly backwards. The force of the shove causes the air to leave my lungs, and they ache before my back hits a tree.

I plummet to the ground, landing on my rump, and struggle for oxygen in a place barren of any. Clutching my throat with one hand, I cough and splutter. I palm the rock, and twist and turn it between my fingers.

The reaper rises a few inches off the ground and floats toward me. Using terrible instincts – instincts which give me pause, questioning my sanity – I chuck the rock at the reaper. The rock thuds against its chest with no effect. It drops to the ground with a thud, the fog swallowing it once more.

On shaky legs, I stand to my feet, using the tree to guide me and support my weight with a fumbling hand. With my other hand, a ball of flames flashes to life, crackling and churning within my palm. My eyes glow, reflecting against the never-ending fog. It highlights the dips and edges of its structure, like a sunrise's hues playing with clouds. A renewed sense of protection overcomes me, and I allow myself a moment to bask in it. This moment for myself quickly fades when another reaper reveals himself, floating in from behind a nearby tree. It's like it came from seemingly nowhere. Then another. And another, until I'm surrounded. I steady my back against the bark, using my other hand to produce another ball of flames in hopes of a more effective defense.

I swivel my head left and right, frantically throwing together a plan. I need an exit. If I can create an exit, I can run. Surely these creatures can't run as fast as I can. Right?

Together, their breathing is vociferous and ragged. It sounds like a semi's engine, roaring, brash, and intimidating.

*I've fought fee*, I encourage myself.

Well, I've sort of fought fee. Surely a group of reapers would be a cinch. They only escort the dead to the death realm. Somehow, this thought doesn't comfort me.

My mother's vision floats in my conscience, whispering words of caution. I squash it down, refusing to let her prediction waver my failing instincts.

A tendril of fog, like a flying snake, zips through the trees to my right, catching my eye. Unprepared for this oncoming threat, whatever it may be, I launch the two flaming balls to the reapers on my right.

The closest reaper combusts into flames, winking from existence with an astounding boom. The tree trunk behind it cracks down the middle from the sound vibrations, splitting in two, and begins to descend to the ground. Another reaper floats out of the way of the falling trunk at a speed I would have never thought it capable. The cracked wood narrowly misses it, it's splinters snagging on the cloth of the reaper's cloak. With a thunderous roar, the ground shakes from the weight as the trunk hits. I bend my knees, my arms flailing as I grasp for a sliver of balance.

With the gap of the two missing reapers, I take the opportunity of distraction. I dig my heels in, pump my arms, and run through the opening I created. Flames light my hands and lick my arms. Without aim, I throw them over my shoulder, continually shooting at what I'm hoping is a reaper. I don't hear an explosion and lower myself to the ground, digging my feet in the soil as I push forward.

The snake-fog zips my direction, and I pause from my assault on the reapers, hurling one at the fog instead, while using my free hand to shoot once more behind me. The flames go right through the snake. I prepare to throw another, to scream in fury if it would scare it off, when I fly through the air, an explosion rocking me off my feet. I bounce against the ground in a thud, most of my weight landing on my shoulder and scraping the skin.

Scrambling to stand, I use my hands to finish pushing my top half up while my feet propel me onward. My lungs are suffocating. I'm dizzy and faint. I weave through trees, jump a boulder, the mist covering the ground whisking away with each reckless step. Trees snag my clothes, rip my skin.

They're getting closer, the heavy breathing behind me gaining in speed, and I chance a glance, peeking over my shoulder. The reapers floating in my direction are quicker than I can run. My muscles are already aching and tired.

I glance forward, my mouth open to gasp for more oxygen than this place has. The fog that was snaking its way through the forest obscures my view, swirling around my head, and I stumble as I attempt to bat it away. I should have found a way to destroy it. I shouldn't have dismissed it. I stumble to the ground, my elbows scraping against dead twigs.

Taking a swing at the fog, it continues to swirl and zip before it stops. My mouth hangs open, gasping for air. I fight with myself, forcing my body to remain human, to not let my fears unleash the dragon within.

The fog takes the opportunity and dives inside the opening, slithering past my tongue and down my throat. I choke and splutter, feeling its cold tendrils working its way inside me. It curls around my organs, and I suck in a deep breath as its coldness penetrates them. My hand flies to my throat, but my gaze snaps to the reaper's advance. Choking for air, I hurl another ball at them, watching in amazement as the hand I lifted to do so and notice it is see-through.

*What is happening?*

My heart beats an erratic rhythm inside my chest; I'm not dead. What did the fog do to me?

The reapers slow as they approach, their cloaks swaying in that unnatural, underwater way. Their breaths are normal, like the trek to track me down wasn't a ragged one. One bends, inches from my face, yet I still can't see any of the features hidden under the hood. I hold my breath, waiting for its wrath. I'm not supposed to be here, and it knows it. What do reapers do with the humans they catch touring amongst the dead?

It breathes on me, rugged and stanching. I close my eyes, seal them shut with every muscle in my face, and turn from it. I wait for the worst to happen, for my fate to be sealed. But, the breathing fades, releasing my face from the feeling of impending death, until I no longer hear it. I frown and peek open an eye, watching the reapers back as they retreat to the place from where they came.

Frozen still, I rapidly blink and blow out the breath I've been holding. The air gushes from my lungs in a harsh torrent and my ribcage screams as my chest expands to capacity.

Why am I still alive? A nudge from inside my stomach humbles me. I can feel the fog swirling in there, holding my organs like a lover would hold a hand. Is it friend or foe? Somehow the creature made me invisible. It knew I was coming, knew I was in trouble, and came to find me. Or maybe it happened to be taking a stroll. Either way, I'm grateful because without it, I'd be dead.

Lifting my hand, I go to place it over my abdomen, curious to see if I can feel the creature inside me, but I'm caught off guard when my hand goes through my stomach, floating there as though I'm nothing but mist.

I twist my hand, testing its boundaries. I'm not dead. My heart still beats. But somehow . . . somehow this creature made me look ghost-like. A shade but with a beating heart.

What kind of magic is this?

# CHAPTER SEVENTEEN

*ELIZA PLAATS*

*DEATH REALM*

My hair snags on the bristles as I brush the red strands in front of the makeshift vanity with an unseeing gaze on the mirror. My soul feels empty, my heart irreparable. It shouldn't matter that Aiden's alive. I'm to marry Kheelan, to be his queen. I have no choice in the matter. I'm the slave here, and Aiden isn't Aiden. Not anymore.

My conscience nudges me, desperate to regain hope, but even I know hope isn't a stable reality. Something inside him was there, but it fled as soon as it crossed his mind. What I would give to know what was going through his mind. Could it be . . . maybe he isn't gone from me forever?

Setting the brush down on the vanity counter, I spin on my stool and take in my small allotted room. There's a double bed in the middle, springs poking out the foot of the mattress. It's terrible to sleep in, practically impossible.

Besides the wooden vanity behind me, an ancient rocking chair sits in the corner. This is all that makes up my belongings. I suppose I should be grateful to have anything. Chances are, this is the last time I'll step foot in here. Will Kheelan make me sleep in his bed? Force me to have sex with him? A shiver runs up my spine, and my shoulders twitch at the unwelcome feeling.

*No*, my conscience screams at me, conjuring pictures of Aiden and squashing images of having sex with a greasy, cruel fee.

I blink slowly, regaining my stubbornness which had fled the moment I realized Aiden wasn't gone forever. He's eternally changed, eternally opposite of me, forever bound to never love again.

But . . . the flash of light that crossed his eyes . . .

A knock sounds on my door, strong and sure, startling me. I don't have time to answer, to even rise from my stool, not that I would have. It swings open. Aiden stands within the door frame, one hand tucked into his pocket. He opened it with such ease. It takes every muscle I have to open the heavy stone door enough to slip through.

Our eyes lock, and his jaw ticks. The translucent flow of moving lava inside his eyes gives me pause, and I bite my bottom lip. I should fear him, but I don't. I wish once more that I could have any form of telepathy. Does he still feel? What does it feel like to be a demon? To feed on someone else. Does he feel what they feel? A sliver of me hopes he feels my inner turmoil, my dread and heart break.

"They're waiting," he conveys, his voice deeper than I remember. I'll never get used to this new Aiden, this stranger.

Swallowing, the lump in my throat feels like I'm gagging on a marble. I stand on numb legs, and the stool I've been sitting on, for who knows how long, creaks under the loss of weight.

Stalking toward him, I start to lift my hand and cup his cheek, curious if his skin still feels the same as I remember.

The rational side of me rips me apart for loving a man so deeply, and I barely knew him in the first place. But the other side of me believes in true love, in soul mates. That's the only way I can explain to myself the pull which tugs on my heart.

My fingertips are inches from his face, feeling the heat radiate from his cheek. He recoils, avoiding my touch, and my hand falls to my side, empty as the numbness creeping through my bones.

"Do you even remember who you are?" My voice is weak, held captive by emotions my body isn't allowing me to feel. It's as if the sound does not belong to me. It belongs to some frivolous girl I don't like, love, or wish to acknowledge.

"I remember everything," he answers simply but slowly.

I curse under my breath, a touch of rage driving my next words. "You're like a robot. A shell of something you once were." I purse my lips, searching his face. "Do you feel anything?"

His throat constricts as he swallows, as if his next response is filled with wishes and the gift of hope he can't present to me. He shakes his head, watching my face carefully. My vision blurs with unshed tears.

I skim my hand to his chest, to his heart, where I know it beats behind his ribcage. I know it's there. Yaris said so. "And what about for me? Do you feel anything for me?"

His gaze searches my face, memorizing it the way he did once before. Plump lips part on his perfectly sculpted face, words beginning to form. It reminds me of the very first dream we shared together.

Footsteps echo down the hall's narrow passage. Aiden's head swivels, and a voice calls out.

"Did you find her?" Yaris asks.

I push past Aiden, rage tickling through my once numb body. My arm touches his as I pass, a new scorching sensation brushing my skin. He sucks in a shocked breath, and I take a chance, glancing over my shoulder while exiting my room. His expression is one of surprise, a shudder rippling down his stocky body. It's momentary, passing all too quickly, and all that's left is a slice of disbelief and possible interest. For what, I don't know.

I bunch my lips and push them to the left, chewing on the inside of my mouth. Frowning at Aiden, I call back to Yaris. "Right here." I quiet my voice to a notch above a whisper. "Are you okay?"

"I —" he tilts his head, words failing him. The lava flowing in his eyes disappears, and the irises I remember, only belonging to Aiden, come forth. My lips part, and the action is enough to pull him back to his demon self. Those beautiful, human eyes disappear, returning to his new, true nature.

I inhale, hope stirring in the pit of my stomach like a swarm of angry bats. Is he — Was that…. Did he feel something?

Yaris barges into my doorway, grasps my upper arm, and my thoughts flee as he tugs me down the hall.

## AIDEN VANDER

## DEATH REALM

Stuffing my hands in my pockets, I watch Yaris lead her away, the two of them disappearing in the dark. I tilt my head, staring at the floor of Eliza's room but seeing nothing.

My thoughts work frantically, trying to come up with what I just felt.

*I felt.*

She touched me – she touched me, and for a sliver of a moment, I felt human again. It was momentary and fled like a bat at first sunrise, but it was there, consuming and short-lived. I berate myself for the weakness yet wish to explore it.

What was that emotion? My heart thudded a new beat; my stomach swirled with an anxious, oily nausea. My eyes narrow as I work out this conundrum. Did I feel hope? Love? Both? Or was it only a mimic of what once was.

It can't be possible. I'm not made for such feelings. The feast of fear is what drives me. But as I stood in this room, I felt no fear wafting from my Eliza . . . It wasn't what I was feeding from.

*My Eliza. . .*

I swallow, thick and difficult.

"Thrice Born, you waver," Corbin divulges behind me. I didn't hear him fade in. I didn't feel his arrival. My thoughts were consuming, throwing me off my game.

I turn to him, a frown dipping my eyebrows. "What?"

Corbin holds Eliza's brush in his hands and twirls it within his fingers, cocking his hip to the side. He looks up, his jaw ticking. "I did not make you for love. Love clouds the judgment, demon." He tucks his chin, his eyes boring into mine, and he lowers his voice. "You cause me worry."

Placing the brush back on the vanity, he slithers over to her bed, looking at it from all angles. He pulls at the edge of the quilt draped over the surface, straightening the wrinkles.

"What do I do with a demon if he grows feelings? I must say, I've never run into such a problem, but then again, you are the first of your kind. I'll have to remember that little hiccup when I pull the new humans from the void, creating more demons in your image." He spins slowly to me, crossing his arms over his chest. "Their deaths will have meaning; I can promise you that." Corbin never hides his true nature from me, the sadistic side of him prominent in my vicinity. "I know you're keeping the full extent of your capabilities from me. Do not cause me worry, Aiden Vander. Worry causes me to take irrational action."

He shimmers from his spot, reappearing inches from my face. His black eyes are hard, his lips tense. "First, I will make her feel fear like she's never known. Her screams will drip in terror. I'll let it consume her, let her pleas fill my chambers until she begs for death. I'll force you to feed from her while I slice her inch by inch, limb from limb, until you're standing in a puddle of her blood. I'll make you drink from her wounds while she takes her last breath. You'll be forced to watch the life leave her eyes just as she will be forced to witness the demon who takes it. I will kill her, Aiden. Slow. Agonizing. *Cruciatu*. Do not force my hand."

He shimmers, leaving me in Eliza's room by myself and with his lingering scent. Anger rips through me instead of the fear he hoped to deliver. I do not fear him. I will never fear him.

*Eliza is mine*, my thoughts snarl.

## DYSON COLEMAN

## DEATH REALM

"Has she arrived?" an unfamiliar voice asks.

A black-haired female vampire on watch slouches against the wall. She scrambles to stand flat on her feet, caught off guard. "Fee Corbin," she stutters.

"Sara Lee," Corbin greets, waltzing to her, his feet thunderous. "Has Sureen arrived?"

Sara Lee swallows in fear. "No, sir," she discloses, her voice weak.

He narrows his eyes, his jaw ticking. "Very well. When she does, have her wait for me. We have much to discuss before the games begin."

I frown, watching his body waver, shimmer almost, becoming translucent before he disappears. Sara Lee stands, her back rigid with stiff posture. She blows out a breath and touches her fingers over her lips, her shoulders visibly deflating. I clear my throat, relieving a tickle, and her glare snaps to me.

I glance to my left, eyeing Sandy when he fidgets in his cross-legged position. His white eyes are impossibly wide, fear-filled, and his thick lips part. He's been turned into a human just as every shade held within the cells, and his skin glistens with the candlelight. My mind takes me back to his screams of pain as the process began. It could be heard all the way in here as Kheelan rebuilt his heart. I remember the feeling of intense agony. It's not something I ever want to relive. My wolf had even perked his ears when he registered the sandman's suffering. I believe he's growing a fondness for him as amazing as that sounds. At least he's stirring.

"What?" I ask.

"My creator is coming."

I shift toward him. "And?"

He looks at me. "Do you not understand? If she's coming, she has a reason to be here. This is a Colosseum, wolf. A place of death, a place of battle and blood. If she's due to arrive, she won't be coming alone."

I narrow my eyes. "And . . . What? Is she bringing more sandmen? I don't really see that working out for her. Your kind seem gentle and uncontroversial."

His large hand slaps against the loose rocks covering the ground, fury driving his wild emotions. "How are you so dense? She would bring protection, perhaps a few contenders to enter the entertainment. She'll bring beasts."

"What kind of beasts?" I scratch my jaw, skeptical.

"I do not know." He shakes his head. "There were none when I was there." He thinks for a moment, his scrutiny flowing across the cell as he peruses his brain. "Someone had to reverse the spell on Katriane. The only one who could do so is Sureen." His eyes widen, and he looks back at me. "They've made a deal with her; to release Katriane in exchange for life."

I jut my chin. "How can you be sure?"

"I know my creator, wolf. I was the one she called upon to bed her when she grew restless. She would speak to me, discussing dreams of creating beating hearts, of becoming 'alpha,' as you would say. Jealous behavior continuously drives her purposes. She desires an army."

"And what? You think she'll come here, bring her new army creatures, and give them a test run?"

His jaw ticks. "Yes. Yes, she would."

"Ah, hell," I curse.

## *TEMBER*

## *GUARDIAN REALM*

"What should I expect?" I ask, my voice rising above the howl of wind. The farther we go in, the more the trees thin. The wind has an easier time passing through, beating against our bodies and swaying our purposeful steps.

"You will remain silent," she declares, quirking a perfect, red eyebrow.

I hold a tree limb for her to pass under, bending it as far as it will go. Jaemes is up ahead, whistling a tune. I don't know if he's whistling to ward off predators or if he's doing it to annoy me. Through this trek, he has made verbal jabs at me, his wit strong for the average elf.

She continues after passing under the branch. "They will not take my suggestions if you are to give your input. The tribes won't take kindly to you being there in the first place."

I heave a breath. "They're not the only ones."

Taking a finger, she catches a stray hair tickling her jaw, and tucks it behind her ear. "Are you referring to me?"

"Yes."

"Ah," she expresses, smiling. "So, you do consider my feelings."

I take a deep, calming breath. "I'm not saying they aren't justifiable, Erma. You sent me there to watch after Kat, to discover what we did not know. I could not do that with wings."

Erma is silent for several strides, my heart aching at the loss of words until she finally speaks. "You chose one human over your home. Over me."

I stop in my tracks and whirl to face her, my hands clenching at my sides. "This one human is stronger than me, than you, than her creator. She should be someone we fear, yet we use her. My actions may have let her down, but my intentions were pure. Can you say the same for yourself? Perhaps it is you whose judgment is disturbed by emotions."

Ticking her jaw, she narrows her eyes before pushing past me. "We shall speak no more of this."

I study the back of her head before my eyes lift to our escort. His ear is tilted toward us. He's eavesdropping, picking up our conversation to find a weakness. The edges of his lips curl in a smug smile, and he turns his attention back ahead of him, his torso swaying with each stride the matua takes.

I pick up a jog, my shoes slipping against the snow, and match my pace to Erma's quick strides. "What do you know about him? Can Jaemes be trusted?" I whisper.

Licking her bottom lip, she responds in the same hushed tone. "He's the son of his tribe's chief. Though he sits high in rank, he's overlooked by his father's eye.

Jaemes does not relay information, not to his father." She pauses, adjusting the fur draped over her shoulders. "He made me this, you know. Back when I lived with the elves, Jaemes was a gentle man and a formidable warrior. His brothers, however, gained the main focus from their father. We spoke on several occasions, Jaemes and I. He does not wish to take his father's place when the time comes - if the time comes. He prefers to protect, rather than guiding."

Jaemes' hand is placed on his thigh while the other holds the wood of his bow. His back is straight, the muscles rippling with confidence and pride. I find myself softening toward him, even relating to him. "I see. And how does this make him trustworthy?"

"Because I believe the bond Jaemes and I once had is still in place."

I sigh and rake my hands through my hair. Without intention, her words return guilt to the pit of my stomach, churning it like butter. I no longer own the trust of Erma, and I'm conflicted about it.

On one hand, I know I did what's right. Perhaps I went about it the wrong way in regard to Kat, but I did my duty. Trying to fight for Erma's affection, when she was in the wrong, isn't something I want to endure. I shouldn't have to. However, I've loved Erma most of my life. She's what I know, she's what my heart beats for, but she's also what's forbidden. If the others were to discover what Erma and I have – had – then the consequences would unfold with brittle results. We have enough going on at this moment. A lover's quarrel should be placed low on our lists of concerns.

Erma tilts her head to the branches above, and her jaw ticks, the muscles rippling against a soft cheek. "Incoming," Erma murmurs.

Bodies drop from the trees, agile and sure-footed. They land, crouched, watching me like I'm prey. A few, but not many, stand upright, their heads in positions which reflect their curiosity, and their eyes sweep my body.

"We're close, aren't we?" I ask, studying the elves.

"Yes."

# CHAPTER EIGHTEEN

*KATRIANE DUPONT*

*THE TWEEN*

Striding through the tween, I find myself miffed and consumed with my thoughts. My hand clutches my stomach in hopes of holding the fog inside me immobile. It seems to be playing a game of ping-pong, using my organs as bumpers.

I've searched my memory, tried to remember my lessons, desperate to discover what this creature is. It helped me, so it's not an enemy, right? I frown, skeptical of its timely aid. I'm surrounded by beings and things who use me – or with the agenda of ending my life. How do I know this thing isn't any different? There's no telling the lasting effect of this little spell it placed on me.

The creature stills, a silent, cautionary demand. I lift my head, my face relaxing. A thick wall of swirling fog, mimicking the sky above and the ground below, churns and sways. It's thick, clouds folding in on each other, like a churning thunderstorm absent of lightning. My eyelids flutter, and I absentmindedly scratch my jaw, considerably fearing it and its undeniable lure.

I sigh, a gust of breath puffing my cheeks and blowing my lips, vibrating them against each other. It sounds like a motorboat, and I almost laugh. The pull it has on me is strong and addicting. All I want to do is heed its desires, and the insanity of it is appalling.

*This is it.* My lips purse. *The portal to the death realm.*

Glancing behind me, I take a deep, calming breath. Of their own accord, my legs gather speed, running before I can slink away like the coward I feel. The fog envelopes me, crackles along my transparent skin like liquid to rock pop candy. My heart thuds, and I bite back a scream. My skin feels like it's on fire, like the fog knows I'm of the living. It contains some sort of acidity, attacking each nerve and leaving behind pain as it travels to the next, inspecting every inch of me, punishing me.

I close my eyes, grit my teeth, and dig my fingernails into my palm, waiting for it to transport me to the other side. This must be some sort of defense mechanism – to have a portal which detects a shade.

The creature hunkered inside me expands, spreading itself from toe to toe, from finger-tip to finger-tip, lessening the pain. I marvel at it, hope replacing the feeling of possible demise; a beacon of relief. Each nerve pulses and throbs. The creature is doing this. It's protecting me, muffling the beat of my heart.

In shock, I open my eyes precisely at the moment I'm shoved out by an invisible force, spit and discarded, deemed worthy. Flying through the air, my palms hit stone, and my knees buckle to a bruise. It's odd – I still have all sensations. Whenever I died and became a shade, I expected objects, emotions, senses, would be different. Maybe it's because I'm not truly dead. What does that make me? One third witch, dragon, and ghost? What's next? Let's throw mermaid in there, too. I could pull off the scales thing.

I shake my head and rake my nails on the back of my forearm. *I'm losing my mind.*

Standing, I use the denim of my jeans to dust the tiny pebbles of stone from the wounds in my hands. I turn my head, absorbing my surroundings. A stone wall is in front of me, an arch for a doorway, and a crumbling white brick path leading inside. It's eerie here . . . quiet and dark. I suppose it's not much different than the Tween. The only difference is there isn't any vegetation, half-dead or otherwise. No breeze, no sunlight, just . . . stone. It reminds me of an ancient roman structure.

I slink to the wall and run my hand along the stone. It flakes and crumbles against my fingertips, dust specks floating to the cemented stone beneath my shoes. Such an ancient and uncared for wall. It makes me wonder . . . Is this wall for keeping foes out or keeping the unfortunate in?

Brushing my hand along my jeans once more, I search for any signs of life, but there aren't any. I twitch my lips and prop my hands on my hips. I don't even know where to find Dyson. The sandman said he's being detained in a colosseum, but I imagine the death realm is large. I know nothing of this place besides the basics. My plan has no plan.

I shrug. *What's the worst that can happen?*

Stepping forward, I shuffle through the archway and into the tunnel.

## *ELIZA PLAATS*

## *DEATH REALM*

Aiden didn't follow us to the throne room, to the place I'm marrying the fee I despise. I find myself filling with relief because he won't be here to witness this. His last memories of us are ones of love. I don't want them to be of me wedding another.

The only reason I don't choose death over this, the only reason I'm holding a sliver of hope, is that Kheelan will be forced to share his magic. His jealousy, his greed, his maliciousness, will be his downfall if it's the last thing I do.

I'm shaking. My emotional nerves quiver my muscles, and consuming revulsion turns my stomach. My cheeks are heated, and every part of me wants to attempt to flee. But instead, I stand my ground with a straight spine, holding the hope that someday I'll be able to deliver justice deserved.

As I stand beside Kheelan, our wrists bound in rope, Corbin is in front of us chanting words I cannot understand. It sounds like Latin. I look at the archway from which we entered. Yaris is the only one who stands there, a look of boredom on his face as he leans against the wall, arms crossed. His tongue slithers out, licking the tips of his fangs. A drop of blood is dried on his pale upper lip.

I breathe through my mouth and turn my attention back to Corbin. He grasps my free wrist and everything inside me pleads to recoil. Kheelan willingly gives Corbin his arm, holding it out toward him. Corbin clutches his fingers around Kheelan's wrist, and Corbin closes his eyes. His lips move, but I don't hear a sound passing through them. It's a silent whisper, a wordless prayer, but to whom, I have no idea. Who is it they must ask permission from, for such a union?

Nothing happens at first, the soundless words seeming useless, but then his eyelids flutter, and heat gathers in my wrist, seeping from Corbin's fingers. It's a painful scorching, one from the pits of hell he surely came from. I grit my teeth as it intensifies, traveling up my veins like hot liquid oil. It reaches my elbow, my upper arm, my shoulder. My mouth opens against my will, and a scream rips from my throat.

Kheelan laughs beside me, a staccato of hyena giggles. His glee for my pain is pure.

245

I feel the heat crawl to my heart, lighting it afire and swelling it to an impossible size. My legs quiver, my body convulsing but powerless to collapse. Something invisible holds me up, forcing me to endure every sliver of agony.

My throat is raw from quickly fleeting wind with each passing scream, and I squeeze my eyes shut, allowing my head to recline, my face tilted to the ceiling. The hair I had carefully and numbly placed atop my head loosens and escapes its clips, cascading down my back in locks of red.

Electric bolts build through Kheelan and my conjoined palms, the tingling sensation a welcome pain compared to the one within my chest. A heart attack has nothing on this; that I am sure.

"Make it stop!" I scream, my words resounding off the walls.

I feel it – I'm aware of what's happening, even as my brain pushes against my skull, allowing more room for what my human body wasn't capable of handling. My insides feel like they're expanding, the stretching a whole new ache. My insides shift, allowing room to substitute for what I'm being granted: Power.

Sweat covers every inch of me, and stars speckle my vision. I can't breathe. I can't fight it off. I can't take it much longer. My feeble human body isn't made to withstand this.

Black takes over the stars in a wave of blessed darkness, and my body thuds to the floor.

# DYSON COLEMAN

## DEATH REALM

My hands are behind my head as I lay my back against the sharp rocks. I study the ceiling, scanning left and right. There's not a single flaw or texture on the entire expanse. It wasn't man-made . . . or vampire made. I guess it's what the King of the Dead gets if he twitches his nose and toots magic from his ass.

Disastrous scenarios surface in my mind, working their way in and interrupting my perusal. Thoughts on ways to fight whatever is before us filter in, distracting me. I was never much of a fighter when I was alive on the earth realm. That was my pack's strength, whereas my brain was the most useful. Strategy plans were my thing. I can't come up with anything though. These kinds of scenarios are uncharted territory. Stuff like this, games of death and toying with lives, isn't in the supernatural histories to learn from. We will be going in blind, and there is nothing I can do about it. It's frustrating as hell. Evo – Ben . . . they'd know what to do. They would already have a plan formed, several versions and back-ups in case one failed.

I suck in my top lip and pull it between my teeth. I wonder what they're doing right this very moment. I release my lip with a sucking pop.

The crackling of the bars of our cell stops, and I frown, lifting my head as Sandy pokes my shoulder. I sit up, my words stumbling as Jane, Tanya, and Gan are shoved into our cell by snarling vampires. You'd think they thought we have a chance at fighting back. Their hostility is irritating, and I'd love to deliver a snarl of my own. Don't these predators recognize when they're herding prey?

Scrambling to my feet, I fold Jane in a hug first. A strand of her hair tickles my eyelashes. "Are you okay? What's going on?"

Jane huffs, her body quivering in fear. "They told us . . . We are to fight alongside one another, Dyson."

I hold her out at arm's length, frowning. That's a good thing . . . right? I'd rather have it that way than having to kill each other.

Gan bends his knees and folds his legs, sitting right where he stood. He wraps his arms around his calves and rocks back and forth, his fingers curling around his forearms. My forehead wrinkles. In the brighter light of lit candles, he's dirtier than I imagined he would be. The human odor and stench wafting from his body curls my insides.

Tanya pulls at her fingers. "They're organizing everyone, putting them in groups that they'll fight with or against. Dyson." She lifts watery eyes to mine. "I don't want to die. Not again."

Dropping my arms from around Jane's shoulders, I grab Tanya and press her head to my chest. "We'll get through this."

"How?" she mumbles, her fingers curling against my shirt.

I run my hand over her hair. "I don't know."

## *TEMBER*

## *GUARDIAN REALM*

Instead of staying at their posts, propped hidden in the trees, the curious Inga elves trail behind us. They talk amongst themselves in hushed whispers filled with hate, and for a moment, I'm glad I don't understand their language. Surely their words are directed at me, or about me, and the reason why I'm attending this gathering.

"When will the council be assembled?" Erma asks.

With the moving bodies close behind us, we've matched pace with Jaemes and his matua, forced to walk beside the animal. Its tail twitches from time to time, the smoke brushing my arm. It's a warm smoke, one unexpected within the texture of vapors.

"They've been assembled for many hours, discussing a shortage of livestock," Jaemes responds.

"Oh?" I quip. "Have you misplaced your resources?"

He blinks hard, and his eyes light with mischief. "Oh. Sarcasm. My favorite." He dips his head, tucking his chin. "I'll tell you if you tell me."

I narrow my eyes. "Tell you what?"

"Your wings." He nods his head to my back. "Have you misplaced them? Or did they abandon you when they came to the realization you're nothing more than a metaphorical wingman?" He cocks his head. "Or is it wing woman?"

A small part of me wants to smile due to the invitation of the banter, but the more dominant and territorial side of me screams for revenge – to knock him off the four-legged creature and watch his arms flail before he thuds in the snow.

Erma ignores our bickering. "What is happening to your livestock?"

Jaemes' face relaxes, and he glances back in front of him. His jaw clenches, rippling the muscles inside his cheek. "Theft."

"The angels?" I ask, a chuckle in the back of my throat.

He doesn't respond, his silence my answer. Perhaps I pushed too far. Stealing their necessities will surely create more problems. Angels have a dark side, and though we are all guardians of this realm, from time to time, some like to antagonize the weaker. Many angels forget how formidable and vengeful the elves can be.

The tree trunks are larger here, protecting the ground from heavy snow drifts and the threat of impassable walking inside the village a few yards ahead.

The tops of the trees intertwining to a point where few flakes fall within the village.

Smoke tickles my nose as we enter, several fires lit outside of each teepee hut. Sticks and tree limbs are stacked vertically, meeting at the top and twined to hold them in place. Skin from animals make up the outside walls, completing the structure of individual homes.

Children, tattooed in the same color as the bark, toddle about, giggling and playing until they notice our arrival. In quick scurries, they flee back to their mothers, the women wrapping their arms around the tiny elves. Like Jaemes, thin cloth covers their external reproductive organs. The chill of this winter has no effect on them, just as me.

The village is larger than I expected. It's built around the trees with expert architecture, fitting like a perfect puzzle piece. As far as I know, I'm the first angel to have stepped foot in any elf village. In the past, our battles have always unfolded in a field.

We parade past the first hut. A large male elf sizzles raw meat over his fire. He stops and twists his torso to stare, his meat forgotten. His shrewd eyes study me before they swivel to Erma. Curiosity sluggishly replaces his disdain.

Another, cradling a stack of arrows in his arms, spits a wad of saliva in our path as we weave between the huts. It narrowly misses me. I snarl at him, half-tempted to hiss like the wild beasts they think I am.

"If you had your wings, I would have sent you back by now," Erma mumbles, her head slanted in my direction. The hostility is thick here.

Glaring at those who glare at me, I retort. "If I had my wings, we'd be unaware of the circumstances you wish to discuss with a council. We wouldn't be where we currently stand."

"Now I see," Jaemes quips, faking clarity. "You're not a team player. You're the mascot to your lover."

"Just get us to the council," I murmur, tired of the games. If he verbally arrives to her aid, he clearly cares for Erma, choosing to use our earlier heated, hushed discussion to throw back in my face.

## AIDEN VANDER

## DEATH REALM

Resting my shoulders against the Keep's external stone wall, I stuff my hands in my pockets and look around, waiting for Corbin to exit. This is where I choose to stay away from the wedding. I fidget in my stance and cross my legs, concerned about this new-found sympathy I've been gaining. It'll complicate things if I don't control it . . . If I let it control me.

The streets are empty, the shades absent. To my right, behind the Keep, the Colosseum rests in full glory. Soon, cries of battle will spill from its top, filling these streets with screams of victory and pain.

Vampires mill in and out the oval structure, chatting amongst themselves in excitement for what's to come. Blood is what they live for, no matter how they gain it.

I lick my bottom lip. I understand that hunger. I was created for the same: to create and feed on the chaos. But it makes me question what purpose I have in Corbin's eyes. I know he meant me for more, especially if he threatens me due to my disobedience. He has something to lose, and I plan to find out what it is – his weakness.

The door slides open, stone rasping against stone, and Corbin exits with his hands in his pockets, mirroring me. The vampire, named Yaris, closes it behind him.

"Ugly place, isn't it?" Corbin suggests, pulling his arms up and crossing them. "Absolutely no color or imagination. Stone. Stone everywhere. You can't even sit in the place without dust coating your ass."

I raise my eyebrows yet follow the trail of his gaze. "Kheelan doesn't strike me as the type to enjoy anything but shades of death."

He puckers his lips. "Fair point."

We're silent for a moment, watching as a shade pokes his head through a wall. His eyes land on ours, and they widen, filled with fear of discovery. I willingly feed on him, on the sliver of fear wafting my way, before he disappears back inside.

"Why do they hide?" I ask, raising my voice over Corbin's chuckle.

"They fear they'll be human next."

Kheelan has the power to make them all human again, and the demon in me salivates at the thought of the large expanse of a human's terror if they were all to be turned. Kheelan would have to tie himself to each and every one. It'd be his downfall – his demise.

Could I do it? Could I allow him to turn every shade, making him vulnerable while I feed? My mouth salivates at the endless buffet, but the part of me, this new part of me fighting to surface, is angry this realm is ruled by a selfish fee. Death could be so much more than blankets of grey and misery.

"What is that stench of sympathy?" Corbin growls.

I clench my jaw, my eyes hardening around the edges. I open my mouth to respond, but we're interrupted by a female vampire running at human speed. She stops before us, her hair whipping in her face as it catches up.

"She arrives," she reports, her upper lip tense.

Corbin claps his hands once, his façade sliding back in place. "And so it begins. Come. We will gather Kheelan."

# CHAPTER NINETEEN

*KATRIANE DUPONT*

*DEATH REALM*

The tunnel was short, shorter than I anticipated. I stand in the last foot of it, taking in what's in front of me. It's a city – a city made of stone. But a city should be bustling, no matter what creatures live there. A single cricket chirp would be louder than this place. Where is everybody?

Buildings reach higher than I can see, fog swallowing their tips whole. There are no windows along these buildings, and the streets are made from the same stone everything else is. This isn't how I pictured the afterlife, but then again, this is Kheelan's domain. Maybe he's as empty in the head as the realm he built.

The fog resting in the pit of my stomach applies pressure against the inside of my bellybutton, urging me onward. It's like an internal GPS with its own destination in mind.

Chewing the inside of my lip, I decide to take a chance. What have I got to lose? If I die, I'll just stay here. It's not like I don't know where 'here' is anymore. This realm doesn't look anything like what I had pictured. Would it kill Kheelan to add a grassy hill or a rainbow?

I chuckle to myself, picturing a unicorn prancing toward Kheelan as he strolls along his patch of grass.

Shuffling forward, my noisy shoes grit against the stone's dust beneath them. I gulp, and squint at the path before me. I don't know where I'm going, but moving forward seems the best course. I bend a corner, gasp, and step back around it.

A vampire heads my direction, leisurely strolling instead of the normal blur of speed. What is it doing? Patrolling? Is that why there's not a single shade strolling the streets? Should I kill him?

My shoulders sag, and I internally groan. *Dyson. I'm here for Dyson. Not to diminish the population of blood-sucking dead people.*

I concoct a ball of flames within my palm and wait for the vampire to bend the corner. Muscles tense and prepared, I'm set to throw it, ready even. I squeal as the fog inside me shoves against my spine, sending me straight into the wall my back rests against and directly through the solid structure.

My stomach rolls like I'm diving a hundred-foot drop while strapped to a roller coaster. I land with a thump and a yelp on the other side. Raising my head, I look back over my shoulder, my fingers curling on the stone floor I'm pancaked against. There are no doors here, and a vampire can't follow me in the same fashion. I heave a sigh of relief, my tense shoulders loosening. It's a small victory, but this place is full of the unknown. I was stupid to waltz the streets like I belonged here.

I wipe my mouth with the back of my hand and perch myself on my knees. A woman stands before me, plump and frail looking, even with her transparency. She wears a hospital gown, and in our confusion, my scrunched eyebrows match hers.

On shaky knees, I climb to my feet, stand, and clear my throat. "Hello," I greet, fidgeting with the hem of my shirt.

Frozen in her shocked stance, her gape flashes, regarding me and the wall behind me. "Can I help you?"

I shift my weight, straighten my shirt, and fold my arms across my chest. "Um. Let's keep this tiny intrusion between us." I inspect the room, seeing no furniture, no other shades, and no death trap. "I'm . . . hiding."

Her lips part, fumbling over her next words. "Who are you?"

Reaching, I hold out my hand to her. "I'm Katriane Dupont. Nice to meet you . . ."

"Wanda Tiller," she responds with reluctance, grasping my hand. Her grip is loose and nervous. I marvel at the fact my hand didn't travel through hers. Can the solidity be turned off and on? "Ms. Dupont, I know it's a scary place out there with the Colosseum and shades turning human, but you should really consider hiding in your own room."

I begin to respond as my stomach heaves, rolling within and contents travel up to the back of my tongue. The fog inside is fighting to get out. I grip my abdomen, my mouth forced open as the snake-like mist exits in the same fashion it entered. My eyes water, and the tail of the creature forces itself from my body, slithering into the open air.

Wanda gasps, both hands flying to her mouth. I'm about to tell her it won't hurt her – that it helped me – but she speaks before I have the chance, watching my body become whole instead of transparent.

"Reaper's Breath," she whispers behind her fingers.

I look over my shoulder, slight fear curling my toes. "Reaper?  Where?"

The snake-like fog slithers its way to her shoulders, caressing her like a cat. Wanda shakes her head. "No, not a reaper. This is Reaper's Breath."

I double blink, remembering their stanching breath . . . "Excuse me?"

"It's Kheelan's creation. Reaper's Breath holds a great deal of power, just as its fee creator. You should know. . ." she nods her head to my solid, human body.

I watch Reaper's Breath. The front end of its body shifts like a head. "Is it safe?"

Wanda glowers, her plump cheeks puffing.

I elaborate. "I mean, if it's Kheelan's pet, doesn't it have some sort of obligation to him? I don't know if you've noticed, but the death realm isn't exactly what I pictured. There are no fluffy bunnies hopping through fresh, green grass and never-ending rainbows out there. This isn't the kind of realm I'd place much trust in anyone . . ." My voice trails off as I listen to my own advice and eye Wanda with speculation. I suppose any realm would have a list of untrustworthy people and creatures living in it.

"I don't know anyone, besides his vampires, who are loyal to only him, Ms. Dupont."

I heave a sigh and scrub my hands with my face. What am I doing? I have no plan.

Backing up, my spine hits the wall, and I slide to the floor, placing my elbows on my bent knees. Wanda shifts her weight uncomfortably. Her fingers pull at one another.

"Is this your home?" I ask. There are no personalized objects. It's hard to get to know someone when they're standing in their room, and it's completely bare. If I didn't know any better, and if this was the earth realm, I'd deem her insane.

She nods her head.

"Where's all your stuff?" I inquire as I arch my neck, stretching the stiff, aching muscles. The small yet terrifying battle with the Reapers did a number on me.

"We aren't allowed belongings here. If we hold belongings, it keeps us tied to our old life. Kheelan doesn't approve of that."

I chuckle, shaking my head. "What? Is he afraid you'll cross over and haunt your loved ones?"

She stares at me blankly, confirming without voicing.

I clear my throat and prop my elbows on my knees. "Right. Okay. So, what do you do here, Wanda? What role do you play in the death realm?"

Her posture stiffens, and the worry lines across her forehead smoothen. "What did you say your name was again?"

"Katriane Dupont."

Reaper's Breath glides from her shoulders to the floor and snakes its way to my ankles, swirling around them.

"Kat . . ." she whispers.

*Has she lost her mind?* "Yes . . ."

"You're her," she hisses, dropping her hands to her side. "You're the witch Dyson was looking for."

"You know Dyson?" I inquire, skeptical. This is a big place. I'm flattered she knows my name, but how many Dyson's live here?

Her body snaps from its nervous stance. "Come," she demands, urging me to stand by waving her hands. "Up. We have much to prepare."

## ELIZA PLAATS

## DEATH REALM

*This is a dream. I know it is. It's dark here, wherever here is. It's not a room but an all-consuming blackness. There is a small amount of light and it forms around me like a spotlight.*

*I blow out a breath, and my frizzy hair tickles the edge of my chin. I'm frustrated that my brain keeps playing tricks on me during my sleeping state. Am I a beacon, such as this spotlight, for all things dream-related and supernatural?*

*Am I dead? Is this the void?*

*Memories surface, suffocating me with reason and conviction. I had fainted during the marriage ceremony, the binding of our souls. That's what this is. It's my brain resetting for my new path – my future.*

*"Eliza Plaats?" A voice calls behind me.*

*I whip around, spinning on the balls of my bare feet, and I almost lose my balance. A woman stands there, long* brunette hair, slender, beautiful eyes. Her face is set in a stern, determined expression, and her short-sleeved, black dress blends with our surroundings. A separate spotlight from mine hovers over her.

"Who are you?" I peek around once more. "Where am I?"

She takes a step forward, confident. "My name is Janine Dupont. I'm a witch who belongs to a coven called Demi-Lune. This," she waves a hand around. "This is a portal between minds. A conjure, if you will."

"What?" I frown, tucking my chin and scrunching the skin along the bridge of my nose. "A portal – what am I doing here?"

"I called you here." She sighs. Her patience is impossibly thin, and she crosses her arms. "We don't have much time. I can't hold this link for long. It's difficult, you see, because you aren't dwelling on the earth realm."

I stare at her, my mouth agape and my arms limp at my sides.

She momentarily sucks on her bottom lip, our eyes locked. "I see the future. It's part of my gift. I've seen your future, Eliza. I've seen what you become - what the effect of your union has and the impact you'll have in the near future, regarding the safety of the realms."

Tucking my hair behind my ear, I reach up and scratch my forehead. "I still don't understand."

Janine advances once more. "My daughter is traveling to your realm. She may already be there. I need you to help her. To prove my visions wrong. Can you do that? Can you keep her alive in the face of the oncoming grief and devastation you're about to endure?"

*TEMBER*

*GUARDIAN REALM*

Jaemes hops off his Matua in a graceful leap. "Wait here," he demands, pulling back the skin of the hut we stand before, and heads inside.

This hut – this teepee - is massive, much larger than the ones we've passed while hiking through the village. His Matua stomps and paws at the ground, shifting the snow beneath its foot. It stares at me with all four eyes. I look to Erma, but she's remained unaffected by all of this around her. I regard the animal, choosing to study its bone structure and build instead of focusing on the group who has gathered around us. They stare, and it makes my skin crawl.

I open my mouth to cluck, hoping to gain a positive reaction from the beast, but I'm halted as the flap opens to the hut. Jaemes pokes his head through. "Creator," he says, dipping his head to Erma. He turns his head to me. "Wingless Mascot. They're ready for you."

Erma's strides are poised as she ducks inside the hut, Jaemes holding the skin open for her. He drops it as soon as I step forward, forcing me to slide it aside myself.

Jaemes is enjoying himself; I can tell. If we were of the same make, he and I may get along. I enjoy those who live life on the playful side. Perhaps we'll always be destined to disagree, simply due to our make.

Inside, four elves sit on the ground, cross-legged. The floor is covered in fur of a variety of colors. One elf runs his long, nimble fingers through the strands, using their texture for comfort I imagine.

The elves are younger than I expected, each built with an impressive stature, each as menacing as the other. They're intimidating, and their stares pin me to my spot inside the door. I twitch my fingers at my sides, feeling unwelcome here.

"Erma," a male elf greets, tearing his sharp, murderous eyes from mine, and squints at Erma to my right. His voice is deep and rumbling.

"Mitus." She dips her head.

Like Jaemes, Mitus has dark tattoos. The resemblance between them is uncanny though Mitus is large with a wider frame and a sturdy, square jaw. The sculpted muscles lining his body leave me no doubt as to why he's the head of the Igna elves.

Next to Mitus, is a Yoki elf, his skin covered in green, sprawling line, matching the forest they harvest.

Uji's are red, like the sand from the waters they fish, and the Kaju elf who continues to glare at me, his top lip in a permanent state of snarl, has yellow tattoos. The yellow is light, almost matching his skin. A long knife, broad at the back, intricately etched hilt rests across his thick thighs. The knife curves, coming to a sharp, jagged point. I marvel at the knife, its make and shape fascinating. It's not long, maybe the length of his forearm. It glints, capturing my undivided, envious attention. The light bounces off the polished metal, and a reflection hovers along the wall.

Kaju elves are my least favorite. They tend to not bend in their ways, often passing judgement before guilt is proven.

"You bring an angel?" The Yoki questions, his eyebrows pulled down toward his large, hooked nose.

Jaemes snickers and folds his arms. The quiver against his back tilts. "A wingless one."

"Jaemes," Erma warns.

"Yeah," he sighs, hanging his head to hide a fraction of a grin.

The Kaju elf lifts an eyebrow, skeptical. "Show me."

Erma peeks at me, closes her eyes in annoyance, and nods her head. Shrugging, I lift my shirt, exposing my naked body to the elf men before me, and turn.

I hear Jaemes hiss quietly. The elves observe what's left of my wings in silence. There's nothing to see but open wounds.

"What did you do to them?" I'm asked, by whom I'm not sure.

I slip my head back through the hole of my shirt and twist to face them. "I disposed of them for my charge."

Mitus licks his bottom lip, his eyes focused on my stomach but his mind elsewhere. He comes to a conclusion, nodding his head as he dwells within his thoughts. "I see. And what charge warrants self-mutilation?"

Erma slips closer to the group, stopping me from answering. "The kind who is more powerful than me."

## AIDEN VANDER

## DEATH REALM

Our gallery to the Colosseum's sandpit is low to the ground. A human could jump off the ledge and safely land on his feet, if he so wished. It's a square platform, and as a spray of red splatters the stone, I understand why it's placed here: front row seats to an endless bloodbath.

The platform has no rails, but it's large enough to hold a small crowd. The stone is unrealistically smooth, and a few large chairs – thrones – are situated in a row at the front, which Sureen had made by the twirl of her wrist. With high backs, they're made of solid wood, delicately carved in swirls and undistinguishable patterns. There's one for me, but I choose to stand behind them.

Sureen, Corbin, and Kheelan are seated, watching two shades fight to their death. They reluctantly clink their swords against each other's with weak blows. The metal

266

against metal isn't a familiar sound but rather a song orchestrated by impending death. Sweat drips from their brows, dropping to the sand below their shuffling feet.

Demons and vampires line the stadium seats, some silently watching while others cheer and beg for more bloodbath. A few fights have already transpired between the vampires and demons, but they've quickly ended once they succeeded in killing the other. The fee isn't concerned over the matches on the benches. They only wish to watch the weak destroy each other, to see the deaths at the hands of friends.

A contestant swings his sword through the air, slicing through his opponent's skin across the middle of his exposed belly. The pain on his face, the fear and betrayal at his own hand's deceit, feeds me, filling me with a sense of contentment. The sword drips blood from its edges as more sprays from the victim. Droplets land on our platform gallery, and a grin lights Corbin and Sureen's faces while agony etches the slave's. Kheelan, however, remains impassive, his elbow propped on the armrest while his chin rests in his hand.

It's curious, why Kheelan is here without his new bride. Why did he wed her if he chooses to leave her unconscious in her room? I resist the urge to shake my head. If anything, Corbin was right. This man is weak. His self-absorption could be his undoing.

Corbin stands as though he's been called and spins to me with narrowed eyes. He slides between his chair and Sureen's, coming to stand before me. I slant my head in curiosity, untucking my crossed arms. He looks . . . caught off guard.

"What is it?" I question.

He leans in, whispering in my ear. "Katriane Dupont."

"The dragon?"

I'm privy to the knowledge he and Katriane are linked in a way I can't understand. He would feel her if she were close. It's a useful tool, especially if she's the only one who could be his demise. I tuck that knowledge away for later use.

Nodding, he hushes his voice. "I'll be back."

He shimmers, his body and scent fading with him. I look to the front in time to see the unscathed human stick his sword through the other's torso, a quick death for a beloved friend. The look on the human's face is easy to distinguish. The reality of his actions is eating him alive.

The demons roar, their fists pumping in the air. Saliva drips from the vampires' mouths, their attention focused on the blood as it dribbles down the fading body and soaks through the sand at his feet. The sword is yanked back, and the dying contestant drops to his knees. Pink organs fall from the wound and into his hands, his fingers gripping them.

Sureen glances back, and long braids trickle over her shoulder. She frowns when her surveying doesn't find what she's looking for. "Corbin?"

"An errand," I answer, watching the sandpits. A vampire grips the dead human's arm and pulls him along the blood-soaked sand. He yanks once, lifting the man's wrist to his lips. The organs which were held within those fingers drop and trail along the body. Exposing sharp fangs, the vampire strikes, his teeth sinking into the veins of the dead slave's wrist.

# CHAPTER TWENTY

*TEMBER*

*GUARDIAN REALM*

"Please! Quiet yourselves," Erma shouts, pacing the hut. Her fingers are clenched into fists at her sides, her arms stiff. "Katriane Dupont is not a danger to us."

Mitus' fist thumps against the fur, his pecs rippling. "You just said she amounts to a power greater than your own," he bellows.

"She is no threat to us," Erma repeats, hissing.

The Yoki elf twists his body to face hers. "Says you."

I cross my arms. "What is the meaning behind your words?"

He shrugs, and his shoulder muscles bunch. "Erma does not excel at caring for those she has created. She allows battle to rip through her lands and does nothing to end the mischief and blood bath."

Stepping forward, I prepare an assault in the form of words, defending Erma. Jaemes holds out a hand, capturing my attention, and shakes his head. He looks at Erma then to his father. "If I may?" Mitus inclines his head. One side of his face is covered with a curtain of hair as it falls over his shoulder. "Creator, if you are so sure Katriane isn't a threat, what is your evidence?"

"No!" The Kaju elf demands, slamming his fist on the ground. The fur muffles the sound, but the vibration reaches my feet. "I won't entertain the notion this dragon would do us no harm. We should take swift action, assemble the tribes, and destroy her and the beast within." Perspiration beads at his temples, his huffs and puffs a sign of his agitation and aggression.

Erma quiets her voice. "Tember almost got her killed, and she still stands before you, alive and well." All eyes swivel to me. "The dragon may be powerful, but she is not vengeful without cause. My reason for being here isn't to discuss the longevity of the dragon's existence. I came to discuss my sister fee."

"Erline?" Jaemes asks, scratching his jaw with the back of his nails.

She shakes her head, and her short, red curls rattle. "Sureen."

Mitus juts his chin and purses his lips at the name of the fee who rules the dream realm. Perhaps he's more aware of her cruelty than I am. Have I been more arrogant than I've realized – as Jaemes suggested – these last few years? "What of her?" Mitus asks through pressed lips.

Erma paces once more, her eyes searching the floor as though she's reliving her time in the dream realm. The elves follow her struts, their heads tilted up and swiveling from their seated positions on the floor.

She pulls the fur closer around her shoulders, grasping it in the center. "She's been given the power to create life."

The atmosphere changes, dipping further on the side of hostility than I am comfortable with. I shift my weight as the Council of Four raise their voices in uproar, arguing the same point. None wish to see her with such talents, yet they're hysterical, closing off their ears to one another even though they speak the same words. They're frightened for their people and what it could mean for this realm.

I knew one day they'd regret the choice to remain home instead of protecting the realms as Erma suggested so long ago. The realms have grown and suffered in the absence of protectors.

Erma whips her hand through the air, swirling full circle and closing her fist at the last. A small, yellow glowing ball exits their esophagi through the skin and travels to her palm. She closes her fingers, capturing the yellow orbs. The voices leave the throats of elves though their lips continue to move before they realize what she's done; she stole their voices straight from their cords.

The bridge of her nose twitches and wrinkles. "You need to be prepared," she begins, her tone raspy and authoritative. She's no longer up for negotiations. "The chances are high of Sureen creating some form of protection for herself and her realm. Like you, she's threatened by the dragon. Do not forget the purpose for which I created you. The dragon will stand beside you – it is the nature of her human side. If you are foolish enough to believe you can do this on your own . . ." her voice trails off as she captures the attention of each elf. "The angels must stand beside you, and you must welcome it. If we are to protect this realm, and the others without absence of innocence, you must set your hatred aside. This is a feat you must overcome if our realm is to survive the near future. It won't be long before the dragon arrives. It's time you overcome your prejudices and take the first step."

*****

"Do you think they'll listen?" I ask.

Walking back through the village with Erma, I make small conversation to dull the sense of a million eyes on my back. Every elf is aware of our meeting by now, and their whispers are difficult to dismiss. We pass a group of elves huddled around a fire. They tend to a pot situated over roaring flames, and the liquid inside bubbles over the edges. The aroma coming from the contents makes my stomach rumble. I don't remember the last time I had nourishment, and it'll surely make me weak if I don't eat soon.

"If they have a lick of sense in them," she mumbles. Her strut is cocky, both feet stomping with barely contained displeasure. She's upset about how that went though she received everything she wished. The elves have developed an abundance of disobedience toward their creator, and I believe this meeting has brought that fact to light. She's been absent, and it shows.

Jaemes pops his head between our shoulders and wraps his arms across them. "No need to fear. The fun is here."

I grind my teeth.

When Erma returned their voices, they were fuming. They don't relish the idea of choices being taken from them. I waited in the corner while they discussed the fate of their tribes and weighed it with the fate of the realms. Their discontent for the angels was palpable, but they saw the bigger picture. The Council of Four came to one conclusion: Jaemes and I are to be a trial run between the angels and the elves. He will be my shadow, following me where ever I go, assisting me in anything I need, precisely as I will reluctantly do for him.

Jaemes slides his arms from our shoulders and drops them back to his sides. He sidesteps to the right, choosing to walk beside Erma. His posture is straight and confident, a strut in each stride. It's a contradiction to his witty personality but telling about his formidable nature. His bow and quiver are strapped to his back, and there's a slight twist of his lips. I don't believe he's ever left the forest, and he's the first elf to attempt to leave this realm. My hardened face softens a bit. Let's hope he can handle the real world.

We pass each hut, each elf, and to my surprise, they look to Jaemes in horror instead of me. However, the sway of his arms, the hard edge of his eye, remain unwavering.

"Can we use the portal this time?" I ask, glancing at Erma from the corner of my eye. There is no point in going through this village if it feels like a walk of shame. I've had my share of shame for a lifetime.

"Yes," Erma responds, breathing out a large breath. Despite the glares around us, her posture relaxes. I do not believe she thought the meeting would come to anything. Meetings with the Elves in the past have proven to be fruitless.

I arch forward, catching Jaemes' attention. "Do you know anything about the Earth Realm?"

He peeks at me and lifts a brow, contorting the skin under the tattoos surrounding his eyes. He nods his farewells to those who glare, cocky but poised. "Very little. But even if I did, I have no doubt you'll force your knowledge upon me anyhow."

Closing my eyes briefly, I inhale a calming breath. This is going to be a challenging experiment.

"He's being sarcastic, Tember." Erma rolls her eyes. "They have more extensive lessons on the human race than you did. Many of their positions – the way they live their lives – are similar to the human race."

"I think I'd enjoy drinking that dark bean beverage," he contemplates, pursing his lips while ignoring Erma's comment.

Erma bites her bottom lip. "Coffee," she supplies.

Scowling, I glance back at Jaemes. "Why didn't you just say yes?"

"Then where would I get my entertainment?"

Erma conjures her portal, calling upon it by a simple thought. Bright yellow rays form like glimmers of the sun prodding through lavender rain clouds, an entrance to our destination.

I sigh, my brown curls whipping in the wind and catching in the corners of my mouth. *I can do this.*

*****

"Oh, look at this décor. It's lovely. It's ancient. You haven't changed a thing," Jaemes comments as we step through a portal. He spins full circle, observing the furniture delicately placed throughout her room before plopping himself on one of the maroon, handstitched couches. He points at the fireplace to his left. "The mantel is still broken."

Erma runs her top teeth over her bottom lip, releasing it with a pop. "So, you've told me once before. Possibly twice. Maybe more. It's hard to keep track."

A large canopy bed, detailed with swirling designs carved in cherry wood and hand-painted, gold flowers, is the focal point of her bedroom. A ruby red comforter is laid across, and an assortment of gold pillows are at the head of the bed.

A fireplace, as tall as I am, is nestled into the wall, hot flames licking the bright red, charred brick inside. Two couches are placed in front of it, facing each other. The trim of the couch is wood, matching the canopy bed, and the button accented fabric is a light cream, emphasizing the gold accents scattered throughout her bedroom.

Above, no ceiling holds us in. Not on the angels' ground. Instead, a black sky expands from corner to corner, as far as we can see. Many stars shine and sparkle the most brilliant shades of yellow, blue, and white. They look to be moving and mingling.

It's a room I've been in many times, but I wasn't privy that Jaemes had. Elves do not visit the Angels' Ground, or so I had thought. Perhaps he visited many times in the past. Erma did convey they had a great friendship once before. It's probable they met in secret, enjoying their friendship behind closed doors and cruel, prejudice eyes.

"Jaemes," Erma begins. His hand caresses the gold flower along the arm of the couch, but his head tilts in her direction. He waits for her to speak. "Do you mind waiting here for a moment? I have a few things to discuss with Tember before I send you two to the Earth Realm."

He inclines his head, distracted with outlining the carved wood. "I make no guarantees about resisting the urge to rifle through your possessions."

Erma rolls her eyes. "You wouldn't be you if you practiced restraint."

She swings out her arm and gestures for me to enter her office. My shoes pad along the marble, and I turn as the doors softly click shut behind her.

"Is it safe?" I nod to the door. "To have him in there unsupervised?"

She points a finger at me, her black orbs boring into mine, and she curls her top lip in disgust. "Stop. Jaemes and I were close once upon a time. He's one of the good ones, Tember. You would do well to hold your own judgments."

I rake a hand through my hair and stretch out my neck. "So much hostility. Will you always hate me?"

Sighing, she shuffles to the front of her large, wooden desk and places her rump against it. Her shoulders slump as she grips the edge of the desk. "No."

"Oh?" I incline my head, considering my next move carefully. Crossing my arms, I glide forward, stopping a foot away from her. Close enough to smell her inviting scent; sweet chocolate.

She sighs, grasping my hand from around my middle and lifting it to her face. Placing her thumb over my heart inside my wrist, she rubs it back and forth, feeling the beat while conflicting emotions rapidly cross her face. I can't determine what they are.

"Erma?" I call, bending my knees to capture her downcast eyes. "What is it?"

She licks her bottom lip, thinking of the best way to explain herself. "I created the angels to be merciful, passionate, and considerate, yet they try so hard not to be." She lifts her head, black eyes meeting mine. "There's a reason I gave you wings, Tember. I wanted the Angels' reach to be farther than my first creations." She holds up my wrist. "Your heart lies here. It's to be a constant reminder of what sins your hands could do. You wear your heart on your sleeve, yet you forget its purpose."

"You feel betrayed," I exclaim, searching her face.

"I do." She nods once. "But, I also feel selfish. I created you to care for others, not for me. Not like this." She waves her hand back and forth between us. "What we have together shouldn't have happened. It's a conflict, bound to erupt in our faces. We're lucky to remain undiscovered. Do you know the consequences – the repercussions - if they were to find out about us?"

Lifting my other hand, I tuck a stray red curl behind her slender ear. "You worry too much." As the words pass my mouth, I recognize them to be a lie. She worries precisely enough, and her reasons are valid. The angels wouldn't see this as love. They'd see it as special treatment.

I search her face, cupping my warm hand to her cold cheek, and lean in. Her breath fans my face as I brush my lips against hers. I get lost in them, in her scent, my attention honed in on everything she is.

"Well, what do we have here," a familiar and sinful voice chuckles behind me.

## KATRIANE DUPONT

## DEATH REALM

I pace the length of her small living space, desperate to form a plan. Any plan would do, but nothing comes to mind. My shoes pad against the concrete, and it echoes throughout the small, bare room. I cringe at each step, biting my nails in the process.

I had no idea so many in this realm knew about me. They think I'm the savior for their realm. I can't save everyone here. I came for one reason: Dyson. A part of me believes it's my duty to save him, especially when I couldn't in the past. I want to get in and get out. Nothing more.

Wanda grows impatient with me, her voice motherly, deep, and direct as her foot taps. "You mustn't keep pacing. There isn't a lot of time. The games have already begun."

Dropping my hand from my mouth, I look to her, my face pinched with anxiety. Standing next to the wall, she waves her hand, beckoning for me to follow. Reapers Breath swirls around me, entering my mouth once more. I gag, my resistance strong. I'm not sure I can do this. I'm not sure I can pull any of this off.

"Come," Wanda demands. "Pull yourself together. We haven't much time."

She turns without a backward glance, travels through the wall, her beckoning hand at the last, and disappears. I fidget in front of the wall, pulling at the hem of my shirt once more. I wrinkle my nose, talking myself into it, but before I'm ready, the Reaper's Breath inside me pushes me through.

It's easier this time, traveling through a solid object. It feels normal, almost.

I release the breath I held, and glance to my left. Wanda is already rushing down the stone path, her head swiveling in paranoia. If she's paranoid, I should be too. We're playing a risky game here.

Biting my bottom lip, I jog to catch up to her. Wanda turns down a small, narrow walkway. I skid to a halt as Reaper's Breath shoves its way out of my body. The air rushes from my lungs like I was punched in the stomach by a fist the size of my head. I bend, gripping my abdomen.

"Ah, Wanda?" I call as soon as I have enough oxygen to croak the words.

She swivels on her right foot, spinning to face me with wild eyes. The Reaper's Breath zips past her, heading quickly to a new destination. A frown pulls her eyebrows.

"Where is it going?" I ask, forcing myself to stand upright. My eyes widen, and I pat myself along my abdomen. "I'm not a shade. Wanda . . . I'm not transparent." I panic inside, my voice hysterical. The only part of my plan I had worked out fled around the corner and disappeared.

"It's going to the Keep," she mumbles, watching it disappear. She sighs, her lips forming a thin line.

"Why? What about me?"

She swivels to me, finger wagging. "Reaper's Breath wouldn't abandon you unless there was cause. It must think you have to travel from here without transparency. You'll have to do this as a human."

With the outside of my palm, I hit the stone wall beside me and curse with tense lips. Tiny pebbles break free and fall to my feet. "This is a bad idea."

She shakes her head and inches closer to me. "No, it's brilliant if you pause and think about it. The shades inside the Colosseum are human."

Tightening my jaw, I scowl and rub my sore hand, relieving the ache I forced it to endure. "You want me to get caught. . ."

She nods, a satisfied beam lighting her features. It's an odd look for her, even if I barely know her. To me, she seems like a ham-fisted motherly figure. "Yes. Yes, it's perfect, actually. If you get caught, they'll take you straight to Dyson, or at least get you close to him. You would be working from the inside. What better way to free them?"

I hang my head, shaking it in shame. "I can't free everyone, Wanda. I don't know how."

She raises her arm to pat my shoulder, thinks better of it, and bends, capturing my eyes instead. "But you can try. There really is no other plan. None without dangerous complications. Come, we must hurry."

Without another word after her brief and failing encouragement, she turns, heading down the alley once more without waiting to see if I follow. She's rushed, possibly frightened. Or maybe she has an adrenaline rush because their 'savior' is here to free them.

I release a pent-up breath in hopes of relaxing myself. Determined to grow a backbone, I straighten my spine and roll my shoulders to loosen my tense muscles. It doesn't matter what they think. I'm here, and I have people I can't let down. If I'm capable of helping because of my nature, then I should at least try. This thing, this beast I've become . . . It's possible I can use it to my advantage, helping those who deserve it. Not for Erline's intentions, not for Tember's, but maybe, just maybe, fate, if there is such a thing, has a bigger plan for me. If I can help, why shouldn't I? It's not about *me* anymore.

I walk forward, the fear gone from my stiff joints, fortitude driving my stride. My purpose clicks, my vision of the future changes. This whole time I've been looking for someone to call my own, to not be lonely and to feel like I belonged. But all along, I was never alone. People need me, maybe even the ones who aren't considered human anymore.

My shoulders touch each side of the walls expanding up into the foggy sky. I imagine if a broad vampire tried to travel through this, he'd have to shimmy. Shades, however, don't need to worry about such things. Their shoulders would only disappear into the walls if they so wished it.

Wanda looks over her shoulder. "We're taking the long route. The vampires . . ."

"I understand." With my beating heart, I'd be a fool to try and dupe them. The closer we get to the Colosseum, the more believable it'll be that I'm an escapee.

"It's up ahead," Wanda whispers. "We don't have far, and then I must leave you."

"Leave me?" I question. I hadn't thought I'd be doing this alone.

"I must get to the Keep. Eliza should be there. I must attempt to wake her. She'll want to be at the Colosseum."

I gulp, having no idea what, or who, she's talking about. "Who's Eliza? Why is she sleeping?"

Wanda licks her bottom lip, looking through an alley. Deeming it safe, she continues in a straight path. The buildings are built father apart here. "Eliza was made Kheelan's Queen last night."

My eyes bug. "You trust her?" I screech.

Mrs. Tiller's jaw ticks one. "She's a slave, Ms. Dupont. Kheelan killed her loved one, imprisoned the rest, including Dyson, and forced her to marry him. After the marriage, she fainted due to the transfer of power. She now shares Kheelan's magic." She glances at me, licking her lips while gathering her thoughts for her next words. "This is no place for the dead, even for the wicked and accused. Whatever happens tonight, whether you're successful or you die, you'll always have my gratitude for trying."

Mrs. Tiller turns. She pulls her arms up to her side, bent at an angle, her hustle faster than before. I curse and curl my fingers into my palms, the nails biting skin. "Right. Okay. Um - How many exits are there in the Colosseum?"

"I don't know."

"How many vampires will be there?"

"I don't know."

I cock my head, frowning. "What else should I expect?"

"I don't know."

I sigh and run a hand through my short black hair. "You're just a wealth of information, aren't you?"

285

She stops in her tracks and spins to face me, faster than I thought she'd be able to move. Shades are so fluid. The aches and pains of their human bodies don't exist anymore. It can be slightly unnerving when I'd expect a limp or a hobble due to age or obvious injury.

Her face is tinged in red splotches, her eyebrows dipped in a scowl. "I haven't been dead long, Ms. Dupont."

"Kat," I correct, trying to smooth things over. She frightens me a little. "We might as well be on a first name bases."

"Kat," she corrects. She points at me again, her voice softening. "Stay focused. Do not panic. Remember: You are their only hope. They will die without you. A painful, bloody, slow death. If you panic, if you freeze due to fright, you will be sealing their last death."

Turning her back to me, I purse my lips. Sarcasm threatens to roll off my tongue, deflecting the seriousness of the situation, but I think I would get the wrath of Mrs. Tiller if I tried.

The closer we get to the end of the alley, the more she becomes agitated and impatient. I get that. I feel that. I am that. Lashing out in anger has been my personality flaw lately. After all, didn't I do that to Tember? Even if she had a major role, she's also the one who saved me. I doubt the fee would have gathered on their own if someone didn't call upon them. They probably wouldn't have known. Tember could have left me to rot and called me a lost cause, but she fought for me.

I bite the inside of my cheek. I've been ungrateful. I've been self-absorbed, more than I realized. I have a bigger purpose, this I'm now aware of. Being this close to yet another death, coupled with my mother's predictions of my very narrow future, it makes me want to apologize to the people who truly matter to me. Maybe I'm being irrational. If I make it out of this alive, if I leave here with more than one beating heart under my care . . .

The alley ends ahead, fog swirling past and missing the small opening altogether. Naturally, it should whirl in, taking the chance for a change of course. But this place isn't natural. She stops before the opening, and I peer around her, pebbles of broken stone gritting under my shoes, obnoxiously noisy.

Ahead, a large square building takes up a large open space. "The Keep," Mrs. Tiller whispers.

Tall buildings where the shade's surely live surround the center, and the most massive circular structure is tucked behind the Keep. The structure is unmistakable, a perfect example of a colosseum in its glory days.

I have a brief flashback of Myla's past – the Keep is exactly where the gallows were placed. Similar to the gallows, the Keep is meant to be a symbol of utmost importance – a reminder for wrong-doers. It's an interesting tactic, frightening people by a carefully placed object or building.

"This is where I leave you," she whispers, staring at the Colosseum.

"Okay." I gulp. "Um, you go first. I'll ah – find myself a vampire to take me hostage."

Wanda nods her head and peeks around the building once more. Her fingers twist in front of her, pulling at one another. She straightens her spine but slinks toward me.

Now out in the open, she hesitates and turns, looking at me with sympathy. "Good luck," she mouths.

Nervous energy surges from her as she makes her way to the center of the opening to the Keep. Her waddle resembles a goose, a teeter of balance. Standing between two large doors, she hesitates before floating through it. It's a miracle she wasn't seen or caught even as suspicious as she looked. If I were to be walking by, my attention would have zoned in on her at the very beginning. She had waddled there in a hurry, clearly nervous about getting caught. That would have sounded alarm bells for me.

Without thinking, I slouch along a wall, inhaling a calming breath but gasp when a rock digs into my shoulder blade. Adjusting my stance, I close my eyes, forcing the temporary fear from my system.

*I can do this. Find a vampire. Don't kill the vampire. Let the vampire lead me to Dyson.*

Nodding once, I open my eyes and push off the wall. A figure stands in the way of the alley exit. I gasp, startled, my hand flying to my chest and hovering above my pounding heart.

# CHAPTER TWENTY-ONE

***ELIZA PLAATS***

***DEATH REALM***

"Eliza," a voice whispers beside my ear. I frown, thinking it's within my dreams. "Eliza.".

"Hmm?" I mumble, cracking my eyelids.

My body is weak, and a pounding headache disguises my thoughts.

*Where am I?*

I blink once, taking in the stone ceiling above my head. The past few days flood my mind, forcing me to recapture the memories in a rapid speed of flicking images. The dream I dreamt shoves the memories aside, plaguing my contemplations. I groan, my hand covering my forehead. Too much . . . It's too much.

A head pops in my line of sight, a familiar face.

"Wanda?" I question, my voice hoarse. "What are you doing here?"

Her eyebrows are pulled down and her lips are firm with anxiety. "You must wake. You must get up."

I shimmy my way to a seated position, my quilt falling from my chest. "What's wrong?"

She looks at the door then back at me. "Katriane Dupont – the witch. She's here."

Cursing, I rub the sleep from my eyes with the heel of my hands, and my stomach growls, reminding me it hasn't been fed. How long have I been out? "Of course, she is. The one Dyson talked about?" Nodding her head, she evacuates my personal space, allowing me to swing my legs over the side of the mattress. Janine's words pop back in my head, asking me to help her daughter.

I clear my throat. "Where is she?"

Clasping her hands in front of her, she pulls her fingers, pinching the nails. "She's going to the Colosseum."

"What?" I bark in disbelief.

"She has a plan." Wanda frowns. "I think."

I rake a hand through my hair, processing this information. "Okay –"

She interrupts me. "Come. Get up. Get dressed. We must go."

## DYSON COLEMAN

## DEATH REALM

Tanya screeches as her body hits the concrete. She is the last to be shoved to the archway, the one leading to the sand of the field we'll battle in. Her small frame smashes against a row of swords dangling from their perch along the wall. Their sharp edges snag on the cloth of her shirt, causing the ripping of fabric. The sound of metal against metal, of cheers and shouts from a large crowd, filter in through the electric bars.

"They have something," the vampire smacks his lips, teasing us, "tasteful for you five." The vampire chuckles and leaves us, his laugh brasher as he marches through the tunnel we came from.

"Dyson, what do we do?" Jane whispers. "What if we're to fight each other?"

Gan shuffles to the electric bolt bars. It's the only wall of sorts keeping us separated from the arena. He touches a bolt with his index finger and screams when the electricity travels through his body.

I sigh, my heart pumping in fear. Gan will be no use in an arena. "I don't know, Jane. I don't know anything. I don't have a plan." I pause, frowning, and lick my bottom lip. "We should prepare ourselves. We aren't walking out of this alive."

They stare at me, their eyes wide with fear, except for the sandman. His jaw tightens, and his expression is an unwavering determination. Nodding once, he reaches over, grasping the handle of his choice in weapon. Dangling from the handle is a spiked ball. He glides back to our circle, planting his feet shoulder-width apart.

The sandman studies the spikes which glint in the light of a single candle. "Even if we are to survive this battle," he begins, his words slow and deep. "We won't make it out of here alive. They will kill us in the end. It matters not if you die there, in the arena, or as a champion."

*TEMBER*

*GUARDIAN REALM*

Our lips smack as I break the kiss, quickly pulling back and recoiling from Erma. My heart thudding in my wrist, and rapid self-reflections rotate through my mind, fear coursing its drive and direction.

I turn slowly, my fingers curling into fists, and my teeth grind against each other. Corbin leans against a pillar, his arms crossed over his chest and his hip cocked to the side in the arrogant way he's best known for. He bites his bottom lip with perfect white teeth, and his lips curl at the edge, smiling. "And to think I left my entertainment for a brief, boring chat, and what I witness is even better than my absence at my own event."

Two angels stand beside him. Their cheeks burn a bright red as the initial shock wears off, replaced with barely contained malice. I recognize these two. They dabble with the darker side of our nature. Their intents are not pure but driven by selfish desires.

"Did we interrupt?" Jax growls. His silky black hair is perfectly spiked, creating a halo on its own. He's tall and thin but not as much as Corbin.

Jax's good friend, and often the one he beds, stands beside him. Dena's knuckles are white from the strain of tight fists, and her veins bulge on her forehead, ticking. "Does everyone receive these favors? Or just the one?" she spits.

Erma remains nonchalant, her expression carefully blank. She pushes her rump off the desk with elegance and grace. "What can I do for you three?" she asks, quirking an eyebrow. Her tone holds a great deal of hostility, reminding those before her who is in charge.

"They came to escort me to your chambers, but it seems there's much more to discuss than I previously anticipated." Corbin chuckles, dropping his crossed arms and striding into the office as if it were his own. He takes a seat on the chair in front of me, his manners gone as his ego swells to a whole new level.

I watch the angels behind him, their eyes shooting daggers in Erma's direction. I prepare to call upon Ire, calculating their next moves by the subtle twitch of the muscles lining their bodies. Jax's fingers jerk, and I know he's thinking the same. His fleeting eyes tip to Corbin, and I study the expression crossing his face as it softens in thought. The corners of his eyelids tick, and his fingers clench and unclench, considering his next move, no doubt. I lean frontward, tensing my shoulders at the ready, prepared.

Angels can fall. We are given choices on how we live the life Erma has granted us. If for any reason they decide to fall, to join a side darker than our nature, Erma is powerless to stop it, free-will her motto. Is this what he's considering? Does he consider betraying his own kind?

The double doors to Erma's bedroom swing open, and Jaemes plods through, his expression blank while he takes in the scene. His features twist in surprise, then a hard edge appears around the eyes as he, too, prepares himself for the hostility smothering the room. As all attention turns to him, he raises a hand and grips the stiff string of his bow which lay across his bare chest.

"And the plot thickens," Corbin remarks, his lips smacking in satisfaction.

"An elf?" Dena hisses, her nostrils flaring.

Jax calls upon his bow and arrow and takes aim at Jaemes in one fluid motion. "So, it is true – the speculations. Our creator has truly abandoned the rest of us." He firms his lips, his eyes narrowing. "What will the rest do, Erma, when they discover you hold an elf in your chambers and you bed an angel? What will they say, when they discover how far you've fallen from grace?"

Jaemes' eyes snap to mine, his free hand's fingers twitching, prepared to grab an arrow. The black tattoos along his hand turn a light shade of brown from the strain. I shake my head once at him, silently telling him to back down. If he were to return the hostility, it would be disastrous. This room isn't large enough for a small battle between an elf, two fee, and three angels.

Erma advances closer to Jax. "I am grace, Jax. If I were anything less than what I am, I would be concerned. But since I have an exponential amount of strength compared to you, since I created you, since I created all of you, your point, theories, and speculation, are baseless." She lowers her voice. "I choose the direction of course, Jax. Either you turn back around and walk out of here, or you release the arrow, and I end the life I've given you."

At the square of his jaw, Jax's muscle ticks as he considers her words. Dena's gaze roams over the creatures in the room, weighing her accusations against the right course for her survival. With one step, Dena makes a decision and backs out of the office. Outside the arch doorway, she spins on her heel and leaves with heavy footfalls. Her wings rustle against her back, a few white feathers breaking free and floating to the marble floor.

Jax remains strong, back rigid, his arrow crackling and filling the space of intense silence. The electricity pulses through the air, mimicking the arrow. Emotions rotate across his face at an alarming speed while I work to quiet my breaths, my hand twitching at my side.

Slowly, he stands to full height, lowering his bow to his side, and the arrow disappears with a pop. He turns to Corbin, bowing his head. "Corbin," Jax greets. "Lovely to see you." Turning, he expands his wings, taking up most of the archway. One, two, the feathered-limbs beat, and billows of wind blow light objects and my hair in swirls. His feet lift from the ground and he soars from Erma's chambers.

She watches him go, her jaw ticking at a furious speed. She twists to Corbin, pinning him with a murderous stare, ready for another battle of wits.

"I think he likes me," Corbin suggests with glee.

Growling, Erma crosses her arms. "What are you doing here?"

He smirks, folding his hands in his lap. "I could ask you the same thing." Turning to Jaemes, studying his features, he adds, "Last I heard, the angels and the elves were at a constant war. Has this changed, or are you challenging the dimensions and dynamics of your realm's limited capabilities?" Erma remains silent, her posture rigid. His smile expands, and he inclines his head. "Is there a reason behind your actions, Erma?"

"There is," she utters through clenched teeth. "And I have no plans to share them."

Reclining into the back of his chair, he nestles his spine against it. "I see."

"Don't you be getting any ideas, Corbin. Things are not what they seem. Now tell me, what are you doing here?"

"Really?" Corbin's left eyebrow lifts higher. "It seems to me you've started something you may not be able to control. I'm excellent at restraining a hostile crowd . . ."

"You didn't answer her question," I mumble. I'd rather not know what Corbin has in mind for restraint. Chances are, it ends in death and destruction.

Corbin doesn't spare me a glance, choosing to keep his attention focused on the only powerful person in the room, besides himself. "Is it unprecedented to pop in for a visit?"

"Yes," Erma quips.

Smacking his lips, Corbin leans and rests his elbows on his knees. "Are you preparing to send your angel and elf to the earth realm?"

I narrow my eyes, Jaemes speaking for me. "If you are here to be an elf devotee, I assure you I don't need another shadow. Tember already reserved that occupation." I snort, and Jaemes' tone dips deep and serious. "What does it matter to you?"

Corbin shrugs. "A few reasons. One," he points to Jaemes' head. "It will be difficult to hide the nature of an elf – the horns, ears, and tattoos - they do not scream discretion. Though the earth realm is filled with costumes and oddities, you will still draw unwanted attention and suspicion." Frowning, I glance at Jaemes, seeing Corbin's point. I hadn't thought that far ahead. "Two," Corbin continues, looking at Erma. "Your charge is no longer there."

Erma's head juts back, surprised. "What do you mean? How do you know?"

"Because he's tied to her," I express, my words a sigh. I scratch my forehead, scraping my nails across the skin. Kat's destiny is so intertwined with the realms and those she encounters, it's difficult to hold that at the forefront of my mind. How can I protect her from the tangled web of this life, from the consequences which follow her like persistent shadows?

"What do you mean?" Jaemes questions, placing a hand on his hip.

"Myla was Erline's daughter. She was inserted into Kat to make her the dragon your people fear," I growl as I begin my backlash. "She was married to him. When she died the second time, she may have gone into the void, but the marriage contract did not. Corbin's blood is still tied to Kat. The contract is still live. He can find her whenever he wishes."

"Very good, little angel," Corbin begins with sarcasm so thick I snort. "A gold star for you."

Erma bends frontward, hostility in her tone. "Where is she, Corbin?"

Shaking his shoulders in satisfaction, he grins. "The death realm."

# KATRIANE DUPONT

## DEATH REALM

"You scared me," I whisper before realizing what stands before me. In the back of my mind, I knew it wasn't another shade, but the reflex was automatic – to reply as if what stood before me was a friend.

The vampire's red irises are locked on my hand where my heart beats below it. Black, long lashes fan her high cheekbones, and matching veins swim under her skin. The fog at her ankles swirls, tendrils of mist like her dusky ebony hair cascading down her slender shoulders. Eyes resembling fresh blood lift to mine. Her top lip curls and she hisses past sharp fangs. Tiny droplets of spittle soar with the sharp, quick passing of breath, landing on the skin of my arm covering my heart.

"What do we have here?" she taunts, sauntering closer. "A lost little lamb?"

A patter of feet echoes behind me. I take a step back from the vampire and swivel my head, peeking over my shoulder. Another vampire, traveling at the speed of light, makes her way through the alley.

The black-haired vampire slithers toward me. "I wouldn't do that," I caution. My voice is deep, foreign, as the dragon within me comes forth. My defense mechanism kicks in, against my better judgement, as though it's natural. I suppose it is. I squash it down, mentally stroking my dragon's muzzle, easing my anxiety. Dead vampires won't be able to take me hostage.

She tilts her head to the side as her companion comes to a full stop, directly behind me. "Do what?" she asks, the words dipped with a sickly-sweet quality.

"How did she escape the Colosseum?" the one behind me asks.

Moving the hand covering my heart, I open my palm facing out. "I wouldn't kill me," I suggest, covering my tracks.

"It doesn't matter how she escaped," she answers, ignoring me as though I'm the cattle belonging to a slaughter house. I half turn my body, allowing her to think she's catching me unaware, and the female vampire with ebony hair grabs me from the side. She wraps her arms around my torso, locking me in her grasp. I feign struggle and force a smug smile from my face. Vampires were never smart. Food drives their motives.

"What should we do with her?" she hisses, the words tickling my ear. The stench of death wafts in the small space between us, and I wrinkle my nose, attempting to avoid breathing in. "We could keep her for a pet." She flicks out her tongue and trails it along my neck. I cringe as it leaves a coat of saliva, moisture dripping down the slope. Skin licking and taste testing wasn't part of my plan.

"You know we can't," the other declares. She crosses her arms and narrows her eyes. "If Kheelan were to find out one had escaped, we'd be ash under his foot."

The vampire lifts her nose from my jugular and whips her head to her friend. A feral growl, a possessive noise, snarls past her exposed fangs.

"Don't even start," she warns, pointing. "We serve Kheelan and nothing more."


## AIDEN VANDER

## DEATH REALM


Behind me, something grasps my attention, diverting my focus even as Corbin reappears back in his chair, pretending he never left. My muscles tense, my shoulders bunch, and I attempt to fight it, to draw back like it's a taunting flame that burns upon touch. It's a pull, a sensual lure, a tug at my broken heart. It's one I recognize. I was a shade the last time I felt that breath of fresh, crisp spring air after a long, unforgiving winter. She was what I breathed when I was drowning, my anchor, the one I left in the unforgiving sea in hopes of saving her from a fate I knew she didn't deserve. She's the pure, the untainted, the savior who was never asked. She was my everything.

A familiar scent travels to my nose, and I draw it in against my will, savoring it, tasting it . . . basking. It pulls me from the scene of death before me, luring me with the promise of a sanity in the face of chaos. I can no longer hold back my curiosity, not when I know who stands behind me, not when I'm interested in why it's happening.

Uncrossing my arms, I slowly look over my shoulder. My tense muscles strain as a war breaks inside me: to look, drown, and fall once more, or to divert and remain who I am – strong, powerful, merciless.

With tentative, carefully placed steps, Eliza walks through the stone archway and onto the platform from which we watch. Her red hair cascades around her shoulders, and her face is pinched in internal pain. Those captivating, sparkling eyes jerk in horror to the field of sand tainted in evidence of death. Her attention swivels between all those fighting in the arena, the slaves delivering futile blows. I know what she's seeing. I gulp as the horror of what I allowed, of what I chose not to stop, settles inside me. Sympathy drowns me, flooding my insides until my eyes widen, and I gasp for breath, desperate to release the pressure.

Below, three vampires toy with half a dozen humans. They slice them with sharp claws, bite them with pointed fangs, and dance away before the humans have time to connect their weapons to the predators' flesh.

Breathing hard, my lips part when our gazes lock on one another, and a hush of wind whistles past them, taking the pressure with it. Watching her, having her undivided attention, releases my guilt and pumps life and humanity back into me. Emotions flood as she saves me, restores me, though she doesn't know it. She simply has to stand there and let me lose myself in those blue eyes that I've spent most of my time avoiding in favor of power. Eliza stands for everything my third birth eliminated yet the only one who can restore it. There's a new draw which wasn't there before, back in her bedroom. It's power. I can taste the power as it mingles with mine.

She stands taller, even with the carnage below us. I purse my lips, contemplating the difference in what she once was to who she is now. What changed?

Shaking her head, she stops me from voicing my questions. I frown, concerned, and fully twist my body to face hers. How could she know what I was going to say?

Pulling a hand from around her middle, she holds it out in front of her. She tucks her chin, and her eyebrows dip. Hair tumbles from her shoulders, and she sucks in her bottom lip, biting the skin. I look to what holds her attention captive – to what concern has her absorbed. My pinched face relaxes in awe. Along the delicate, silky skin of her palm, slivers of electric bolts play with the lines and indents, silently crackling between each finger. Unlike a storm, these bolts are slow, taking their time from finger to finger, like a cat rubbing along an owner's leg.

Her head snaps up, and her wide eyes find mine, sparkling with unshed tears. I watch her throat constrict, and fear wafts from her pores. The invisible smoke tumbles my direction, and it's then that I fully understand what I am. It's a choice I'm all too willing to make…if for nothing but her.

Gritting my teeth, I squeeze my eyes shut, my hands clenched at my sides, chanting to myself. I won't allow this. This isn't what I want. My demon side screams in fury for turning my back on my nature, lighting my nerves on fire, and threatening to consume me. I allow the waft of fear to pass, refusing it access to my pores. I won't feed from my anchor, from the keeper of my heart.

# CHAPTER TWENTY-TWO

*KATRIANE DUPONT*

*DEATH REALM*

Forcefully marching along a hallway, we pass many humans huddled or standing inside cells. I frown at the construction of them. Instead of bars, they pulse with an electric current, each human keeping a safe distance from them.

Shouts and battle cries filter through the alleyway stretched between the cages. It's an echo, so I know it isn't anywhere close. I gulp, hoping I'm not too late.

"You'll be in the front," my ebony-haired vampire usher hisses, shoving me from behind.

Burning candles along the walls light our path. I stumble anyhow, the vampire's strength surprising.

Humans stand to their feet, coming as close to the cell's electric bolts as they dare, watching my march. I don't make eye contact with them, instead, choosing to bite the inside of my lip and gaining as much information as I can about the inside structure. It's difficult to concentrate while I'm forcing myself to squash sympathy. Seeing the large spread of humans, I know I won't be able to save them all.

Turning a corner, we approach a tall, lanky vampire. His black, greasy hair is disheveled atop his head. He leans against the wall with his arms crossed and an ankle overlapping the other.

"Yaris," my vampire escort mumbles, her voice dense with guilt.

He smirks and puffs his chest. "Did you let one get away, Sara Lee?"

Sara Lee, shoves me once more, hissing like a feral kitten. "I don't know how she got out."

"Right." He unfolds his arms, pushing his back from the wall. "Taking her to the front?"

"Yes."

Yaris narrows his eyes, sweeping me from head to toe. "Very well." We pass him but not before he takes a sniff in my direction, his jaw almost bumping my shoulder. I recoil, goosebumps lighting my nerves, and the muscles along the back of my neck stiffen.

We pass many more blood-sucking men and women, and a sense of pride surges within me. The Reaper's Breath was right. Getting caught was a good plan. There's no way I could have made it in here undetected. These creatures of the undead roam this place like an angry ant hill.

We bend a sharp curve, and Sara Lee shoves me into an archway where light filters in. I fall, my hands scraping against the stone floor.

"You're with the next batch," she snarls with distain. Her footsteps echo as she leaves, and a hand grasps my upper arm.

"Are you okay?" a male voice asks.

I glance up, my eyes meeting another's. My heart sings, skipping beats to an irrational tempo. My plan is working far better than I had hoped. Not only did I gain access to the inside, but I found the man I was looking for. "Dyson," I whisper.

He frowns and blinks hard. "Kat?" He pulls me to my feet and curses. "You're here?"

Sliding my bleeding hands along the thighs of my jeans, I nod. "It would seem so."

Dyson rakes a hand through his hair, pulling at the strands, and jolts, pacing, giving me a chance to realize we aren't alone. I swivel my head, taking in the others around me.

Two women and two men stand before the electric bars leading to an opening. I'm guessing beyond the bars is the main attraction. The shouts are deafening here, coming from inside the narrow walkway just beyond.

Swords line the stone wall, axes and weapons I've never seen before.

I look to the humans watching me with frightened eyes. They're still, almost too still, waiting for introductions, or possibly a rescue. One of them I recognize. "Sandman?"

He inclines his bald head, and my eyes widen as the single candlelight on the wall reflects on his shiny skin. He's human. I wasn't expecting that though I don't know why.

My gaze tips to the weapon in his hand. His lengthy fingers grip a long, wooden handle, and a chain attached to the top, dangling a spiked ball inches from the ground. It looks heavy . . . an omen of a painful, blundering death.

"Beasty," a high-pitched male voice babbles.

I spin to the voice as the people part and look toward him. The owner sways, rocking back and forth while seated on the floor. The man's arms envelop his calves in a tight vice. I recognize him immediately. Anger rips through me like heat rolling from a blazing oven. I take a step forward, my hands balled into straining, tight fists.

"You!" I shriek. The sandman places a cold palm on my shoulder, stopping me. "You're him. You're the peeping human who got Myla killed."

"Easy, dragon," the sandman rumbles. "His name is Gandalf, and her discovery wasn't his fault."

"I know his name," I snap.

Gandalf shimmies his rump along the floor, his back hitting the pristine, white, stone wall, and the edge of his head bumps the weapons. The metal swords sway as he curls in on himself. Peeking over his hairy forearms, he cackles an inhuman laugh. "End-inning."

I cock my head to the side, my hostile emotions fleeing as fast as they came. He rocks, tucking his face back inside his arms and chanting the same word. He's insane I realize. A small part of me finds glee in that.

I look up and glare at the sandman. Though his height is intimidating, I'm directing my outrage and tension on the next available person. "What do you mean it wasn't his fault? How long has he been here?"

"A long time." The sandman glances over his shoulder to Gandalf. "I was forced to place a false dream upon him, creating suspicion in hopes he'd expose Myla."

A lightbulb goes off in my head. "He didn't die in the past, Sandman. How did he get here?"

"Corbin and Kheelan," he mumbles, his jaw ticking.

"So, her death is your fault?" I cross my arms and cock my hip. He inclines his head. My anger deflates for reasons I can't fathom. My heart has a soft spot for my sandman, and I'm not sure why.

Huffing, Dyson spins to face me, cutting off our conversation. "You might be too late."

I untuck a hand and wave it in the air, swirling it in the space around us. "Doesn't look that way to me."

He glares, his lips tense. "Do you fully understand what we are walking into?"

"Sure, I do." I nod once. "Our death."


**TEMBER**

**GUARDIAN REALM**


Erma paces the office while rubbing her arms. The action is becoming repetitive as her stress level rises. "I will go retrieve Katriane," she mumbles, her voice weak with the weight of the situation.

My attention is still glued to the chair Corbin sat in. He disappeared shortly after dropping his one and only smug secret. He enjoys his mind games, his trickery, and disappearing in a timely manner, leaving behind chaos and fear. It never fails.

Jaemes shakes his head. "You will do no such thing."

"You must stay here," I add and then frown, finding myself supporting Jaemes' statement. I shake it off and continue. "There will be repercussions for what Jax and Dena witnessed. You need to address the angels. Discuss with them what you have discussed with the elves. Ease their worry and get them on board. Your job is to protect this realm. You let me care for my charge."

Jaemes places his hands on his hips and slightly bows to whisper in my ear. "Our charge." I purse my lips and pretend as though I didn't hear him. It's better this way, to refuse to encourage him and instead, think of him as a fly on the wall, bothersome and intruding . . . something to squash with the heel of my palm and watch in satisfaction as he plummets to the ground in a crumpled heap of guts and twitching wings. I allow a small smile.

Erma scratches her scalp and rakes a hand through her hair, snagging at the ends. "This is a disaster."

Jaemes nods. "A swirling mess of doom and gloom." Standing beside me, arms crossed over his chest, his feet wide apart in a confident stance, he adds, "I trust the Wingless Mascot's assessment. The arrogant fee is untrustworthy, and so are your angels. You must stay. I will go, retrieve the dragon, and save the day." He looks to me, sweeping his stare from my head to my toes. A nostril flares. "Tember can help . . . maybe."

I roll my eyes and throw my hands in the air. "I can't do this." I whirl to Erma, raising my voice. "I can't work with him!"

Jaemes swivels his head back to me, one side of his face pinched with a smile of satisfaction for ruffling my non-existent feathers. "If I would have known I'd be escorting a toddler prone to tantrums, I would have brought a rattle to distract you from potential meltdowns."

My nostrils flare. If looks could kill . . .

Erma takes a deep breath and rubs her temples. "Do we know why she's in the death realm? How she arrived there? What her purpose is?"

"No," I grumble while keeping my eyes on Jaemes. Before he had me riled, I had been questioning that myself. I cannot fathom the logic behind her actions.

"Then go," Erma says, exasperated. She rolls her delicate hand in the air and dismisses us without another look. "Be discrete; do not get caught." To the left of Jaemes, a portal forms in the shape of a brilliant yellow orb. "I won't know if you land in his dungeons. Hide your natures." She turns, glaring as she catches our eyes. "If either of you kill one another, I'll dangle the survivor in the East Ocean and summon Corbin's Pyrens to feed from your toes."

Jaemes leans to me once more. His silky black hair falls loose from behind his shoulders and sways in the small space between us. "Interesting imagery," he murmurs. "I haven't had a conversation with the octopus-headed fish people in a while, but I've never asked them if they enjoyed the flesh of an angel. Perhaps . . ." I swing my arm out, punching him in the abs. My fist might as well hit a brick wall.

Unaffected, he straightens his posture and raises his voice as though what had transpired between us never happened. "Shall we blend in by our wit? Tember's personality may be transparent, and certainly as dull, but it does nothing for our solid form," Jaemes adds.

Erma bites her bottom lip, growling with scarcely contained exasperation. "Go!"

*****

Exiting the portal, Jaemes places his hands on his hips and swivels his body to get a full view. The trees look lifeless and brittle, crooked yet tall. I've never seen trees like this. A thick fog blankets the ground and the branches above our heads, obscuring any view we could have for a sky and possible vegetation.

"The Tween," he declares, and whistles in awe.

"Very observant," I mumble.

He turns, his eyes bulging. "Tember? Is that you?"

"What?"

"I –" he stutters, placing his hand over his chest. "You look odd dressed in sarcasm."

Pressing my lips, I run my tongue over my teeth and stretch my neck. "Ironic. You'd think someone who speaks only sarcasm would recognize their language when spoken."

He tilts his head back and laughs, throaty and deep. "A battle of wits it shall be."

Taking the moment, I twist my torso, stretching my spine, and swinging my arms, preparing for a hike. I don't know how long we'll be in the tween, but hundreds of years of experience has taught me to always remain limber. Jaemes blows out a slow breath, impatient as he waits for me to finish.

I plod onward, my shoes crunching against the tree's bark cluttering the soft ground. "How about we play a game? Hmm? Let's see how long you can remain silent."

"Now that just hurts," he huffs, traipsing on a twig and snapping it in two.

"Then my job here is done."

Snorting, he retorts. "A mascot's job is never done."

"Right," I respond dryly.

We hike in silence for several minutes, studying the eerily quiet forest, our bodies tense and rigid. It's nothing like the guardian realm where life happens so vibrantly; it's difficult to miss. Here, nothing exists. The fog swirls against our ankles, the chill tickles our arms, and the crunch of dead wood fills the silence. We should have nothing to fear, yet loneliness emits in the absence of life.

The distress soaks through my pores and creeps into my bones, making me regret my inconsequential game of attempted retribution. I applaud him for his efforts, and

I'm shamed he'll be victorious. I cannot stand the silence any longer. "Tell me about yourself," I demand.

He chuckles. "It's exactly like a wing-woman to be alarmed enough to lose at her own game."

"Do you ever stop?"

"For you, my shadow, only this once." He huffs, stepping over a rock's jagged edge which pokes above the fog. "I'm the son of a chief."

"I already know that." I take a moment, chewing on his lack of words. "You hide behind your sarcasm, but there is more to your story than you care to share. You're overlooked, aren't you?"

Hearing his smacking lips, I squint at him, distractedly ducking to miss a low branch. "Are you calling me an underdog?" he asks. "I believe those are your shoes. My feet wouldn't fit."

My forehead wrinkles. "Deflection?"

"That's not a nice thing to say," he tsks, wagging a finger at me.

"I'm not a nice person."

"Subtlety isn't your strong suit, is it?" He puckers his lips "You are comparable to an Oxtra let loose in a village." I shake my head at the mental image of the large creature they use to pull wood, wreaking havoc through their feeble teepees. I grab what I can from his words and the ones he doesn't say. There is more to this elf than meets the eye, and I'm making it my mission to discover what's behind the mask.

I drop the subject and ask another question. "Do you think this experiment will work?"

He hoists his leg over a log, fallen from one of the dead trees. The trunk is split, the remains abandoned to the forest floor. Something large hit this tree to cause such substantial mutilation. "This one?" he gestures with his hand, pointing to me, then to himself. I nod my head and he shrugs. "I suppose we will know if we don't kill each other first." Tilting my head, I acknowledge and agree.

"There," he points, cutting off my thoughts. Ahead, the swirling fog dips from the trees and raises from the forest floor, creating a wall of billowing clouds. "That's our entrance."

"How do you know?" I ask, watching the fog dip into itself.

"Do they not teach you anything in angel school?"

We reach the wall and he runs his hand through the fog, testing it, feeling it. "Wingless women first? Can't have the hero dying before the rescue is attempted. It'd brand a deprived tale."

"Coward," I mumble under my breath. I search the wall, inhale through my nose, and skulk through.

The fog licks my skin, tingling, lighting it afire, beating against it. My heart thuds in my wrist, heightened by the assault. This wall is an entrance for the dead, not the living. My breaths come in harsh wheezes as the fog dips inside my nostrils, filling my lungs. It doesn't hurt – I don't feel pain - but if I don't move, I'll die.

Gritting my teeth, I push forward, my arms swaying as I blindly feel around. I'm not willing to wait and see how it spits me out. I have no plans of dying here today. A scream rips through my hoarse throat, my eyes pinched, and I use all my force to shoulder through. It's like wading in a tar pit.

My foot lands on blessed solid ground, and I stumble against white stone. As soon as I catch my balance, I wipe my hair from my face with an annoyed swipe. Jaemes exits with grace, barging as though the portal was nothing but descending stairs. His bow twirls within his in hand as he surveys the new landscape. His face holds such seriousness, a profound edge, and it transforms his features. It renders his witty personality unrecognizable, replaced by the determination of a warrior.

I bend, placing my hands on my knees, heaving heavy breaths, and looking up at him through my fallen, disheveled, brunette curls. Did the fog not affect him the way it did me?

I study his steel features, this new expression, and it takes a moment for me to understand why he lifts his bow from a dangled angle. A flexible twist of his narrow hips, the ripple of bicep, the stretch of defined abdominal muscles . . . he reaches over his shoulder, grasping an arrow from the leather quiver against his back. In one swift, fluid motion he settles the arrow between agile fingers, pulls the string back, and without aim, releases it with precision. It feels almost slow motion. My hair brushes my cheek as I turn my head, following the arrow.

A male vampire hisses, deep and feral, before the arrow imbeds in his chest with a wet thud. The force of the impact is strong, sending the vampire into a stone wall behind him. He screeches and clutches at the wood, ripping the fabric of his shirt and scraping at his chest. His skin peels and flakes, like a freshly baked croissant, until he's nothing but a pile of black ash along the stone floor, and the arrow settles on top of it.

Hissing comes from my left, and I twist, spinning on the balls of my feet. I call upon Ire as a hoard of vampires speed our direction. Their arms pump at their sides, and their feet blur as they run, the group traveling as one. The familiar weight of wood settles in my palm, crackling to life against my curled fingers.

In his native tongue, Jaemes curses next to me. He bends his knees, ducking to the ground, pulls the string, and releases another arrow. The string vibrating as the arrow whistles, departing from his bow. I follow his lead, picking off the vampires one by one, until only a few are left.

They gather speed and one slams into my shoulder, popping the joint. Her mousy brown hair obscures my vision as we drop to the ground, my back hitting stone. We land with a thump and tiny stones dig into the exposed flesh of my hip. She falls on top of me, and the breath leaves my lungs in one rushed wave. The female's hissing turns feral and spittle splashes against my cheek. Her hair tickles my skin as I hold her jaw with a tight grip, inches from my neck.

Screaming in fury, I wrap my leg around her calf and pull, twisting my torso and flipping us over. I grip her neck and slam her skull into the stone, the rock cracking under the force. Her teeth crunch inside her mouth, her limbs flail in surprise, and her scarlet eyes roll. Black sludge seeps from the fresh wound, mixing with her hair and puddling around her head like a halo. She's not dead yet, though I marvel that she isn't.

I look to my left, Ire laying not far. Holding out my free hand, palm up, an arrow appears, forming the long shape of crackling blue electricity. I curl my fingers around it and raise it above my head, gathering strength in my biceps. With a scream, I embed the arrow in her chest.

Quickly, I scramble from her torso as she combusts into quick, consuming flames. Her screeches reach above others, and I turn to the next, catching Jaemes in my peripheral vision.

For a moment, I marvel at his hand-to-hand combat. He's fluid and graceful like a cheetah taking down his prey. His limbs are formidable weapons, fatal as his aim. He bends, ducking from the swipe of his opponent, and slams his shoulder into the vampire's abdomen. Each movement he makes is quiet, subtle, and effortless. Elves are legendary for their grace in combat.

# CHAPTER TWENTY-THREE

**DYSON COLEMAN**

**DEATH REALM**

The crackling electric gates retreat with a pop, and we stand, staring at open space. My heart constricts in fear amidst visions of my red, hot blood splashed and steaming across sands that victor no champions. No one moves. No one breathes. Our bodies are rigid, our minds focused on our last and final rest while a crowd watches the life leave our eyes. Their cheers will be the last thing we hear as we stare, unseeing to a foggy, dejected sky.

*There's no place for the twice dead.*

I swallow thick saliva, wishing not for the first time in any of my lives I could go back in time and correct every mistake I've ever made. I would have done things differently, loved with my whole heart, devoted myself to the right crowd, walked down the correct path . . .

It's the tunnel to our death, the parade to our expiry. My heart pumps, fluttering butterfly wings, and blood rushes, heavy, to my face. Tears prick my eyes, memories held captive within their liquids, and my cheeks burn with regret.

Kat looks at me over her shoulder, her face carefully blank.

"Grab a weapon," I whisper to the group. "Anything. Grab anything."

Snapping from my stupor, I go to the wall, hobbling on numb legs, and wrap my fingers around the hilt of a sword at the same time Kat does. Our fingertips brush, a stroke of heat, a caress of clarity . . .

I tuck my chin as an odd sensation overcomes me. It multiplies, and the cheers from the crowd filtering through the tunnel, the stone walls, and the shadows from the one glowing candle, fade. It's a zone, a spotlight, held only for one.

My lips part, and I swallow once more, my Adam's apple straining against the tense muscles of my neck. It's a feeling I can't place, a mental touch – an internal nudge – a flooding emotion that has no one word to supply a definition. It starts at our fingers, traveling up my arms in sprawling heat, and wraps around my chest like the comfort of a lover's embrace.

My wolf stirs from the buried position he's placed himself in, curious, observing our brushing skin.

My heart fills, heavy yet captive with the consuming emotion. I lift my eyes to hers, holding them, refusing to blink for fear it'll be the last time I ever see their shades of brown and gold flecks.

I brush my knuckle against hers once more, feeling the last stitch, an invisible knitting of my heart, mending the shambles of my broken life. I am the cloth, and she the seamstress. What is this?

*Mate*, he declares inside me, standing on all fours. His posture is certain, unwavering. I bite the inside of my cheek.

*Shit.*

"You okay?" she asks. The specks of gold in her eyes sparkle as she double blinks. Did she feel it too?

Wolf mates are supposed to be exactly that – wolf and wolf. Not dragon and wolf. Is my second life messing with the rules of nature? Or is her existence doing this?

I lick my bottom lip and remove the touch of my hand from hers. My mind frantically searches for reasons, incoherent thoughts and questions flicking through and disappearing before I can explore them. I'm about to stagger to my death, to fight for my life, when I've finally found my purpose.

"Get a move on!" a vampire yells from behind us.

"I'm fine," I grunt, angry at my situation and placing the blame on Kat's undeserving shoulders. I grab the hilt of the next, one sword for each hand, in case I have to defend Kat as well. Two swords kill faster than one.

I spin to the group and stiffen my shoulders, swinging the swords in a circle at my sides. "Let's go."

Slowly, they turn, taking small, frightened shuffles through the tunnel. Kat's strides are large as she leads the group, her gait confident and unwavering. The very real possibility of her death, of everyone's deaths, doesn't seem to affect her. She has something up her sleeve; I just haven't figured out what. Every plan I tried to come up with, she's shot down, refusing to add her own advice to what's to come. I don't know if she'll turn into a dragon. I'm not even sure if she can do it at will, but I'm not banking on it.

I twist the swords in my hand once more as the few stray sand particles grind below my shoes. The light filters in from the end of the tunnel, casting deep shadows from everyone's shuffling. It was a much shorter walk than I anticipated it to be, and as soon as we enter the large area, our feet sink into dry sand. Our heads swivel, and our bodies' turn in full circle, taking in the scene.

The Colosseum is large, causing my heart to drop to my toes. Less than a minute ago, I had imagined a much smaller area, surrounded by small groups and crowds of people. The arena is large, football field size, and those definitely aren't people.

The walls are made of ascending stone benches. Rows and rows of creatures I've never seen before line the seats that make the walls. On one side, a slab of stone sits low to the sands, Kheelan sitting with two others I don't recognize.

I look behind them and gasp, the twirl on my swords halting in my hands. Aiden stands behind a lean, tall fee, and Eliza behind him. Fresh tears run down Eliza's face, her cheeks red and shining, while Aiden's arms ripple with agitated muscle. What did I miss? How is he alive? Squinting, I attempt a closer look. Instead of normal irises, some sort of red – lava – ripples in their depths. What is he?

The crowd raises its collective fists while most shout "mortem." I tear my eyes from Eliza and Aiden, dropping my gaze to the two fee I don't recognize. One is undoubtedly the fee of the dream realm. Her resemblance to Sandy is unmistakable. The other has his black eyes locked to something next to me, his jaw ticking and his face beet red. The female fee's eyes widen as she, too, gazes at what he sees.

I look beside me, curiously concerned. My heavy breaths drown the cheers of the crowd as adrenaline courses through my body, pumping blood in my ears. Kat stands there, locking eyes with them, a smug smile puffing her cheeks. She switches the hilt of her sword to the other hand, twirling it within her palm.

"What's going on?" I ask her. "Do they know you?"

"We're about to have a party, Dyson." She mumbles, knowing I'll be able to hear. "Get your party hat on."

"Open the gates!" Kheelan yells, throwing his arms in the air. His voice echoes as though there are speakers built throughout the structure, booming and menacing.

Chains rattle, and metal scrapes against metal. The unknown dangers ahead stir my wolf, his attention moving from his mate to impending threat. He paws inside me, muddled at my distress. All it takes is a mate and a battlefield to rattle the chains he confined himself to?

I glower to Kat, the group forming a circle, back to back. The sandman sways the handle of his weapon, the spiked ball swinging. Gan holds two, short knifes in his hands, his chuckle cackling and mad. Jane and Tanya each grip a sword though I can tell they're heavy in their grips. The tips tilt too far toward the blood-soaked sand.

"Get ready," Kat yells to us, her eyes glowing an infuriating orange. Dark, black circles emerge on the skin around her eyes, her features contorting to a hell-bent witch. Smoke curls from her flared nostrils and she grunts, her voice deeper. "We have a few uninvited guests."

We stare at the lifted gates, and a rumble rocks our feet, stirring the sand in a trembling wave. The crowd's cheers swell at the sound of wild beasts. I nod to Kat, ready, and stretch my stiff neck. Though I have no wish to see what's about to exit this wall, I know I have no choice but to endure it.

Survive . . . or die. Fight, or cease to exist. I'll be damned if this is the end.

I look to Kat, concerned for whatever creature is heavy enough to feel like an earthquake when it walks. "Think we could get a little help from a dragon?"

She puckers her lips. "I'd prefer not to play all my cards just yet." Her eyebrows wiggle with salutation and she bends her knees, lowering her body. "Here it comes."

In what feels like slow motion, the breath rushes from my lungs as I swivel my head back to the opening, my cheeks loose and eyes wide.

Hoofs exit the shadow of the tunnel first, mid gallop, before the full creature emerges, a beast riding its back. It's the largest four-legged animal I've ever seen, and its rider is more massive; skin a dark blue, tusks exiting large lips, white sparkling eyes, and a bald head. Its skin looks like worn blue leather, flawed with imperfections as though it was sewn together. The muscles roping its arms are beyond imagination. I'm positive if its forearm was placed next to my body, the bulging bicep would be taller than me.

"An Orc," the sandman yells, gripping his weapon tighter, twirling the spiked ball in a circle. "Sureen created an Orc."

The orc rides a horse almost as large as he is; four hoofs, an elongated neck and muzzle, two ears, but the comparison from a horse to this creature ends there. A three-foot-long, rigid and pointed horn juts from the horse's forehead, its body made of bones with no eyes or skin. There isn't even muscle, which baffles me, yet I feel fear for the unknown, for this creature who breaks the laws of nature. But there is no law here. None which warrant any sense.

My wolf snarls inside me while I gulp. "Is that a unicorn?" I ask, my voice cracking.

Kat's eyebrows lift, and her chin juts with calculation. "Some sort of dead one." We watch as the Orc and unicorn gallop around the field, a show of display to rile a feral crowd. "It's an interesting twist, don't you think?"

"What is wrong with you?" I spit.

She doesn't answer me, which infuriates me more. Every bone in my body wants to take her and run, to protect her from even herself. There's no way we will all survive this. Not with the giant and his steed of bones.

My wolf growls, snarling and scratching inside me. He wants free. He wants to defend. I don't know what the hell he plans to do against this opponent. Besides . . . no one is walking out of here alive.

Two more orcs riding the skeletal unicorns exit the same tunnel, their hoofs kicking up dust and sand as they ride past us. Any hope I once held, fades, my stomach dropping with it.

The first Orc roars, and I fight to cover my ears to keep them at my side with my swords at the ready. The soundwaves bounce off the walls, and those seated along them, rebounding back and vibrating the ground.

## DEATH REALM

Kheelan turns to Sureen, a brow quirked. "Unicorns?"

Distracted, her head barely moves as she shakes it, her attention remaining on the sands and those who now roam it. "Necrocorns," she corrects.

I hold my breath with tense lips as Katriane is the first to act. I marvel as her free arm lights with a blazing red and orange flame, and Kheelan's back stiffens in surprise. She jerks her arm through the air as though she's throwing a Frisbee, and hurls it at a necrocorn's hooves, erupting like a bomb. Sand sprays the walls and crowd, and black smoke rises in puffs. The animal screeches a sound I've never heard. It's raucous, a noise that tickles my eardrums. Scrunching my nose, I cover my ears and watch as the necrocorn drops to the ground, the orc thudding after it. A cloud of dust rises from the sand, obscuring the view with billowing, rounded shapes.

The orc skids to a halt, face buried in the sand. Waving her sword in the air, she digs her feet in and runs toward the orc, breaking free of the group and the circle they formed.

A blur passes her, a ball of grey. It takes a moment for my eyes to adjust, for the dust to lift enough to see a massive wolf encase its jaw around the Orc's thick neck. With a yank of his head, the wolf rips it out with one fluid motion. Thick droplets and streams of blood stray from the open wound, coating the ground like a hose spraying a thirsty garden. The cheers erupt in the crowd, some relishing the reminiscence of the Orc's liquid life force splashed against their face.

Sureen's fingers grip her thighs, her knuckles flexing, and the nails dig into her dewy, mahogany skin. She's watching her creations wither by the hands of her enemy.

My observation snaps to my mother, to Aiden's mother, and the sandman who stands with them. An orc dismounts his necrocorn, jumping from it to land in the sand. His weight shakes our platform, and I widen my stance to keep my balance. He swings his arm to the side, hitting the creature in the ribs, deeming it useless. The necrocorn soars, landing in the rows of seats. Its weight crushes a portion of the crowd's demons and vampires, and the wall creaks, a crack running from the impact to the sands.

The Orc picks up a large foot, his four fingers balled into fists, and runs toward the group. He's easy to watch, every detail, his movements slow due to his massive size.

I squeal, deadly, bloody, gruesome deaths and scenarios playing out in my head. My hand hovers over my mouth, and I bite my bottom lip. Aiden partially turns his torso, his eyes wide as they lock with mine, and his lips part. He doesn't know how to stop the impending deaths any more than I do.

With a swing of the sandman's weapon, and timely precision, the spiked ball connects to the orc's temple mid-run. The orc staggers back and shakes its head with an abundance of pain etched around the skin of his large eyes. His leathery skin jiggles with each shake, and black blood floods down his cheek.

A man I don't recognize sits on the sand in the middle of the arena, rocking back and forth, his daggers at his side. The last necrocorn and orc gallop his direction, taking advantage of the weak, the hoof beats thunderous.

I gasp. The man doesn't see them; he's unaware. He won't be able to move in time. What I witness, what I see, will be forever burned into my mind, haunting me for the rest of my second life.

I can hear the crunch of bones, of body, from here. The hooves of the large animal run directly overtop him, crushing the man beneath as though he was transparent, nothing but a wisp of wind, a twig in the road.

A cloud of sand dust settles as the necrocorn reaches the other end of the arena, rearing its skeletal head in the victory of its kill. The Orc turns his upper half and the skin along his hard stomach wrinkles. His wild eyes glance at the damage they've done and a slow grin spreads across his face, revealing large, yellow teeth. He raises his arms and beats his chest like a drum, whipping his head along his shoulders and roaring to the sky.

What's left is a man who no longer resembles one. He's a pile of skin. The organs were ripped from his body by piercing hoofs and lay next to him, haphazard and catastrophic. His entire blood volume soaks in the sand, swallowing what once fed his heart. A crushed face, an open mouth, pleads with the fogs of the sky, forever screaming the injustice of his demise to a heaven that will never hear.

Aiden faces me once more. His face is carefully blank, murderous I realize, as his thoughts whisper in my mind, mirroring my own.

I was right before. There is something of Aiden left, and it thrives with each passing second his mother fights in the pits below. He fears for her, for her life, especially after witnessing the first death of a man more deserving than most. They killed him without consideration and deterrent, without conscious effort. It was all too easy and the man all too helpless. They're down there, my friends, my family, fighting for a few more minutes to a borrowed heart, but they'll die as slaves of entertainment.

I've had enough.

Fury beats against my sympathy until my internal walls shatter, bursting through me like the cracking of an old, frail dam. This isn't right. This isn't fair. I had promised justice.

I scream, the heavy noise leaving my throat in a roar. It doesn't sound like it belongs to me. I feel the rush of power within sparkle and slither along my skin, feeding me the promised righteousness. It's a quenching need, a thirst, a hunger for vengeance, a cool downpour on a desert sand.

My hair sparks with static. It lifts and floats wherever it chooses, swaying around my head.

It's darkness. Pure, undiluted dusk. A black, patchless hole. It's the downfall from which I may never return. It's the call to a side everyone restrains with a lock, choosing to bury it beneath a mental cement.

I won't stand aside while everything is taken from me.

Blue bolts of lightning light my skin as though I am the storm ready to unleash my fury on an unsuspecting town.

I'm the center. I'm the sun. I choose what lives. I choose when I erupt. I choose what I consume.

Lifting my arms, my power feeds me, filling me to capacity as it gathers. My feet leave the flat platform, and I hover.

A whisper tickles words inside my head, a slithering tone using my voice. It's the power, the expanse of mind, a second consciousness which should never be allowed access. It's alluring, convincing . . . evil. *You want the darkness. You need it . . . This is who you are.*

I listen to the voice, feel its call, and accept its request.

Aiden's eyes widen, and his crossed arms drop to his sides like dead weight. The fee in front turn, their expressions matching Aiden's.

## TEMBER

## DEATH REALM

I glance at the scratch on my shoulder, sluggishly bleeding blood. A vampire's claw caught my skin when he swiped at me. Standing here, chest rising and falling, I chastise myself for the miscalculation which caused such a blemish.

"All dead?" Jaemes asks, kicking a pile of ash.

"It would appear so." I sigh, dropping my fingers from probing the wound. It'll heal soon. "Where did you learn to fight like that?"

"I have brothers," he responds with a dry tone. He places his hands on his hips and spins to face me. Through all that exertion, Jaemes doesn't have a drop of sweat or a scratch on his body. In fact, his breathing is normal. I bite the inside of my cheek, nervous, refusing to believe it's a very real possibility that I may be losing my touch.

"Right." I clear my throat. "Shall we?"

We lumber onward to an archway, the only entrance there is. Crumbling, brick walls hail our path, our shoes echoing and bouncing off, vibrating my ears. It's disrupting my ability to listen for another oncoming assault.

"That won't be the last of them," he warns. "I still don't know how we are to accomplish this undetected."

"I don't either," I murmur.

Up ahead, I see a break in the walls, and I know we've reached our destination. Jaemes grips the curve of his bow which is settled over his shoulder, his gait confident as he crosses. His foot is the first to land in the death realm, but he halts, cocking his head instead of continuing on.

"This may be easier than we thought," he whispers.

My eyes narrow. "Where is everyone?"

The streets are quiet; no shades or vampires roam them. This wasn't what I imagined death to be like. I knew Kheelan was a cruel man, but this place is empty. There's no meaning here; it's dark, gloomy, and full of despair.

"I don't know," he mumbles. He slants his head to the side, his pointed ears twitching. "Do you hear that?"

Frowning, I hold my breath to get a better listen. Shouts – many shouts are raised off in the distance, whispering through the streets of tall buildings with no windows. "Yes. What is it?"

"Some kind of gathering? What would be happening in the death realm to warrant such a cheer?"

I take a deep breath and grip Ire tighter in my palm. My skin squeaks against the rub of sturdy wood, a comfort to a circumstance I've never endured. "Come on."

Sidestepping close to the wall, Jaemes leads the way, silent and deadly. He holds an arrow in the other, our bows swaying with each stride, our hands at the ready.

The cheers escalate the deeper we travel into the realm, encouraging excitement as adrenaline pumps through my body. The stone beneath my shoes grits with each footfall, hundreds of years old dust and crumbling stone pebbles kicking out behind us. It's impossible to stay invisible here, even as we stay close to the wall. Not even a shade could hide, unless they walked through the buildings.

I briefly wonder what it's like, living in a realm with bloodthirsty creatures. It must not be too bad if the shades are gathered somewhere, cheering. There's not a vampire in sight, and this fact alone gives me mental pause. I shake my head. If I had to choose, I'd wager they're with the cheering crowd. Perhaps those cheers aren't of pure happiness.

The road we've been walking on splits and spills out into a large opening. At the center is Kheelan's home, which he calls the Keep the last I heard. Behind it, a perfect circular wall, resembling a . . .

My eyes widen, wrinkling the skin on my forehead. "Is that a Colosseum?"

Jaemes' teeth grind, his eyes roaming the surface and the many arched entrances. "Yes."

Another round of cheers resounds, complimented by a roar of a creature I don't recognize. It's deep, rumbling, and aggressive. It accents the Colosseum which is constructed only for blood, a performance of the unwilling and pleasure for a sick mind. The cheers of delight, the battle cries, spill over the top as one and slither through the streets like the fog.

"What are we walking into?" I whisper.

"Death," he responds, thick and clipped. His posture is frontward, his muscles rigid, and he twitches his top lip. As his large eyes narrow, the black tattoos surrounding them darken.

I look back to the structure. "Kat is in there. She wouldn't be her if she let innocents die."

"I hope you're ready, angel," he grunts, taking the first step.

## KATRIANE DUPONT

## DEATH REALM

The brittle, snapped, and protruding bones of what's left of Gan's body are the white flags buried in the field of a losing battle. His blood is puddled around him, soaking into a thirsty sand. It drinks it, craves it, and begs to subdue an unquenchable appetite.

I don't know why I am, but I'm overcome with the loss of life. I hated Gan and everything he did to aid in ending Myla's life, but he was my last tie to her. He's from her time, he's seen her, and just as I, he's heard her voice and possibly listened to her wisdom. And now he's gone.

Sorrow swells in my heart, fury pumping the beats, and heat floods my extremities. These emotions ground me, and my earlier pride and bravado flee. Impenetrable, overriding revenge takes its place - a splash of fuel to an already raging fire.

This isn't how I saw this playing out. This isn't what I envisioned. The orcs were unexpected, and the death even morose. I've tried turning the tables in our favor by refusing to play all my cards, but it's not working.

I glance at my sword which is held in my hand at my side. The crowd fades as though they were never there. Gan's body becomes nothing but a blur of red, and time seems to slow. My inhales and exhales are dense, lurid, and foreign. The flawless sharp edges are all I see, and I turn my wrist, examining it with a fine eye. A glint sparkles at the tip, the weapon speaking to me as if it has insight it wishes to share. It knows . . . It knows it'll never be enough, that it won't crown me a conqueror, or be an extension to my victory.

I inhale and exhale once more, my blinking unhurried, my vision obscured as another wave of sand sprays my side and bites my skin. A few of the tiny rocks hit the blade, a tyrant to the less privileged.

Uncurling my cramped fingers, one at a time, I allow gravity to take the blame for abandonment. It falls, spinning, a final farewell for my betrayal. With a thud, it hits the sands and the grains soar, attempting to swallow its rival. Yet, the sands forget – it bites the hand who feeds it. The edge of the sword catches another reflection, a glint that weeps for my treachery.

I turn my back from it and grind my teeth. Swiveling my head, I take in what's left of our enemies roaming the field. The crowd cheers, their fists raised and shaking, their bodies bouncing on toes supported by anxious, twitching legs.

A large grey wolf nudges my abdomen, and a cold, wet nose settles in my palm. I look down and run my fingers through his fur. "Go," I whisper to Dyson, knowing he'll hear me.

I catch the eyes of the sandman, and we hold the contact long enough for a silent communication to pass between us. I nod to him, a slow incline of my head. With a battle cry from deep within his chest, the sandman turns back to his group, who deals with an orc of their own, and lifts his swinging spiked ball. He arches his back, the muscles rippling along his spine, and swings forward, catching the orc in the thigh. The spikes imbed and the orc roars with rage, spittle soaring from his mouth.

Dyson whines, his rose-red tongue slipping past his canines and licking away the blood along the light grey fur surrounding his lips. He nudges once more, and I push against his shoulder blade. Yipping, he digs his paws into the ground and kicks up sand as he takes off in a low-to-the ground sprint. His ears lay against his skull, and his tail sweeps behind him. My moment of comfort is gone as his warmth disappears.

The orc swings his massive arm, knocking Jane and Tanya from their feet.

If I don't do something and quick, none of us will survive. I shift, my feet digging further into the ground, and turn to the Orc who ran over Gandalf. His skeletal steed paws the sand, his roar of victory deafening.

A slow smile spreads across my face, and I unleash the fury within. It floods through the mental gate I've secured in hopes to contain the side of me I fear. I'm about to do something I told myself I'd never do, that my mother cautioned me to resist. I'm about to allow the dark freedom.

I hold out my arms from my side and spread my legs farther apart for better balance. The rushing wave of dark intentions overcomes me, and I hold back a relishing moan as my intentional innocence is consumed, taking my fears and concerns with it. My smile widens, a smile promising vengeance and certain death.

As the first to crack and reshape, my ribs disconnect, my back arches, and my shoulders hunch, ripping my shirt at the seams. The transformation lengthens my spine, and my skin pulls along my back as though it's an itch I can't scratch. A blazing heat slithers along my muscles, and scales slice through, replacing the shell of my human skin. My eyelids flutter closed, and my head tilts frontward in ravishment. This feeling of ecstasy is unlike any other.

The rest of my body continues with the transformation, the bones crackling as they break and reform, and the muscles stretch, snap, and knit back together. The sensations are caressing, a release, like a deep tissue massage after a long week of hard labor.

When I open my eyes to vision so sharp, I can see each individual grain of dust floating in the air. I'm taller, my head reaching to the same height as half of the colosseum's wall. The cheers erupt with wild vigor at my transformation, fueling my dark side. A rumble of leashed malice tightens in my chest, waiting to exclaim my wrath.

The ground shakes as my front feet drop to the sands and I extend my long neck toward the ground. The spikes along my spine flatten, my muscles rippling, shifting each scale like a row of tipped dominos. I open my muzzle and expose sharp, pointed teeth. The swell of my chest travels, rumbling up my throat, and a roar exits my mouth.

Seconds ago, I was human. Minutes ago, I was reluctant. My entire life, I've been hiding from fate. I flick my tail, sliding the tip along the loose, gritty sand. The unfamiliar, yet climactic, sense of dark disobedience and merciless revenge settles in its new home, feeding me adrenaline.

If the tide doesn't turn, light the bitch on fire and watch as it burns. The ill-fated will claim their victory. The neglected will speak. Today, the slaves will teach the master.

I inhale, filling my chest with fire straight from the pits of hell, my eyes blazing, my heart racing.

*Burn it to the ground.*

# ALSO BY D. FISCHER

| THE CLOVEN PACK SERIES |

| RISE OF THE REALMS SERIES |

| NIGHT OF TERROR SERIES |

| OTHER |

*Cure the Enemy*

*Christmas Stranger*

# ABOUT THE AUTHOR

D. Fischer is a mother of two busy boys, a wife to a wonderful and supportive husband, and an owner of two hyper, sock-loving dogs and an attention-seeking fat cat. Together, they live in a quiet little corner of a state that's located in the middle of the great USA.

Follow D. Fischer on Twitter, Facebook, Goodreads, Pinterest, and Instagram.

DFISCHERAUTHOR.COM